THE BODYGUARD'S RUIN

GALACTIC CLAN WARS
BOOK ONE

SAMANTHA CHARLTON

He thought he could deny himself forever … until fate threw them together. A diplomat and her bodyguard embark on a daring rescue mission in this steamy space opera romance adventure.

Malik swore an oath to protect the Mir-Brennan clan-lord and his family with his life. But that doesn't stop him from wanting the sister of the man he serves—a woman he can never have. Ambassador Jenna Mir-Brennan is married and barely acknowledges his existence.

However, when Malik escorts Jenna on a peace mission, the line he never thought he'd cross starts to blur.

Jenna's marriage is over. After two years of hell, she's dragged up the courage to leave her bullying husband. Now she's focused on negotiating a ceasefire with the enemy.

But from the moment she sets off on her mission, she finds it hard to keep her mind on the job. The man leading her security team both unnerves and fascinates her. She doesn't want any romantic entanglements, especially with her bodyguard, yet now she's at risk of losing her hard-won composure.

When disaster strikes, Jenna and Malik are thrown together in a fight for survival. Passion ignites, tearing down the boundaries between ambassador and bodyguard.

Out of her depth, Jenna's sure that Malik will be her ruin.

But he fears she will be his.

Book One of The Galactic Clan Wars series, THE BODYGUARD'S RUIN is a stand-alone romance in an exciting new space fantasy series.

There are thousands of clans throughout our galaxy.
They range widely in power and influence, yet only three
dominate in the Rith sector. For decades now, the Mir-
Brennans, the Mir-Ferrins, and the Mir-Leliths have
jostled for supremacy. It is a struggle that has left the
pages of our history awash in blood.
—*The First Book of Rith*

"It matters not how strait the gate,
How charged with punishments the scroll,
I am the master of my fate,
I am the captain of my soul."
—*Invictus, William Ernest Henley*

In another time …
In another galaxy …

1. GLORY IS THE REWARD OF VALOR

JENNA'S PULSE QUICKENED when the door to her bedchamber whispered open behind her.

There was only one person who'd enter her private space without buzzing first.

Dragging in a deep breath, she straightened up from where she'd been packing. Her shuttle was leaving shortly. She didn't have time for this.

Steeling herself, she glanced over her shoulder.

Her husband stood just inside the doorway, arms folded across his chest. A scowl twisted his handsome face.

"Good morning, Tian," she greeted him mildly, pretending not to notice his thunderous expression.

A muscle bunched in his jaw. "So, it's true then?"

"What is?" Jenna took the shawl her droid passed her and carefully folded it, placing the item in her suitcase. Anxiety fluttered up under her ribcage. This was *her* space; she didn't like Tian invading it. A few months earlier, they'd moved into separate bedchambers. Her husband had never set foot in here, until today.

"Cathal's agreed to negotiate a ceasefire with the Mir-Leliths."

Jenna stifled a sigh. She'd known Tian would be angry about her brother's decision. "Yes ... finally."

She twisted around to face her husband fully then. Tian had moved to stand before the window, his lean form silhouetted against a wide pink sky. Harsh red-hued sunlight streamed into the room, although the triple-glazed glass and air-conditioning prevented the planet's blistering heat from entering as well.

Tian met her eye, his lip curling. "Cathal's making a mistake. Instead of sending his simpering sister to treat with our enemies, he should be striking a blow they shall never recover from. Show Aran Mir-Lelith mercy, and he will despise you for it."

"You're wrong," Jenna replied, deliberately ignoring his slight. "Aran knows ... as we do ... that an escalating conflict will just weaken both our clans. He's humbled and ready to talk. And that's why I'm going to meet his delegates ... maybe we can mend some of the bridges we burned."

Tian snorted. "What would *you* know? Your brother should be listening to me. *I'm* his military advisor."

"One that has sent us into open war with the Mir-Leliths," she countered, her temper rising now. "Cathal no longer looks to you for counsel, Tian. Instead, he's sending *me* to fix the mess you've made."

That was the truth. For months, she'd watched Tian push her brother and his other advisors toward the point of no return. Now, the Mir-Lelith clan-lord wished to negotiate a ceasefire, and she was leading the Mir-Brennan delegation.

Someone had to do something—before it was too late. The balance of power between the sector's three most powerful clans had always been a fragile one. Over the past years, the Mir-Brennans had grown in strength—and Jenna's father had decided to use his position of power to work toward peace with their rivals: the Mir-Ferrins and the Mir-Leliths.

Jenna's marriage to Tian had secured an alliance between the Mir-Brennans and the Mir-Ferrins, ending decades of feuding. Her clan had also been working toward a treaty with the Mir-Leliths, one to divide mining rights upon Staturine II, a mineral-rich planet the two clans had been in dispute over. But everything had unraveled when the Mir-Lelith ambassador tried to assassinate her brother on Jenna and Tian's wedding day.

Peaceful communications between the Mir-Brennans and the Mir-Leliths had ended then, and their relationship spiraled into military conflict just weeks later.

Tian's gaze narrowed. "Stuck-up bitch." His gaze raked over her from the crown of her head to the hem of her golden ambassadorial robes. "You always think you know best, don't you?"

Silence fell in the bedchamber, broken only by the hum of the climate control unit on the ceiling above them.

Jenna stared back at her husband—and as she did so, something gave way inside her. This man had brought her nothing but misery since their wedding day. She'd tried to like him—and when that had failed, she'd tried to get along with him—but Tian Mir-Ferrin's scorn was poison.

Every encounter between them left her feeling diminished. Whenever they were alone, he did his best to erode her self-confidence, to grind her into the dirt. Cruel words left bruises no one could ever see, yet they scarred all the same.

Jenna inhaled sharply. "Enough," she murmured. "We're finished, Tian."

Her husband tensed, his dark brows crashing together. "Excuse me?"

"Our marriage ... it's over."

Tian moved then, so fast he caught her off-guard. Three paces brought him across the chamber. A moment later, he was looming over her, his gaze burning into hers. "You don't get to decide that," he snarled.

Jenna tilted her chin back to meet his eye properly. Tian was a lot taller than her, and she was used to his intimidation tactics. Even so, her pulse trebled, her mouth going dry.

She had to free herself of this bully.

Sucking in a deep breath, she focused on keeping her voice steady when she replied, "When I get back from Aura Terminal, I want you gone. I suggest you start packing up your things today. If you're still here when I get back, I'll have the Lord's Watch march you out of the tower."

Tian reached up then, his hands clasping her shoulders. His grip was bruising, although Jenna managed not to flinch. Gods, she wanted him out of her life

A muscle worked on her husband's jaw. "Are you threatening me?"

Jenna continued to hold his gaze. "I don't speak idly," she replied, her voice surprisingly steady. "Test me and see what happens."

His grip on her shoulders tightened, his fingers biting into her flesh.

Jenna's pulse started to thunder.

Tian had never actually lifted a hand to her, but she could feel he was on the brink of doing so now.

The comm next to the door buzzed then. A second later, a man's baritone vibrated through the chamber. "Ambassador, the shuttle is ready to depart."

"Thank you," Jenna replied, her gaze never leaving Tian's. "I'll be right there."

"Very well, Your Excellency." The comm then clicked off.

Long moments passed before she murmured. "Let me go."

Tian's lips thinned, his gaze still smoldering.

Victory ignited in the pit of her belly. She'd defeated him, and they both knew it.

He released her then, stepping back from her.

Turning to the bed, she closed the suitcase and set it down at her feet. "Hand me my bag, Daisy."

"Yes, Mistress," the droid bleeped its acquiescence, amber lights blinking as it swiveled around and plucked the large bag from the chair behind it. Daisy—DA15Y—was a D4-class utility-droid who'd been with Jenna since she was eight. In the two empty years of her marriage to Tian, the droid had provided much-needed companionship. However, Daisy couldn't ease the knots of misery in her stomach whenever she contemplated her future with this man.

She hadn't planned on ending their marriage today, but now she had, she suddenly felt light, free.

Glory is the reward of valor, Jenna.

Resolve hardened under her ribcage as she reminded herself of the Mir-Brennan clan motto. There was no going back now.

Taking the bag, Jenna slung it over her front. She then turned to face Tian once more.

He was still watching her, and she didn't care for the glint in his dark eyes. It was calculating—a further reminder of why she wanted out of this marriage.

"I'll contact my lawyer as soon as I get to Aura Terminal. Expect to receive divorce papers within a day," she told him, marveling at how calm she sounded, despite her racing pulse. Years as a diplomat and then as her brother's ambassador had served her well.

Without awaiting a response, Jenna grabbed her suitcase and headed toward the door.

Stepping out into the corridor beyond her quarters, Jenna found Captain Malik Mir-Draven waiting for her.

Clad head-to-toe in gleaming black armor, his face partially shielded by a helm, the man seemed out of place against the elegant gold-hued walls, sparkling pendant lights, and pots of desert succulents lining the wide spider-vaulted corridor. The captain, who led her brother's team of elite bodyguards, wore a breastplate with a blood-red sand-scarab embossed upon it. A heavy crimson cloak rippled from his broad shoulders.

Trying not to let the relief show on her face—for she couldn't believe she'd just had the nerve to leave her husband—Jenna nodded to the head of the Lord's Watch. "Captain."

"Your Excellency," he greeted her. "Your brother is waiting for you downstairs."

Jenna eyed Captain Malik warily. She'd always found the man intimidating: her brother's silent, watchful shadow.

Together, they set off down the corridor toward the bank of elevators. "Cathal must be impatient," Jenna noted, wishing her voice didn't sound so breathless. Truth was, Tian scared her, and she was relieved to be out of his presence. "If he's sent you up to fetch me."

Indeed, her brother's trusted bodyguard rarely left his side.

In response, Captain Malik swung his visored gaze her way. However, he didn't answer. That didn't surprise her. He'd served her family for years now, and she'd only ever heard him utter a handful of words. Not that she and the captain had spent any time together—they hadn't.

Stepping into an elevator, Jenna fought the urge to sag against the golden wall behind her. Everything glowed gold in Mir-Brennan Tower—it was their clan color.

The adrenaline that had pumped through her while she'd faced Tian down ebbed, and her legs suddenly felt wobbly. He'd been furious when she left him, but it didn't matter. His days in Mir-Brennan Tower were numbered.

Anxiety tightened Jenna's stomach then. Now, all she had to do was tell her brother.

Don't worry, Cathal will understand.

Closing her eyes, she did lean back against the wall then, listening to the whoosh of the elevator as it descended to the ground floor. She was about to undo everything her father had worked so hard to achieve—an alliance between the Mir-Brennans and the Mir-Ferrins— but the past two years had proved that this marriage had done nothing to bring the two clans closer together.

All it had done was place Tian, the Mir-Ferrin clan-lord's youngest son, amongst them—making it easy to cause trouble from within. Surely, Cathal realized he'd been played?

"Are you well, Your Excellency?"

Jenna's eyes snapped open to find Captain Malik watching her. Staring up at the gleaming visor was disconcerting; it made him seem like a cyborg rather than a man.

Shifting uncomfortably, she dropped her gaze. His formality with her—and his insistence on using her ambassadorial title rather than calling her 'Lady Jenna'—was unsettling. "Yes, thank you," she replied coolly, "I'm fine."

2. CAREFUL, YOUR EXCELLENCY

THE ELEVATOR CAME to a smooth halt then, the doors springing open.

The captain stepped back and gestured for her to move past him.

Gripping her suitcase's handle, Jenna nodded, striding out through the entrance hall and another set of doors into the cavernous space beyond.

The landing bay took up the entire ground floor level of Mir-Brennan Tower. Great metal beams arched overhead like the ribcage of a massive beast. At the heart of the vast, echoey hangar reared the building's central core—a gilded column covered in ventilation hatches and climate-control panels.

A narrow, fenced walkway with several service corridors leading off it lined one side, and a number of craft—including the clan-lord's fleet of gleaming shuttles—sat on platforms facing closed doors. Outside, the temperature was already climbing; they'd keep those hangar doors closed until a shuttle needed to depart.

A mid-sized, gilded vessel sat ready to go. Her aide for this diplomatic mission, Pelicon Mir-Barus, robed in black and gold, stood before the ramp, flanked by black-armored figures: members of the Lord's Watch.

A few yards back from the shuttle, Jenna's brother, sister-in-law, and niece waited.

"There you are," Cathal greeted Jenna with a grin. Clad in flowing gold, with a black cloak hanging from his shoulders, her brother sported their clan insignia upon the breast of his tunic: a shooting star above a clenched fist. "I was beginning to worry you'd slept in."

Jenna pulled a face. "I was on my way ... but Tian delayed me." She paused then, summoning her courage. "I'm divorcing him."

Her brother's broad shoulders tightened, his dark-brown eyes widening. "What?"

"I can't pretend any longer, Cathal. I hate him. I've told him to leave."

Her voice carried high into the metal rafters above, causing a technician working on a nearby shuttle to stop work and turn to stare at her.

Surprise rippled across the clan-lord's face. "But the alliance we—"

"This marriage was supposed to bring peace, but all Tian's ever done is agitate. I know you no longer trust him … isn't it time we ended this farce?"

Silence fell, and Cathal's gaze narrowed.

Jenna tensed. Gods, she hadn't wanted to be so blunt, but it was the only way to get through to her brother. She'd hoped to have a quiet moment alone with him to say all this, but in the end, she'd blurted out her personal business with an audience. She could feel the gazes of everyone upon her.

However, her attention never wavered from her brother.

Moments passed, and then Cathal sighed heavily. "Very well, sister. You're right about Tian … I regret that I ever took his counsel." His expression softened then. "And I would never force you to remain wed to someone you loathe. Don't worry, I'll take care of him."

"Thank you," she murmured, her voice growing husky as her throat tightened.

It was a relief to know that she could count on her brother at a time like this. There had been moments, in the years since they'd lost both their parents, when she'd felt alone.

"How long will you be away, Auntie Jen?"

Jenna turned to her six-year-old niece, Beatrix. "I don't know, sweetheart," she replied, grateful to change the subject. "It depends on how long it takes to negotiate something both parties are happy with."

Bea stared up at her, blue eyes wide. The stark overhead lights inside the landing bay made the girl's pale skin seem almost translucent against her curly black hair. "Can I come?"

Jenna moved closer to her niece and hunkered down so she was at eye level with her. Maybe Jenna had once been excited about voyages—she couldn't remember what she'd been like at six—but she'd long since lost her enthusiasm for space travel. Takeoff and the jump into hyperspace always left her feeling sick, and staring out at the emptiness beyond the windows was unnerving. As determined as she was to conduct successful negotiations, she wasn't looking forward to the journey to Aura Terminal.

"Of course, you can't, Bea," she replied softly. "But I need someone to look after Daisy while I'm away … can you do that?"

Bea's expression was a blend of pleased—for she didn't yet have a droid of her own—and disgruntled. "I suppose so."

Jenna enfolded her niece in a hug and then rose to her feet, nodding to Cathal. "Time to go."

"Have a safe journey, Jen." Isla stepped up next to her daughter. Reaching out, she took Jenna's hand, squeezing firmly. "And may the Gods favor your negotiations."

A rueful smile curved Jenna's mouth. "They'd better."

"Keep me updated." Her brother's expression was serious now. "I'll want a daily report." His brow furrowed then. "Don't let them push you into anything."

"I won't," she assured him. Part of the difficulty in the coming negotiations wouldn't just be dealing with the Mir-Lelith ambassador's demands, but her brother's. Cathal didn't like to compromise. "Don't worry. When any decisions must be made, I will consult you first."

Her brother's face relaxed just a little before he reached out and put a hand on her shoulder. "If anyone can negotiate this ceasefire, it's you."

Captain Malik Mir-Draven watched the ambassador step away from her brother and his wife and continue toward the shuttle.

The clan-lord's sister was usually difficult to read, yet not so this morning. He'd noted the flush upon her face, her rapid breathing, when he'd fetched Lady Jenna from her quarters—and upon hearing that she was leaving her husband, he now knew why.

The news shouldn't have surprised him, but it did. The ruling-class often married for political reasons rather than love. Seeing Lady Jenna and her husband together of late, the tension between the couple was clear. However, this decision would have political ramifications.

Pelicon Mir-Barus bowed as the ambassador approached the ramp, the loose wattles that hung from his long neck swaying. "Good morning, Lady Jenna."

She favored him with a tight smile. "Greetings, Pelicon ... and sorry for keeping you waiting."

"No apology is needed, My Lady." The ambassador's aide paused then before gesturing to Malik. "Captain Malik will be leading your security team on this mission."

Lady Jenna glanced Malik's way before giving a stiff nod. "Captain."

"Your Excellency." Was he imagining it, or had the news he'd be leading her security team displeased the ambassador? He couldn't understand why. The pair of them barely had anything to do with each other.

In the fifteen years he'd served the Mir-Brennan ruling family, this was the first time Malik had ever accompanied the clan-lord's sister on a diplomatic mission. This wasn't his choice now either—for his place was at Cathal's side—but the clan-lord had insisted.

Malik stepped back to allow the ambassador to climb the ramp into the shuttle.

Back ramrod straight, her chin held high, Lady Jenna carried a bag slung across her front and pulled a small, gilded suitcase behind her. She took two steps up the ramp and tripped over the hem of her flowing ambassadorial robes.

In an instant, Malik was there, catching her before she sprawled face-first across the shuttle's entranceway. Gloved hand closing around her upper arm, he hauled Lady Jenna upright, while he caught her suitcase with his free hand. She staggered, falling back against him— and a sweet, spicy scent wrapped itself around him.

Malik stiffened, taken aback.

Desert Rose. It was the perfume of Idral, yet a scent he associated with the pleasure houses in Melor, the busy port town twenty klicks from Mir-Brennan Tower. Not with a noblewoman.

Not with Jenna Mir-Brennan.

Even so, he dragged the scent deep into his lungs. It brought back memories of his early childhood, of his mother—and of the narrow alleyways of Melor, where he'd run wild.

"Careful, Your Excellency," he said, gently pushing her upright.

"These damn robes," she muttered, her cheeks flushing. "Thank you, Captain."

Picking up the skirts of the flowing golden fabric that draped over her small, shapely form, Lady Jenna hurried up the ramp and disappeared inside the shuttle.

Malik watched her go. Mir-Barus moved past him, climbing the ramp in long strides. The Nandoon was so tall there was no risk of him tripping over the hem of his robes.

Ensuring his expression was neutral—although it was easy to look impassive when wearing a helmet that covered half his face—Malik turned to where the small party gathered at the base of the ramp. His gaze settled upon the clan-lord.

Cathal Mir-Brennan's face was sterner than usual. "Look after my sister, Captain," he instructed. "Much depends on these negotiations going well … but keep an eye out for anything suspicious, as we discussed."

Malik nodded. He knew what was expected of him. "I will take all the necessary precautions, My Lord." He paused then, nodding to the black-clad figure standing behind the clan-lord. "Lieutenant Anan will be your shadow while I'm away. I have briefed her on your requirements."

Cathal's mouth quirked. "Thank you, Captain. Thorough, as always."

"Of course, My Lord," Malik replied. The clan-lord might tease him over his seriousness, but Cathal Mir-Brennan headed one of the most powerful clans in this sector. It was Malik's role to ensure his safety.

He then ducked his head, acknowledging the clan-lord's wife and daughter, before turning on his heel and following the others into the shuttle.

Inside the gold-paneled entranceway, Malik hit a button and the ramp lifted with a hiss of hydraulics. Moments later, the deck beneath his feet started to vibrate. The pilots had just engaged the engines.

Striding out of the entranceway, Malik walked down a sleek, brightly lit corridor—between rows of berths—past the gleaming galley, which had booths set into the walls, and into the spacious passenger cabin behind the cockpit. Soothing Idralian pipe-music drifted out into the space.

Malik tensed. Just like the scent Desert Rose, the pipe-music took him back to his humble roots— something he didn't need when in the company of the nobility.

Especially with the clan-lord's sister nearby. Although they'd barely spoken more than a handful of words to each other over the years, Lady Jenna Mir-Brennan affected him.

She always had.

Ignoring the tightening in his gut, Malik glanced over at his team. Most of them—six of The Watch who would be joining them on this mission—had buckled themselves in, as had Mir-Barus. But the ambassador was digging through the suitcase she'd towed after her.

Malik stopped before her, irritation feathering through him. Why couldn't the woman sit down and buckle herself in like everyone else? "We shall be leaving shortly, Your Excellency."

He noted how Lady Jenna tensed at his use of the honorific. They weren't yet at Aura Terminal, and she hadn't yet stepped into her role as ambassador, but he insisted on using it. It was a mark of respect, and seeing that it annoyed her surprised him. It also made Malik want to continue using it.

"I know," she muttered, snapping her case shut. She then cast him an imperious look. "Very well ... please stow my case, Captain."

Malik picked up her luggage and shoved it into the overhead compartment, while the ambassador sat down and started searching through her bag now.

"Have you forgotten something, Your Excellency?"

"Evidently," she replied, her tone clipped. She didn't look up from her riffling. "I was sure I'd packed my space-sickness pills."

"We have some onboard," he replied. "I shall retrieve them."

3. A GREAT START

WITHOUT ANOTHER WORD, Malik retraced his steps to the galley, where he retrieved a glass of water and a bottle of space-sickness tablets. Lady Jenna wasn't the only traveler he'd encountered whose stomach rebelled at space travel. This shuttle had a cabinet full of nausea medicine.

The task gave him a moment to compose himself. He was always careful to keep his visceral reaction to the clan-lord's haughty sister buried, hidden from sight. However, her proximity unsettled him all the same.

Not for the first time, he wished Cathal had put someone else in charge of this mission.

Returning to the seating area, he passed Lady Jenna the water and tablets before lowering himself into a seat next to her. He'd just clicked his harness into place when the shuttle's rumbling engines rose to a whine, and the craft rolled forward.

Small windows lined both sides of the seating area. In front of them, the hangar doors rolled open to reveal bright sunlight. Scorched red earth lay beyond, shimmering in the heat.

The shuttle cleared the doors, sliding out onto the launch pad beyond. As they lifted off, Lady Jenna swallowed a space-sickness tablet. Jaw flexing, she then shifted her attention to the window. Malik noted the light sheen of sweat covering her face. This was the first time he'd ever traveled with the woman; he hadn't realized she disliked space travel. It wasn't ideal in an ambassador, for her role called for frequent trips throughout the sector.

The shuttle gained height, and then, moments later, they were accelerating away from Mir-Brennan Tower. Craning his neck, Malik caught a glimpse of the retreating fortress—a wide, thin, gilded blade piercing the dusky sky—and then they were flying over a sea of rocky pinnacles and deep chasms. Idral possessed a brutal beauty. The planet consisted of one large mountainous continent studded with thriving towns and a great, deep ocean that pounded its rocky shores.

They were gaining height now. Below, Malik caught sight of the coast. Lines of white surf crashed against rust-colored cliffs. Vicious waves, some of them enormous, battered the coastline, thanks to the pull of Idral's two moons: Mira and Elda. For that reason, most of the planet's inhabitants lived inland.

The shuttle climbed higher still, shuddering as it hit turbulence. And then they were looking down upon the planet's curve, silhouetted against the inky depths of space. Mira, the largest of the two moons, hove into sight then, silver and pock-marked with craters.

Malik continued to gaze out the window. It didn't matter how many times he flew, he never tired of seeing Idral from the sky.

He caught sight then of a large, crab-shaped battle-cruiser that also orbited the planet. It's pale gold surface gleaming against the glittering void, *The Star Siren* was one of three ships that warded Idral. With the escalating conflict between the Mir-Brennans and the Mir-Leliths, Cathal kept security tight—even here, far from Mir-Lelith territory.

A murmured oath drew his attention then. Lady Jenna's face had paled, lines of tension bracketing her full mouth.

"Brace yourself," he warned her. "We'll be making the jump into hyperspace in a couple of minutes."

She swallowed hard before nodding.

The pilots would be maneuvering the shuttle into a lane. The route to Aura Terminal—a border station that sat on the boundary between the Rith and Eos sectors—was a well-traveled one, and being a clan-lord's ship, the shuttle could make the journey faster than most: twelve hours instead of the twenty-four it would have taken a passenger liner.

"I usually try deep breathing if I feel queasy during the jump, Lady Jenna," Pelicon Mir-Barus spoke up from the opposite aisle. "It helps."

"That works for me too," Malik murmured.

"Thanks, but I've tried that," Lady Jenna replied, her voice strained. "It's not just the jump that bothers me … it's being stuck in here." She gestured to the spacious yet spartan interior of the shuttle. "While just outside the walls there's … nothing."

"Try not to think about it, Your Excellency," Malik advised her. He knew the emptiness of space scared some people, for it was as cold and inevitable as death. Nonetheless, he'd have thought the clan-lord's sister would have taken it in her stride, as Cathal did.

The shuttle jolted then, throwing them all back in their seats—and then the stars beyond the windows changed from sparkling pinpricks to flowing streaks of light.

"Gods," Lady Jenna gasped. "I'm going to be sick."

Malik reached into the pocket on the back of the seat in front of him, yanked out a bag, and handed it to her.

The ambassador clutched the bag tightly, her face ashen.

Leaning back in his seat, Malik shifted his gaze to the panel lighting overhead. The pilots preferred the passengers remained harnessed for a few minutes after making the jump into hyperspace, otherwise he'd have gotten up and given Lady Jenna some privacy.

He frowned then, knowing the visor he wore hid his expression, and waited for the retching to begin.

Serves you right for fantasizing about her.

It was true. Lady Jenna might barely notice his existence, but that hadn't stopped him from taking himself in hand at night to thoughts of what she looked like naked. He'd been twenty when he'd been promoted to The Watch. Lady Jenna was an awkward teenager then, although she'd matured into a sensual beauty.

She'd worn a revealing gown to a charity function recently that had all the dignitaries gawking. Malik had found it hard not to stare at her curves too. His role demanded rigid discipline—but he wasn't made of stone. That night he'd lain in bed imagining ripping the silky material off that lush body and taking her hard up against the wall.

But now he was escorting her on an important mission, and he had to focus. Perhaps seeing Lady Jenna as a fallible human being rather than his fantasy woman would prevent any more inappropriate thoughts.

Moments passed, and then Idralian pipe-music started once again.

Glancing the ambassador's way, Malik's gaze settled upon a pinched, wan face. Lady Jenna sat rigidly in her seat, holding her bag—which she hadn't yet used.

A 'ping' sounded, letting them know it was safe to move about the cabin.

Unlatching his harness, Malik rose to his feet and turned to her. "Do you need anything else, Your Excellency?"

Lady Jenna swallowed before shaking her head. "I should be fine … now we've made the jump," she said huskily. Her grip tightened on the sick bag once more. "I'll hold onto this for a bit longer though … just to be sure."

We're off to a great start.

Taking a sip of water, Jenna swallowed down the sting of bile in the back of her throat.

It had been a while since she'd actually thrown up during takeoff or the jump into hyperspace—but she'd come very close to embarrassing herself today. She was on edge, more so than usual. A lot was riding on these negotiations, she'd just left her husband, and Captain Malik's intimidating presence had only made her anxiety worse.

The gleaming black helm he wore covered half the man's face—leaving only a full mouth, a strong jaw with a slight cleft in his chin, and bronzed skin visible—yet she'd seen the way his lips compressed when he'd handed her the sick bag.

He'd been judging her; she was sure of it.

Pulling a face, Jenna took another gulp of water. What did it matter what the Captain of the Lord's Watch thought of her?

"Are you feeling better, Lady Jenna?"

Glancing left, she caught Pelicon Mir-Barus's eye. The Nandoon's long body was still folded up in the seat. It must have been uncomfortable for him, for the seats had been designed with humans in mind. Nonetheless, her aide didn't seem to mind. Pelicon had an unflappable, easy-going temperament that she appreciated more than ever today.

"Yes, thank you." She unclipped her harness and rose to her feet, swallowing as her belly churned once more. "Although, I think I'll go and lie down for a bit." She then moved out into the aisle between the rows of seats.

Pelicon nodded, a gesture that caused both his long proboscis and the wattles upon his neck to waggle. "A wise idea ... however, I'd like to talk to you later, if you don't mind? We need to prepare for our preliminary meeting with the Mir-Leliths."

Jenna swallowed a sigh. "Of course." This journey was long enough to give them plenty of time to plan for the negotiations. "I'll see you later."

Turning, Jenna walked straight into a hard wall of muscle and steel. The impact jarred, and she bit down on her tongue as she reeled back.

Gloved hands caught her by the shoulders, hauling her upright.

Tasting blood, Jenna looked up into Captain Malik's visored gaze.

"Careful, Your Excellency." His tone was low, almost a drawl.

Heat rose to Jenna's cheeks, yet again. What was the matter with her today? Ever since greeting this man, she'd turned into a clumsy, jumpy idiot. Nonetheless, the way he said 'Your Excellency' was really starting to grate on her. The title wasn't necessary—it was a formality used in diplomatic settings.

Was he using it to goad her?

"Yes, well … I didn't realize you were standing right behind me," she muttered.

"I wasn't. You ran into me."

A cough sounded behind Jenna, a muffled laugh from one of The Watch. The warmth on her face increased to a burn.

"Excuse me," she replied coldly.

Nodding, the captain moved aside. Jenna then dragged up what little dignity she still possessed and strode past him, out of the seating cabin.

Ensconced in the largest of the berths and hidden behind closed doors, Jenna sank down onto a bunk and covered her scalding cheeks with her hands.

She really needed to get ahold of herself.

Her encounter with Tian couldn't have knocked her off-balance so badly, could it? His aggression had shaken her, yet she was still relieved that she'd had the guts to finally rid herself of him.

No, it wasn't Tian. Instead, Captain Malik unnerved her.

Jenna's daily routine at Mir-Brennan Tower didn't bring them in direct contact, but that didn't mean she hadn't noticed him over the years. The tall, broad-shouldered man clad in black and crimson—a silent, watchful presence always standing two steps behind Cathal—was impossible to miss.

She didn't understand why he disturbed her—none of the other bodyguards did. If only her brother had sent someone else to head her security team.

Straightening up, Jenna surveyed the berth. It was simply yet elegantly furnished: soft white carpet covered the floor, a gilded mirror sat upon the exterior wall, and small golden lights studded the ceiling. Like inside the cabin, gentle pipe-music drifted through the berth— music she always requested for her shuttle journeys— providing a calm, serene environment.

"I just need to rest," she murmured, dimming the lights before stretching out on the bunk. She'd stayed up late the night before, writing notes for the upcoming negotiations, and hadn't slept well afterward; fatigue was clearly affecting her. "Everything will be easier to deal with then."

4. DESERT ROSE

JENNA AWOKE WITH a headache and a metallic taste in her mouth. Blinking, she rolled onto her side and checked the time on her tablet.

She'd been asleep five hours. Indeed, she'd been tired.

Her stomach growled then. The nausea of space-sickness had passed, as it always did eventually, and she was now ravenous.

Getting up, she crossed to a gleaming white basin in the corner of the berth, splashed water on her face, and undid her hair. She'd been wearing it up in an elaborate knot upon the crown of her head, but the bun now listed drunkenly to one side. Braiding it so that her hair hung in a plait down her back, Jenna frowned at the image in the mirror.

She was only twenty-seven, but she looked older these days. Her face bore lines of strain, and her eyes had dark circles under them. The conflict with the Mir-Leliths had preyed on her mind of late, but her marriage to Tian Mir-Ferrin had also taken its toll.

Jenna sucked in a deep breath, reminding herself that she didn't have to worry about Tian any longer. *When I return to Idral, he'll be gone.*

She exhaled slowly then, tension draining out of her.

It was over. Never again would she have to sit opposite him at the dinner table and weather his barbed comments. Never again would she have to suffer his touch. Their wedding night had revealed Tian to be a rough, insensitive lover. Right from the beginning, he'd tried to dominate her, control her, both in private and in public. And when his efforts met resistance, she saw a side to him that scared her.

Pushing thoughts of her soon-to-be-ex-husband aside, Jenna turned from the mirror, adjusted her clothing, and exited the berth. Beyond, the hum of the life-support greeted her. She turned left, walking from the berths down to the galley.

To her surprise, she found it empty, save for Captain Malik. Seated at one of the booths, he was eating what looked like flatbread, salted cheese, and dried fruit. The man still had his helmet on, visor pulled down. Did he ever take it off?

"Captain," she greeted him politely.

"Your Excellency."

Clenching her jaw at his drawled greeting, she turned from him and focused on the food replicator. The arrogant captain was the last person she wanted to see right now. However, her hunger forced her to stand her ground. "Poached monet and flat-bread," she instructed the machine before hesitating. "And a glass of pori-pori."

The dispenser before her whirred, and then a cloche-covered tray slid out onto the ledge.

Picking it up, Jenna turned.

She was about to move down the gangway and pick a booth as far from Captain Malik as possible when stubbornness rose within her.

Jenna was tired of men trying to intimidate her. She'd shared a bed with a bully, had weathered his scorn, and wasn't going to let another man cow her. She hadn't risen to the role of ambassador because she was the clan-lord's sister. Jenna was a natural diplomat. She knew how to charm, and when necessary, how to manipulate. She'd have this man eating out of her hand by the time this diplomatic mission ended, even if it killed her.

And so, she slid into Captain Malik's booth, opposite him, and flashed him a disarming smile. "May I join you?"

If her move surprised him, he hid it well. Only the slightest tightening of his mouth betrayed him. "You just have, Your Excellency."

Jenna kept smiling. "You don't have to keep calling me that, you know?" she said sweetly. "*My Lady* or *Lady Jenna* will suffice outside of negotiations."

Captain Malik didn't reply.

Satisfied she'd made her point, Jenna lifted the cloche off her food. The fragrant scent of fish poached in herbs wafted over the booth.

"Monet," her companion murmured, his sensual mouth curving just a little. "You like Idralian peasant food?"

Jenna stiffened. *Peasant food?* "Yes … as do you," she replied, gesturing to the tray before him and the glass of amber-hued pori-pori at his elbow. The juice was made from a desert fruit that only grew on this planet.

"I grew up in Melor's southern ward," he replied, his voice carefully bland. "What's your reason?"

Jenna caught the challenge in his voice and wondered if he had a chip on his shoulder about their differing classes. He'd always treated her brother with respect, but perhaps he nursed a hidden resentment. "I might have been born into a ruling family, but Idral's my home too," she pointed out, keeping her tone light. "I love the planet … its rust-colored mountains, the strong iron tang of the air at dawn … the scent of musk-melon and spices wafting through the streets of towns, and the chime of temple bells, echoing across the rooftops as the sun sets."

Her voice trailed off there, as embarrassment rose. She hadn't meant to speak so openly—but he'd gotten under her skin.

Yes, they came from different worlds, but she was as much a citizen of Idral as he was. Once her grandfather had seized power from the Mir-Ferrins, he'd allowed Mir-Brennan citizens from all over the territory to settle on Idral. Located at the geographic heart of the sector, the planet was a bustling trade hub. As such, many Mir-Brennans had chosen to move from damp, cold Staturine II, which had over-crowding issues, to Idral.

Indeed, the seat of the Mir-Brennan clan now resided on the desert planet.

"You have a romanticized vision of Idral, My Lady," he replied after a long pause. "Those of us who grew up sheltering from its searing heat, and defending ourselves from its wildlife, view it a little differently."

"You don't share my connection to the planet then?"

"Of course, I do … I'm a Mir-Draven. We *hail* from Idral." He took a sip from his glass. "You're wearing Desert Rose."

Jenna stiffened. It wasn't a question, but a statement—and it had caught her off-guard. It surprised her the captain recognized the perfume she wore. Nonetheless, she had been in close quarters with him twice since nearly face-planting while boarding the shuttle—and the scent was a distinctive one.

"Yes," she admitted. "It's my favorite perfume."

His visored gaze remained upon her. "It suits you."

Silence fell, and Jenna picked up her fork. This conversation wasn't going as she'd envisaged. Instead of establishing control, she was starting to feel self-conscious. She needed to steer their exchange in another direction. "Why are you wearing your helmet while eating?" she asked. "Surely, it's uncomfortable?"

"I always wear it on duty."

"Can you remove it please."

Captain Malik, who'd been about to take a bite of flatbread and cheese, froze. "Excuse me?"

"Take off your helmet, Captain. I find it off-putting talking to someone when I can't see their eyes."

Tension rippled across those broad shoulders, his jaw tightening. Victory thrilled through Jenna. Finally, she'd put this man on the back foot.

Moments passed before the captain put down his piece of bread and reached up with both hands. He removed his helmet and placed it on the table next to him.

And then he raised his chin, his gaze fusing with hers.

Jenna observed his face frankly.

Violet eyes, framed by dark brows, high cheekbones, and a proud aquiline nose—no one would ever mistake this man for anything but an Idral native. He had jet-black hair, tousled by removing the helmet, and skin that was bronzed even without going out in the blazing Idral sun. Of course, as he'd just reminded her, the Mir-Dravens had originated here. Nonetheless, his looks were also distinctive, and that gaze would give him away anywhere. The only humans she'd seen with purple eyes hailed from Idral.

No one in Jenna's family had eyes of that color, for the Mir-Brennan ruling-family were from off-world. They'd only been living on Idral for around fifty years. Her family hailed from Staturine II.

Seconds passed, and discomfort feathered down Jenna's spine. Perhaps it had been a mistake to ask him to take off his helmet. The man's violet gaze speared her with such intensity, it was difficult to hold his eye.

But she did.

"That's better," she murmured. "There's a man under there, after all."

Jenna then took a forkful of fish and began to eat. Often synth food lacked the flavor of the real thing—the Mir-Brennan food replicators weren't as good as the Mir-Ferrin ones—but this was tasty. Hunger hollowed out her belly. Even Malik Mir-Draven's brooding presence couldn't prevent her enjoyment.

The captain eyed her. "You've recovered from your space-sickness then?"

Nodding, she took another mouthful of poached fish, chewed, and swallowed. "Yes, thank you for your concern, Captain … it always subsides once we're underway."

His mouth lifted at the corners. He picked up his glass and drained the contents.

"Lady Jenna." Pelicon Mir-Barus appeared in the gangway, the hem of his black and gold robes brushing the deck as he bowed. "Did you enjoy your rest?"

"I did," Jenna replied, reaching for her own glass. "I was more tired than I realized."

Her aide's long snout twitched. "Are you ready to discuss the negotiations?"

"I'll be right there … I've almost finished my meal."

"Of course, My Lady. I shall await you in the cabin." With a swish of robes, Mir-Barus retreated.

"An ambassador has many demands on her time," Captain Malik observed when they were alone once more. "Mir-Barus is eager to get to work already."

Jenna picked up her fork and speared another chunk of fish. "As am I."

The shuttle came out of hyperspace with a lurch, its fuselage shuddering.

The jolt didn't bother Malik. He'd gotten used to it over the years. Nonetheless, the woman seated next to him bristled with tension. The ambassador would never be a spacer, that was for certain.

Outside the windows, the stars morphed from streaks of glittering light to familiar bolts of fire. However, Malik wasn't interested in what lay beyond the shuttle at present.

Instead, Lady Jenna kept drawing his attention.

Despite her rigid posture, the ambassador's face was a picture of composure. She was full of contradictions. Until this journey, he'd seen her as the beautiful yet aloof sister of the man he served. He'd entertained a few inappropriate fantasies about Jenna Mir-Brennan over the years, but he'd also dismissed her as stuck-up. She clearly thought herself better than the likes of him— something that just added to the fantasy.

But, from the beginning of this journey, she'd surprised him. Her space-sickness aside, she had a vulnerability to her he hadn't expected. Nonetheless, when she'd slid into the booth opposite him in the galley a few hours earlier, he'd noted the Mir-Brennan pride.

Like her brother, she didn't like to be bested.

He'd been taken aback that she wanted him to remove his helmet, yet he'd done as ordered.

"Ambassador," the pilot's voice crackled through the comm, interrupting Malik's train of thought. "The landing bays are congested at present so tower control has put us in a holding position … we should be able to dock in around ten minutes."

Glancing out the window, Malik caught sight of a bristling outline starboard. They were approaching Aura Terminal.

"Thank you, Captain," Lady Jenna replied.

Moments later, the shuttle veered left and began a slow circuit above the border-station. Named after 'Aura', Goddess of Prosperity, the space-station lived up to its name, for a great deal of inter-sector business was conducted here.

Lady Jenna stared down at it. "I always forget just how big Aura Terminal is," she murmured.

"Population three point four million … and steadily climbing," Malik replied. "It's popular with those wanting to live, and trade, outside sector politics."

The ambassador nodded, her full lips compressing. "I'm not surprised … what with the war going on in the Eos sector."

"And in ours too," he reminded her.

Lady Jenna nodded, her attention remaining upon the station. "It's perfect for political negotiations … neutral territory." Her gaze narrowed then, and she leaned closer to the window. "I never realized there were so many trees down there."

Malik unclipped his harness, moving closer so he could look over her shoulder. That was a mistake, for the sweet, spicy scent of Desert Rose wrapped itself around him, causing his pulse to quicken.

Jidea preserve him, he really had to shut down his attraction to this woman. Lusting after her from afar was one thing, continuing to do so when they were in close quarters was another.

Trying to focus, Malik gazed down at Aura Terminal's 'upper-side'. A transparent shield protected a city of high buildings, green squares, and yes—trees. Long avenues and parks full of them.

The upper-side was where the station's wealthy lived, while everyone else resided on the lower-side. And as the shuttle turned, angling now for one of the loading bays, Malik caught sight of Aura's underbelly. Blinking lights, snaking tubes, thick steel plating, and antennas covered a bloated hull. The residents of the lower-side didn't get to live amongst greenery like those above.

The shuttle nosed its way closer, and before them yawned a huge landing bay. The pilot hadn't been exaggerating—it was busy. Spacecraft of all shapes and sizes packed the brightly lit space.

Turning from the window, Malik switched into work mode. He rose to his feet and moved out into the aisle where the six bodyguards he'd brought with him were forming a line. "Tenet, Zara, and Cor … you are to lead us out," he ordered. "The rest of you will bring up the rear." He paused then, his gaze sweeping over their helmed faces. "As the station's busier than usual, we'll need to be vigilant on the way up to the conference center."

"Are you expecting trouble?"

Malik turned to find the ambassador standing behind him. She'd slung her bag over her front and retrieved her case from the overhead locker.

Now that he was wearing his helmet again, Malik let his gaze roam boldly over her face. "Not especially," he replied, "but it's my job to be prepared."

"And I'm relieved to hear it, Captain." Pelicon Mir-Barus unfolded himself from his seat and pulled his suitcase down. "You can never be too careful in these border stations… they attract all sorts."

The ambassador eyed her aide. "I thought the Aura Garrison kept law and order well here?"

"Oh, they do," Malik replied, turning away as the shuttle trembled. It had just touched down on the docking station. A moment later, the rumble of the engines slowed to a halt. "But it pays never to be complacent."

5. UNDER ATTACK

JENNA PICKED HER way carefully down the ramp. The spectacle she'd made of herself upon boarding was still fresh in her mind, and she didn't want to repeat it. She was usually confident and dignified on diplomatic missions, and she wished to keep her equilibrium.

Captain Malik flanked her left side, Mir-Barus her right—with three bodyguards leading the party, and another three following. Bright overhead lights reflected off gleaming black armor.

Officials waited for them at the edge of the docking station, tablets in hand, to check their papers. It was noisy inside the landing bay: the clang and whirr of machinery, and the hiss of hydraulics, blended with the rise and fall of voices, echoing in the vast space.

Jenna didn't mind the noise though; she was just relieved to get off the shuttle. Aura Terminal wasn't a planet, but it was so big she no longer felt like the vacuum of space was pressing in on her from all sides.

Once the paperwork had been done, they headed off the docking station and out of the landing bay. An even busier terminal greeted them, filled with crowds of travelers waiting to board passenger liners.

Jenna breathed in a lungful of the warm, scented, and oxygen-rich air as soon as she entered the terminal. A smile then curved her lips. Of course, the upper-side's greenery extended to the spaceport as well. The huge space resembled an enormous hot-house garden. Lush green foliage, festooned with tropical flowers, climbed the metal walls, and a domed roof decorated in swirling silver and blue arched overhead.

Unlike the stations within the various clan territories, no banners hung from the ceiling bearing insignias or mottos. This was neutral territory. Instead, a fountain depicting a tall, robed female figure, her hands reaching for the sky, dominated the center of the terminal. Aura greeted and farewelled travelers.

Citizens of all galactic clans were welcome here—it was a place where you could leave clan allegiances behind, where you could start afresh.

As Jenna moved across the floor, a group of Nandoon loped past, pulling huge trunks behind them. A few yards away, a family of Gibbits argued noisily by the ticketing-droids, furry hands gesturing and pointing.

Jenna's escort cut a path through the crowd. Travelers smartly side-stepped to avoid them, and loitering groups parted to let them through. It was hardly surprising, for Captain Malik and his team were an intimidating sight.

Jenna continued to look about her with interest, spying figures patrolling the verdant edges of the terminal. Lean, fit, and clad in dark-grey uniforms, laser-rifles at the ready, the Aura Garrison emitted an air of cool vigilance.

Of course, Captain Malik and his team also carried weapons—for they had special status as bodyguards to a diplomatic envoy—but the sight of the sleek rifles the garrison wielded unnerved Jenna just a little. Was it really necessary?

"The Aura Garrison are an intimidating lot, aren't they?" she murmured to Pelicon.

Her aide nodded. "They are … but I find their presence reassuring."

"The garrison won't bother you, if you don't bother them," Captain Malik rumbled. "All the same … it's best to keep out of their way."

Exiting the terminal, the Mir-Brennan party crossed the entrance hall and made their way to the transpod station. They'd been waiting a couple of minutes on the wide platform when a sleek transpod, bound for the Business District on the upper-side, glided to a halt in front of them. Transparent doors sprang open, and a wave of passengers disembarked.

Stepping onto the long capsule-shaped pod, Jenna and Pelicon settled themselves down on a padded bench seat near the rear doors while their bodyguards took up positions around them.

A soft hum vibrated through the pod, and then it glided away from the platform, whisking through the network of narrow tunnels. The transpod moved swiftly, but it was a lengthy journey upward, all the same, for they had to stop regularly to load and off-load passengers. By the time they reached the end of the line, the pod was packed.

The doors opened, and Jenna rose to her feet, letting the security team flank her as she stepped onto the platform.

Moments later, she'd left the transpod station behind and was standing on the upper-side, looking up at a starry sky through the transparent dome.

"Lady Jenna." Captain Malik's voice held an edge of impatience. "I'd prefer we didn't loiter."

Casting the bodyguard an exasperated look, Jenna resumed walking. He could relax a little; she'd only stopped for a moment so she could get her bearings.

She followed her escort down a wide path, flanked by spreading trees. Aura Terminal's Business District was a blend of leafy and austere. Indeed, the air up here was light and fresh. They passed tinkling fountains and a large moonstone statue depicting two galactic goddesses—Fara and Nain—in combat. It was a scene Jenna had gazed upon many times of the two sisters: the Goddesses of Light and Darkness locked in an eternal struggle.

Well-dressed citizens drifted by, taking a break from work, and Jenna viewed them with envy. She'd always wanted to explore this station during past visits but never seemed to find the time. What would it be like to be able to wander the avenues of Aura Terminal as a tourist? Without bodyguards. At her own pace. She suddenly craved the freedom.

Glancing right at Mir-Barus, Jenna flashed him a smile. "Do you know Aura well, Pelicon?"

The diplomat swung his head toward her. "Very well … my family comes from a nearby system."

"Once negotiations are over, I'd like to stay on an extra day and explore. Would you be my guide?"

Pelicon smiled back, his small dark eyes crinkling at the corners. "It would be an honor, Lady Jenna." He paused then. "As long as your brother permits it, of course."

Jenna flashed him a smile. If these negotiations were successful, Cathal wouldn't deny her a short break. "Let me worry about him."

The avenue ended, and they walked out onto the central plaza, the heart of the business district. The conference center loomed on the far edge, its smooth sides gleaming. Gaze lingering upon it, Jenna wondered if the Mir-Lelith delegation had already arrived.

A milling crowd filled the square; the plaza was busier than she recalled from her last visit. It was lunchtime. Citizens of many galactic races perched on stone benches, chatting as they ate, while others crossed the crowded plaza on their way to meetings. Meanwhile, brightly lit screens hung from the facades of surrounding buildings, advertising exotic vacations and luxury beauty treatments. The latest news headlines scrolled underneath.

Jenna glanced at where Captain Malik walked at her shoulder. Her bodyguard's visored gaze moved right and left, surveying his surroundings.

They were halfway across the plaza now, and Jenna looked up at the screens once more. The vid-screens were incongruous with such park-like environs, garish even, a reminder that she was on a bustling space station. However, as she watched, the advertisement for holiday homes in the Manix System froze.

The screen went blank for an instant, and then a newsreader appeared.

The man's voice was muted, although subtitles scrolled underneath—and as Jenna read them, she went cold.

Skidding to a halt, she grabbed hold of Captain Malik's arm. "Look!"

The entire escort stopped then, their gazes flicking to the news broadcast unfolding above them. Likewise, many of the office workers milling around them swiveled to watch.

Behind the newsreader, a familiar landscape of rust-colored mountains and a dusky-pink sky filled the screen.

And then the words started to scroll: *Just hours ago, the Mir-Ferrin space fleet launched an attack on planet Idral in the Gastira System, in Mir-Brennan territory.*

One of the guards behind Jenna whispered a curse.

It's reported that after a violent exchange, Mican Mir-Ferrin has seized control of Mir-Brennan Tower. A Mir-Ferrin blockade is now in place around the planet.

Jenna's heart started to kick against her breastbone. "Gods ... no."

Aghast, she watched as the newsreader paused, one hand rising to his earpiece.

We have a live broadcast from Mir-Brennan Tower.

The image changed then, and there was the Mir-Ferrin clan-lord, standing in Cathal's solar, flanked by two towering bronze battle-droids. Lean and clad in flowing robes the same color as his intimidating metal bodyguards, Mican Mir-Ferrin wore a rare smile. His lips then began to move.

Fifty years ago, the Mir-Brennans robbed us of this planet. Now clan Mir-Ferrin has launched a successful military operation and reclaimed what is rightfully ours.

The camera panned out, revealing Tian standing at his father's side.

"You bastard," she whispered, her stomach clenching.

Mican Mir-Ferrin resumed talking. *We have the Mir-Brennan clan-lord, and his wife and daughter, under house arrest.*

The camera panned out farther still—and there was Cathal, Isla, and Beatrix. All three of them were wearing wrist restraints. Isla and her daughter's faces were chalk-white. Cathal's forehead was bleeding, and his expression was thunderous.

The camera zoomed in on Mican Mir-Ferrin's face once more. The clan-lord's gaze narrowed. *Lord Mir-Brennan will now be put on trial for the crimes of his clan.* He paused then, his gaze narrowing. *If found guilty, he will be executed.*

Jenna stared up at the screen, barely able to believe what she'd just read—just seen.

Was this some elaborate hoax?

Her pulse thundered in her ears. No, it was real.

The Mir-Ferrins had launched an unprovoked attack on her people—their allies.

Nausea rolled over her then. *Merciful Syr, this is my fault.*

Tian had done this because she was divorcing him.

But how had he organized the attack so quickly? She hadn't even been away from Idral a day.

Jenna started to sweat. *He's been planning for this … waiting for the right moment to strike … and I was the catalyst.*

"Lady Jenna." Captain Malik's voice intruded, low and hard. "We need to get you inside … now."

Jerking her attention from the screen, Jenna nodded.

She was just about to resume her path toward the conference center when the high-pitched whine of detonating laser bolts ripped through the plaza.

Screams erupted, and the crowd scattered.

Next to Jenna, Pelicon Mir-Barus grunted, clutching at his side. An instant later, his long body folded in on itself and her aide sank to his knees upon the pavers.

"Pelicon!" Jenna let go of the suitcase she'd been towing and dropped to a crouch next to him.

"Run, Lady Jenna!" the Nandoon wheezed, clutching at the dark, wet stain that flowered through his robes.

"Not without you."

Chin kicking up, she realized that her bodyguards had formed a circle around her and Mir-Barus. They'd drawn laser-pistols and were firing back at the unseen assailants.

"Who's attacking us?"

None of the security team answered.

Two of them fell, sprawling to the ground, and a scream clawed its way up Jenna's throat.

Her aide staggered to his feet, his breathing labored. "Come ... we ... must—"

Pelicon Mir-Barus never finished his sentence, for a laser bolt hit him in the back. The Nandoon lurched forward, colliding with Jenna—and the pair of them went down.

Pinned under his body, she struggled to free herself. Her breathing came in pants now, fear thundering through her. Pelicon had been right. She had to run—flee like a rock-bounder.

Scrambling out from under the Nandoon on her hands and knees, she saw that three more of her bodyguards were down—their black-armored bodies spread-eagled upon the ground. Just the captain and one of his guards remained. They both had cyan-shields up—glowing blue spheres that projected from their wrist-comms—yet they wouldn't hold off the hail of laser bolts for long.

Captain Malik and his companion were edging back, stepping over the bodies of the fallen, as they fired into the crowd—at the figures who were closing in on them.

Nothing about them identified the attackers. It was difficult to get a proper look, but it appeared they were men and women dressed just like the workers surrounding them—in well-cut tunics and pants.

The captain reached her then, grabbing Jenna by the arm, and hauling her to her feet. "Time to go."

Chaos reigned in the plaza now, as workers fled, their screams echoing high into the sphere. In the distance, the wail of sirens cut through the din.

The plaza was rapidly clearing, making it even easier for their attackers to surround them.

An agonized cry sliced through the air as the last of Malik's guards fell.

Now there was only Jenna and the captain left.

Malik unhooked something from his belt. He then hurled the object at their attackers and threw himself at Jenna, knocking her to the ground once more.

An explosion rocked the space station, causing the ground beneath Jenna to buck and shudder. A wave of searing heat broke over them, and then debris rained down. Jenna cringed under her bodyguard's muscular form, her ears ringing.

Moments passed before Captain Malik climbed off her and rolled smoothly to his feet, pulling Jenna with him.

Thick dark smoke billowed around them, momentarily obscuring their surroundings. Jenna coughed as acrid dust caught in her throat. Her ears were still ringing, and she felt unsteady on her feet.

"What was that?"

"A pyro-grenade," he replied tersely. "Come on." With that, he took hold of her arm and hauled her after him.

Jenna stumbled as she ran. Her legs suddenly felt rubbery, as if they might give way from under her at any moment. Terror had rendered her clumsy; her feet wouldn't seem to cooperate. After a few meters, Captain Malik was dragging her through the panicked crowd. Jenna didn't care. She was desperate to get away from their attackers; she didn't mind if he threw her over his shoulder, as long as he got her to safety.

Leaving the square behind, and dodging workers, who were also trying to escape, they headed between two buildings.

"Wait!" Jenna gasped, clawing at the captain's arm. "Shouldn't we be heading for the conference center?"

"Whoever wants us dead is blocking our way."

"But we—"

"Go anywhere near that building and you'll die before you step through the front door."

They were still running, down a street lined with benches and low shrubs. After a block, they left the chaos behind.

The wail of sirens grew louder, reaching a crescendo above them. Craning her neck, Jenna spied a group of sleek hoppers speeding toward the plaza, lights flashing.

"Who were they?" she gasped, her voice cracking as panic seized her by the throat.

"No idea," Malik replied. Jenna's lungs were heaving now, yet he hardly sounded out of breath.

"They looked like Aura citizens."

"They did … but they moved like trained killers."

They sprinted out onto a wide avenue where a shunt had just drawn to a screeching halt. The long silver caterpillar, perched upon a single slender rail, shuttled citizens from one end of the upper-side to the other. With a hiss of hydraulics, the shunt lowered a ramp, allowing a flood of passengers to disembark and alight.

Captain Malik slowed to a halt and slid into the line, pulling Jenna with him. Those already waiting for the shunt were looking around, curious as to what was going on. Yanking off his helmet, he then cast a look over his shoulder, scanning their surroundings to ensure they hadn't been followed.

It seemed they hadn't, and moments later, they were aboard.

The shunt was narrower than the transpod. It was also crowded, standing room only. Faces swiveled toward the tall man clad in black wearing a tattered crimson cape and the disheveled woman at his side.

Breathing hard, sweaty, and splattered in blood and dust, Jenna knew she was drawing attention to herself. She tried to slow her breathing, tried to keep the fear from her face, but it was nearly impossible.

The doors slid shut, and the shunt rolled off the platform, gathering speed as it headed down the avenue toward its next stop.

Peering over Captain Malik's shoulder through the window, Jenna looked back at the street they'd exited from. Her blood still pounded in her ears, yet so far, there wasn't anyone pursuing them.

"Do you think we've lost them?" she whispered.

The captain's mouth thinned. "That grenade would have killed a few," he muttered. "But they'll still be hunting us."

Jenna moved closer to him, placing a hand upon the breast plate of his armor, pretending to show affection to her companion so others wouldn't overhear their conversation. "Who's after us?"

His purple gaze bored into hers. "Think, Lady Jenna … who'd want you dead?"

Her throat closed, cold sweat beading on her skin.

If she hadn't just witnessed her planet, her family, captured by the Mir-Ferrins, she'd have blamed the Mir-Leliths for this. Perhaps they didn't want a ceasefire after all. They had nothing to gain by killing her, but these ceasefire negotiations could have been a ruse.

However, she'd seen that newsreel, had read the words that scrolled across the screen above her.

"Tian Mir-Ferrin," she whispered.

6. ALL FOR NOTHING

THE SHUNT TOOK them into a far more densely populated area of the upper-side. Thick crowds lined the sidewalks, and shops crammed in on the ground floor level, with high-rise accommodation rearing above. Even from inside the shunt, sirens reached them.

The Garrison would be looking for those involved in the attack.

Malik waited until they were in the busiest shopping area before he took Lady Jenna's arm and steered her off the shunt and down the ramp.

After their initial words, she'd fallen silent. Now, her face was bloodless, her mahogany eyes haunted—and the arm he held trembled.

He needed to get her to safety before shock hit.

Outdoors, the blare of the sirens grew louder. Some of the shoppers stopped, craning their necks upward. Moments later, a squad of silver hoppers streaked past.

Jenna's arm went rigid against Malik's. "Shouldn't we contact the garrison?" she whispered. Her voice was hoarse, subdued, as if she was on the verge of tears and only just holding it together. Malik didn't blame her. He was a trained warrior, but even he was reeling from seeing Jenna's aide and his team mown down in cold blood.

"It's not safe," he replied tersely, glancing around him as he walked, steering her through the crowd. "They'll be stirred up like sand-stingers right now ... I'd prefer to get you back to the shuttle ... and off Aura Terminal."

They kept walking. The aroma of roasting nuts, blended with incense from streetside shrines, wafted over the street, and the chatter of excited voices rose and fell around them.

Malik frowned. News of what had happened in that plaza was rippling through Aura Terminal with frightening speed.

"However, before we return to the spaceport, I need to get us some kind of camouflage." He gestured to their blood, dust, and sweat-stained clothing, which was drawing looks from passersby. "We're attracting too much attention."

Jenna's throat bobbed, before she nodded, accepting his plan. Malik hoped that if they moved fast, they could escape on the shuttle. The pilots would still be onboard; the pair of them would be residing on the shuttle during the negotiations.

They had to reach their ship.

Halfway along the street, Malik pulled Jenna toward a clothing store crammed next to a shrine to Aura. An elderly human male knelt before the statue of the deity, murmuring a prayer as he lit a candle at the feet of the Goddess of Prosperity.

Malik's mouth thinned as they moved past. Aura wasn't much good to them right now. Instead, he could do with protection from Jidea, Goddess of Fortune. Reaching up, his hand pressed briefly against the amulet he wore around his neck—a reminder to the goddess that they could do with her blessing.

A short while later, Malik and Jenna emerged wearing matching deep-green hooded cloaks. Malik had tossed his helmet and plate-armor aside—they were too distinctive—although he kept his close-fitting body-armor on under the cloak. Jenna had lost her suitcase during the attack, yet she still carried her bag slung across her front. She'd dug into it for some hard credits to pay for their new clothing. The cloak was long enough to cover her golden robes, with a deep cowl that shadowed her face. Malik would have preferred a better disguise than just donning cloaks, but it would have to do.

Farther along the street, they entered a transpod station, where a brightly lit underground passage led to a row of platforms. Climbing the stairs and stepping out onto a crowded platform, Malik spied grey-clad figures sporting laser-rifles, on patrol.

His pulse quickened. Jenna's earlier suggestion wasn't a foolish one—they *could* go to the Aura garrison for help. However, Malik had just thrown a pyro-grenade into an upper-side plaza, causing extensive damage. Even though, as a diplomat's bodyguard, he was permitted to be armed, they wouldn't have expected him to carry something so dangerous. The garrison wouldn't be happy with him at all.

No, it was best they stuck to his plan and got off Aura Terminal. They needed to catch a transpod before one of those guards spied them.

Jenna squeezed his arm, letting him know she'd seen them too.

A pod arrived then, and they stepped aboard. The doors whispered closed, and they were off, beginning the long journey back down to the spaceport.

Seated next to Jenna near the front doors, Malik glanced her way occasionally during the journey. He couldn't see her face, although he could feel the tension vibrating off her. They didn't speak for the duration of the trip—instead, Malik kept a close eye on the surrounding passengers, and who was getting on at each stop—but when they finally exited the transpod, he leaned close to Jenna. "Walk slowly," he murmured. "Before we head through the gate, I need to make sure it's safe."

Jenna nodded.

Grateful that she was letting him do his job without interference, Malik guided her out of the transpod station and into the spaceport terminal.

If anything, it was even busier in here than when they'd arrived. However, the crowds worked to their advantage. As earlier, grey-clad members of the Aura Garrison lined the vast green space, their helmed gazes surveying the throng.

Malik led Jenna into the terminal, and they did a slow circuit, weaving in and out of seats and crowds of travelers waiting for the next passenger liner to depart. Moving close to the viewing platform that looked out over the landing bay, Malik's gaze swept the docking area, traveling over ground staff and droids to where the gleaming ambassadorial shuttle sat.

However, the moment his attention rested on the ship, his stomach clenched.

Bright orange tape covered the door of the shuttle, and a pair of grey-clad guards stood in front of it.

"Shit," he muttered. "They've impounded your ship … we won't be getting off Aura that way."

Panic beat in Jenna's breast. The sense of disconnection that had settled over her since they'd narrowly escaped death shattered. Once again, she felt hunted.

"Come on." Her bodyguard turned from the window. "We need to get out of here."

"Wait," she gasped, reaching out and grabbing his arm. "There has to be another way … what about a passenger liner?"

Her bodyguard halted, his hooded face turning toward the queue of passengers that had formed at one of the gates. They were about to board. "We can't travel on our IDs," he said, stepping close to her and lowering his voice. "The garrison will stop us from boarding."

"Why are you so worried about them?" she hissed back. "They're the good guys, aren't they?"

"They are … but they're upset right now and will have a lot of questions for us. I just set off a pyro-grenade, after all." He paused then, his gaze boring into her. "Besides, once we're in custody, your husband will know exactly where we are. What if they hand you over to him?"

Pulse roaring in her ears, Jenna considered his words. "They wouldn't do that … would they? I've got diplomatic immunity, anyway."

Captain Malik continued to hold her gaze. "You do, but this is still their turf. Are you willing to take that risk? The quicker we get out of here to safety, the better."

Dizziness swept over Jenna. "All right, have it your way. Where to now then?"

"Back to the transpod station," her bodyguard replied. His arm linked through hers, and he steered her off the viewing platform. "Try to look relaxed, My Lady."

Jenna's mouth compressed. "Easier said than done," she muttered.

Sweat slid down her back as they wove their way through the press of passengers. Beyond the terminal windows, a large diamond-shaped passenger liner sat ready to disembark, while ground crew scurried around underneath its belly, unfastening cables, and removing coils.

The lightheadedness returned. How she wished she were safely on that liner, bound for the other end of the galaxy.

Instead, she was trapped. Aura Terminal was a big station, but those hunting them could be anywhere.

They circuited a delegation of robed Daksari who'd just stepped away from a ticketing-droid. Tall and slender with glittering grey-green skin, neck gills, and protruding brow-ridges, the Daksari hailed from a water planet. Dressed in heavy emerald cloaks, they were deep in discussion while they waited, their sibilant voices cutting through the rumble and chatter of the surrounding crowd.

Some of them glanced Malik and Jenna's way, their gazes drawn by the sight of two more green-cloaked figures approaching. However, an instant later, upon realizing they were human, and not Daksari, the delegates glanced away.

Gaze riveted on the doors leading out to the transpod station, Jenna concentrated on putting one foot in front of the other, when all she wanted was to bolt.

Waiting on the platform for the next pod, she made the mistake of turning around and glancing up at one of the vid-screens behind them.

And when she did, Jenna clutched at her bodyguard's arm, her fingernails digging into his body-armor. "Look!"

Captain Malik swiveled, his gaze alighting on where a reporter stood before the wreckage of the plaza on the upper-side. Smoke still drifted across it, and the wail of sirens almost drowned out the reporter's voice.

"I'm here in the Central Business Plaza, where a detonator has caused considerable damage … and loss of life," she shouted at the camera before waving her hand toward where officials and garrison guards swarmed behind her. "A Mir-Brennan diplomatic delegation has been attacked by a group of unknown assailants. All members but two were gunned down … Ambassador Lady Jenna Mir-Brennan and Captain Malik Mir-Draven are reported missing." Two images flashed up on the screen then. "The garrison is urging anyone who has seen the ambassador and her bodyguard to please come forward. There is great concern for their safety."

Malik muttered a curse under his breath and yanked his hood down over his face. "Great … this is all we need."

Swallowing, Jenna also drew her cowl forward before glancing nervously around the platform. Luckily for them, it was empty.

They needed to hide before someone recognized them.

By the time they stepped into one of the pods—this one bound for the lower-side shopping ward—sweat ran down her back, and she was struggling to breathe normally.

This transpod was packed with commuters, and Jenna found herself pushed up against the far wall. She clung to Malik's arm, too unnerved to care about propriety. Right now, this man was the only thing standing between her and death. After the attack in the central plaza, it didn't look like those after her wanted to take her captive.

Heat ignited in Jenna's belly then, rage cutting through paralyzing fear.

She couldn't believe Tian had hired assassins to ensure she never made it to the conference center, never met with the Mir-Lelith delegation. She'd always known he was ruthless, but this took it to a new level. She was Cathal's deputy—and the Mir-Ferrins didn't want her claiming her brother's seat once they executed him.

The fire in Jenna's gut roared hotter still. And they would kill her brother. The coming trial would be a sham, just like Mican Mir-Ferrin's 'military operation'.

Reaching their destination, they followed a stream of passengers out into a dimly lit street.

The streets on Aura's lower-side were nothing like the spacious, leafy avenues of the upper-side. For one thing, no transparent sphere stretched overhead, providing a starry backdrop. Instead, a ceiling of dull-grey steel tubes, grating, and coils formed the sky, around fifteen meters above—and the buildings that rose beyond the shop fronts were ugly metallic boxes.

The shrines to galactic gods and goddesses were ornate on the upper-side, decorated with gilded statues; but down here, they were cramped alcoves with little more than a shelf and crudely made clay figurines. Someone had just lit fresh incense inside the shrine to Wis, the Seer of Truth. The cloying scent drifted across the street, catching in Jenna's throat, and making her cough.

Nonetheless, the residents of the lower-side had done their best to inject some cheer into their drab surroundings. They'd hung lights over the streets, and gaudy, illuminated shop-front signs added much-needed color to the shadowy underworld.

Carefully keeping her hood covering her face, Jenna glanced around her. It was even busier down here than above—although the residents of the lower-side didn't dress in the expensive robes of the rich. Many of the human faces that passed them were pinched and tired, and those who were fair-skinned were pallid—a result of living permanently on a space station.

Jenna lengthened her stride to keep up with Captain Malik's long one. She glanced up at his cowled face. "Do you have a destination in mind?"

"Not yet," he replied tersely. "Can I borrow your tablet?"

Wordlessly, Jenna dug into her bag and withdrew the device. However, she was careful to switch off the geo-locator before she handed it over.

If Tian was behind this—and she'd bet her life he was—he'd be waiting for her to surface. She wasn't going to make it easy for the bastard.

Captain Malik took the tablet and did a quick search before leading them out of the shopping ward and into a warren of backstreets.

A short while later, they checked into a squalid hotel in the poorest end of the lower-side. The lights and colors of the heart of the district gave way to shadowy streets, illuminated by orange streetlights, as they walked. The residential ward was a dormitory for the thousands of souls who kept Aura Terminal working. There was little to recommend the area, no parks or plazas, and few shops save a large, bustling market, where the residents shopped for their daily food supplies.

The Spacers' Retreat sat in a poorly lit alleyway. The name was an irony, for the hotel looked about as welcoming as a detention block. A squat utility-droid welcomed them at reception. Perched upon a seat at the desk in a cramped, unadorned lobby, it didn't ask to see any ID, as most hotels would have.

Digging into her bag, Jenna withdrew her PCSD: a small Portable Currency Storage Device. When she went on diplomatic missions, she always liked to travel with a PCSD, rather than accessing her accounts on Idral. Having funds on her person made her feel more secure—and freed her up if she wished to go shopping. And now, it provided them with anonymity. No one could track hard credits—as the funds were downloaded onto portable devices rather than accessed from a bank account.

Swiping the device over the reader, she took a keycard from the droid.

"Third floor, Room 37," it chirped.

They took the elevator upstairs, and as soon as the doors closed, Jenna pushed back her hood and glanced at her companion. "Nice place … I can't believe they only had one room left."

Her bodyguard shoved back his own cowl. "It's a dump … but it's safe … for now at least."

Stepping out onto a narrow, dimly lit corridor, they made their way down to their room, an equally depressing-looking cubicle. The room was windowless with hard grey floors, stained walls, and a large bed covered in stark sheets. A tiny bathroom led off the cubicle.

Jenna's mouth thinned when her gaze settled on the bed. It was just her luck that the only room this fleapit had left was a double room, not a twin.

Pushing aside her discomfort, she walked over to the bed and sank down onto it. Now they'd finally stopped running, her limbs felt weak and shaky. If she didn't sit down, she'd fall over. She didn't even have the energy to remove her bag or cloak.

"Are you carrying any water on you?" Captain Malik asked after a pause.

Woodenly, she nodded, reaching into her bag, and withdrawing a bottle. She then handed it over to him. He unstoppered it and took a couple of gulps. "I'll go out and get us provisions," he said after a pause. "This isn't the kind of hotel that provides room service."

Jenna nodded once more. She then shifted her gaze to the wall.

A moment later, a tall figure moved between her and the stained paneling. And then, to her surprise, Captain Malik lowered himself so that their gazes were level. A frown marred his forehead. "Lady Jenna?"

"I'm all right," she murmured. "It's all just hit me … that's all."

"Do you have any sedatives in that bag of yours?"

She shook her head. "I don't like them. I prefer to keep clear-headed." She paused then. "This is my fault, Captain … Mir-Barus and your team are all dead because of me."

Those startling violet eyes narrowed. "How so?"

"This is Tian's revenge for me leaving him."

"It's possible … although the Mir-Ferrins' attack on Idral is hardly *your* fault."

Jenna swallowed. "I should be there … with my family."

"If you had been, you'd be imprisoned and standing trial alongside your brother … how would that help?"

Jenna didn't answer. She appreciated her bodyguard's practical response, yet it didn't ease the ache in her chest. Pelicon Mir-Barus had been a loyal advisor to her family for nearly twenty years.

Images of her aide sprawled upon the ground, of her security team falling, returned, so vivid she could almost taste the acrid smoke in that plaza. Jenna's throat constricted, and her eyes started to burn.

Captain Malik cleared his throat. "You need to rest, My Lady."

Nodding, Jenna reached up and dragged a hand down her face. "What about my family? I can't let them execute Cathal."

The bodyguard pulled a face. "One thing at a time," he murmured. "Your own life is still in peril … let's focus on getting you off Aura Terminal first."

Jenna stared up at him. "How are we going to do that?" she whispered, despair pressing down like heavy hands upon her shoulders. "You don't want the garrison finding us either … and they'll be watching every gate."

The captain's mouth quirked. "There's always a way … and we'll find it." He picked up the keycard from where Jenna had tossed it down on the bed and rose to his feet. "I'm going out to do some shopping ... and to have a scout around."

"Here," Jenna said, digging into her bag and withdrawing her PCSD. "You'll need this."

He nodded, taking the device from her. His gaze met hers once more, holding firm. "Try and get some rest while I'm gone ... and don't open the door to anyone."

7. THIN WALLS

ALONE IN THE room, Jenna covered her face with her hands.

Now that Malik Mir-Draven wasn't present, she could let her shields down.

Tears stung her eyelids, leaking out onto her cheeks.

In the space of just a couple of hours, her world had shattered. All the security she'd taken for granted, the privilege, had just been ripped away from her. And now, she was on the run with her bodyguard, while her brother was about to be put on trial for a crime he didn't commit.

With shaking hands, Jenna wiped her wet cheeks. She then reached into her bag and withdrew her tablet.

Switching it on, she brought up the Rith sector newsfeed. Images from Idral assaulted her.

The violent skirmish in the planet's orbit.

The swarm of Arrow fighters circling Mir-Brennan Tower.

Squads of battle-droids and cyborgs storming the stronghold.

The blockade of Mir-Ferrin battlecruisers that now guarded Idral.

The images of Cathal, bleeding and captured, yet defiant.

The terror in Isla and Bea's eyes.

Mican Mir-Ferrin's pitiless face. His cunning words.

And Tian standing at his father's side, smug and victorious.

Despite that the ambient temperature in the room was pleasant, Jenna started to shiver.

Righteous and devoted—that was the Mir-Ferrin clan motto. The Mir-Ferrin clan-lord had nursed an old grievance—from fifty years earlier. Her father's dream of lasting peace between their clans had, in fact, been one-sided.

When Mican Mir-Ferrin agreed to the marriage alliance, he'd been planning this all along. He'd placed Tian at Cathal's side—and his son had likely been feeding back intelligence for the past two years.

Jenna's belly twisted, and she switched off the tablet, tossing it back into her bag. Once again, rage burned, sweeping away the grief, the shock.

She had never loved Tian, hadn't even liked him, but his betrayal still cut deep.

Malik moved purposefully toward the lower-side's shopping ward. As promised, he would buy supplies—plus a few other items they'd need to get out of Aura Terminal unnoticed. But first, he needed to know exactly what he was dealing with. Who had Tian sent to kill his wife?

Senses on alert, he glanced around as he walked, peering into the shadows. Down here on the lower-side, it seemed like perpetual night. The streetlights illuminated the various wards, but most of the station's resources were clearly used to keep the upper-side functioning.

The atmosphere down here was subdued compared to above. Malik passed a few beggars hunched on street corners. Children, poorly dressed and barefoot, sprinted past him. He watched them go, the sight bringing back memories of his youth in Melor.

Malik's mouth thinned. He, too, had lived on the streets and ended up in a gang. Evading the police and their droids was a game, until the day he got caught thieving. The beating he'd received for that, both from the police, and his mother, had made him rethink his choices. Malik had grown up with nothing but had somehow managed to claw himself up the social hierarchy. How many of these children would though?

Eventually, he reached the heart of the ward. Slowing his gait, he approached the transpod station, surveying the milling crowd.

The station was even busier than earlier—workers flowing in an out—for it was 1800, and shifts were changing.

Malik noted the fatigue he saw on the workers' faces. They were trudging back to their homes after a grueling shift somewhere on the station. It was a hard life. These citizens spent their days working in the landing bays, cargo terminals, and on the engines of Aura.

A squad of grey-clad figures emerged from one of the pods then and marched through the terminal. The guards had laser-rifles slung across their fronts and moved with military precision.

Those on the platform stepped aside to let the members of the Aura Garrison past, their manner respectful.

Malik tracked the guards' path from within the shadow of his hood. They were hunting those responsible for the attack on the upper-side. However, he knew they were also searching for him and Lady Jenna.

He'd have to be careful to avoid them.

Frustrated he hadn't yet caught sight of anyone suspicious, Malik was about to leave the terminal, and make a start on his shopping, when three men emerged from one of the pods.

Watching them, the fine hair prickled on the back of his neck. At first glance, they looked like any of the workers who filed in and out of the transpods. Dressed in loose tunics and pants, they wore cloaks about their shoulders. However, these individuals didn't have slumped shoulders or exhausted faces like many surrounding them. Instead, they were alert.

The trio made their way out onto the street, gazes swinging left and right.

Malik broke away from the crowd and followed the men. Years of training, as well as a childhood living amongst criminals, had honed his instincts. He kept a discreet distance back, observing their stalking gait. All three had the quiet intensity of dangerous men. He noted how they talked together, their lithe forms tense with purpose, before they headed up the street.

Eventually, they reached the end of the shopping ward's main street. Here, the three companions split up, each heading down different side streets, widening their search.

In the shadow of his hood, Malik allowed himself a thin smile.

Jidea be praised. The Goddess was gazing upon him at last. He'd hesitate to take on all three killers at once—but not one.

Turning left, he slid into the shadows.

The hours passed, and Captain Malik didn't come back.

For a while after he left, Jenna sat upon the bed, too exhausted and shaken to move. Then, eventually, she'd dragged herself to her feet, unslung her bag, and made her way into the bathroom.

Locking the door—for she didn't want her bodyguard returning and accidentally bursting in on her—Jenna undressed. Her once pristine golden shift dress and over-robe were dirtied and crumpled. Nonetheless, these were the only clothes she had.

She turned on the shower and stepped under the hot water. She quickly washed her hair before closing her eyes. The heat restored her, and Jenna was just starting to relax when the water went ice-cold.

Snarling a curse, she switched off the water, staggered out of the shower, and wrapped herself in a towel. She then dried herself off, put on her sweaty robes, and returned to the room.

Still no Captain Malik. She wondered what was taking him so long.

Jenna retrieved her tablet and turned it on. Three hours had passed since he'd left. Now that her shock was starting to fade—and after the warmth, and polar blast, of the shower—she was beginning to feel hungry.

Sitting down on the bed, she lay back and stared at the paneled ceiling.

She hadn't thought she'd be able to relax enough to nap, but after a few moments, she grew drowsy. Jenna was just dozing off when the sound of loud groaning jolted her awake.

Heart hammering, she sat up, glancing around her.

The groans—deep and male—continued, and Jenna realized they were coming from the next room.

Gods, the walls are thin in here.

Jenna's brow furrowed then. She knew Malik had chosen this hotel on purpose, for it was far from the center and provided the secrecy they needed. However, she wished they'd spent a few more credits on better lodgings.

Someone was having sex next door.

The groaning grew louder, joined now by female cries.

In between grunts of encouragement, they were murmuring to each other.

Jenna listened, her breathing growing shallow.

No one had ever growled such things to her.

A rhythmic thumping began then, as the head of their bed slammed against the wall. The woman's cries grew louder, drowning out her partner's. She begged, groaned, and screamed—and Jenna listened, envy spiking through her chest.

Lucky bitch.

Whoever the woman's lover was, he clearly knew what he was doing.

Jenna's mouth compressed as unwelcome memories surfaced.

Sex with Tian had been an ordeal, right from their wedding night. Unlike her previous lover—a delegate she'd met on a diplomatic mission—he was rough. They'd shared some wine on their first evening together, both unnerved after their disastrous wedding day. There had been a short spell when Jenna had dared believe she might be attracted to her husband. After all, Tian was good-looking, his body toned from a career in space fleet. But the moment he started undressing her, the sparks of attraction died.

He hadn't kissed her, hadn't shown any desire to please her or put her at ease. Instead, he'd torn off Jenna's wedding dress, pushed her back on the bed, and mounted her. Then, without any preliminaries, he'd thrust his way inside his wife, and pumped away until he collapsed.

It had hurt.

In the aftermath, Tian rolled off her and promptly fell asleep.

Meanwhile, in the next room, the woman's pleading reached a sobbing crescendo before a male cry finally echoed through the wall.

And then everything went silent.

Jenna exhaled sharply.

It was over, thank the Gods.

The door clicked then, drawing her attention.

It swung open, and a tall, cloaked figure stepped inside. Her bodyguard carried a bag over one shoulder.

"I was wondering where you'd gotten to," Jenna muttered, climbing off the bed and rising to her feet. "You missed the show."

Captain Malik pushed back his hood and cocked an eyebrow. "What?"

Jenna nodded toward the wall. "Our neighbors," she replied, lowering her voice lest they overheard her. "They're both screamers." She halted then, arching an eyebrow. "This is a hotel, isn't it … you didn't accidentally check us into a pleasure house?"

The captain's mouth curved. "*The Spacers' Retreat* is a hotel all right, My Lady." His gaze glinted. "However, lovers often choose hotels like this." He glanced at the wall, his expression turning speculative. "They're likely upper-side nobs who want their affair to remain a secret."

Jenna made a face. "You don't know that."

Captain Malik lowered his bag to the floor and shrugged off his cloak. "I grew up in a pleasure house, My Lady … you'd be surprised what I know."

He turned away then and hung up his cloak. Underneath it, he wore black, close-fitting body armor. The captain then undid his heavy utility belt and laser-pistol holster, hanging them up too. He had a soldier's orderliness—a habit drilled into him after spending years living in barracks.

"How is it you grew up in a pleasure house?" Jenna asked.

Her bodyguard glanced over his shoulder, his expression shuttered now. "My mother was once a priestess at the Temple to Jidea in Melor … but after she took a lover, she was cast out. Eventually, she found work as a whore. I was brought up by all the women who worked in the house … and became their errand boy when I was old enough." Bending down, he picked up the bag he'd brought with him and carried it over to the bed. "I spent the rest of my time looking for trouble in Melor's backstreets."

Jenna met his eye. "And now you're Captain of the Lord's Watch."

Captain Malik snorted. "Growing up in the gutter turns you one of two ways. You either become part of the underworld … or you try to rise above it. I joined the Melor Guard when I was sixteen and later managed to get an assignment to work at Mir-Brennan Tower in the House Guard. Two years on, I applied to join the Lord's Watch … and I was accepted."

"You must have been young?"

"Just twenty."

Jenna stilled. She would have been in her teens when Malik Mir-Draven joined her father's bodyguard. He'd been with them for years, but she'd never noticed him until he became captain.

Captain Malik was watching her in that frank, direct way she found unnerving. Jenna cleared her throat and motioned to the bag. "What do you have there?"

"Food and drink." He flashed her a disarming smile then. "And our way off Aura Terminal."

8. FOOLHARDY AND FLAWED

"YOU HAVE A plan?" Jenna shifted forward, peering into the bag. "Already?"

"Half of one … at least." Reaching into the bag, Captain Malik withdrew a small plastic box. "Contact lenses … to turn our eyes golden." He then pulled out a larger container. "And body clay and paint."

Jenna cocked her head, mouth pursing, her excitement ebbing. "What kind of plan is this?"

His smile widened. Damn him, her bodyguard was enjoying her discomfort. "Those Daksari in the spaceport gave me the idea," he replied. "They looked our way because at first glance our green robes made us look like them."

"It didn't take them long to realize their mistake though," Jenna pointed out.

He gestured to the two containers sitting on the bed. "That's where the contact lenses and body paint come in." He paused then, his expression sobering. "It won't be a disguise that'll stand up to close inspection … but it should get us through the gates and onto a passenger liner." He reached into the bag once more, withdrawing two cards. "Our new IDs."

Jenna took them from him, looking down at the two faces staring back at her: grey-green skin, neck gills, and protruding brow-ridges above penetrating golden eyes. "We're going to have to do a good job with those paints," she murmured. Glancing up, she met her bodyguard's gaze. "What are we going to do about our voices?"

"Try not to speak."

Jenna inhaled deeply, her fingers clenching around the ID cards. "Okay," she murmured. "This *could* work."

Captain Malik reached into the bag and pulled out two neatly folded jade-green garments. "Those robes you wear are impractical … I bought you a pair of pants and a tunic to go under your cloak."

Jenna took the clothing, her mouth curving. The material was silky and finely woven. "Thank you … I need something clean to wear."

Her bodyguard dug into the bag once more and took out two food containers and some bottles of water. The savory odor of something fried and heavily spiced drifted toward Jenna, and her belly growled. "Come on," he murmured. "Let's eat."

Taking one of the containers and a fork he passed her, Jenna smiled. "Thank you, Captain. I do appreciate all of this."

Instead of accepting her thanks, her bodyguard's expression shuttered. "Just doing my job, My Lady," he replied curtly.

Jenna's smile froze upon her face. She didn't expect them to be fast friends, but his off-hand response stung. She knew their relationship was a professional one, but he didn't have to be rude. She'd never seen him respond to Cathal so brusquely—in fact, he always talked to her brother with the utmost respect.

However, Jenna swiftly recovered; years of working as a diplomat served her well.

Perching on the bed, she placed the container on her lap and carefully opened it. She wasn't sure what the name of the dish was he'd brought her—a mélange of fried strips of meat and spiced, steamed vegetables— but it smelled good.

Meanwhile, her bodyguard lowered himself onto a chair in the corner of the room and started on his meal. They ate without conversing, each withdrawing into their own thoughts. It wasn't a companionable silence.

After the captain's blunt response, Jenna was now wary of him.

"The Widow Makers are hunting you," he said eventually, shattering the quiet.

Jenna froze before lowering her fork. She'd heard of the Widow Makers—few in the Rith sector hadn't. They were reputed to be the best, and the most expensive, assassins in this corner of the galaxy.

"While I was out shopping, I tracked three men who drew my attention," Malik continued, meeting her eye. "They split off, and I followed one of them … and ambushed him." He paused then, gaze glinting. "It took some persuasion, but he eventually revealed his identity … and that Tian Mir-Ferrin hired him."

Jenna's fingers tightened around her fork. There was a hard edge to her bodyguard's voice that made a chill feather across her skin. She didn't want to know what methods Captain Malik had used to *persuade* a hardened assassin to reveal his identity.

Her belly contracted, the greasy meal she'd just consumed churning uneasily. "Gods, Tian really does want me dead," she murmured.

"Don't worry, the assassin won't be telling anyone about his chat with me," her bodyguard assured her. "I dealt with him."

Jenna swallowed. She had no doubt he had.

He'd deliberately been blunt in his telling of the incident, as if he wanted to remind her who he was, and what his role was.

A trained killer. Her protector.

Glancing back down at her half-eaten container of food, Jenna forced herself to keep eating. Even so, her stomach had closed. Abandoning the last few mouthfuls, she wiped her hands clean on a paper serviette and helped herself to one of the bottles of water he'd brought. Sipping it, she pulled out her tablet and brought up a browser.

"What are you doing?"

Jenna glanced up to find Captain Malik watching her.

"Checking the newsfeeds." Dropping her gaze, she started to scroll. A moment later, she murmured a curse under her breath. "My picture's *everywhere* …

Ambassador Jenna Mir-Brennan, missing, presumed kidnapped."

"Kidnapped?"

She sighed. "Since we haven't come forward … the Aura Garrison has assumed the worst."

Her bodyguard didn't reply, and Jenna's mouth thinned. She understood why he didn't want them to go to the garrison. However, at the same time, she was frustrated not to be able to ask for assistance.

Closing the newsfeed, she brought up a list of upcoming departures from Aura Terminal spaceport. "They've canceled all passenger liners to Idral, I see."

"You wouldn't want to go there, anyway."

"Where then?"

"Best you choose a destination as far as possible from your husband."

Jenna's jaw clenched as she stared down at the tablet screen.

Damn it, she didn't want to flee, to let Tian destroy her family, her clan. If she did that, she'd always be running, always looking over her shoulder.

Fire ignited in her belly. *I'm a Mir-Brennan—not a fugitive.*

An idea stole upon her then, one that caused both her pulse and breathing to quicken. It was audacious and reckless.

Raising her chin, she met her bodyguard's eye, and announced calmly, "Change of plan, Captain … we're leaving Aura Terminal, but I'm not running away."

Captain Malik stared back at her, and she had the momentary satisfaction of seeing her protector struck speechless.

"I'm not letting them execute my brother and imprison Isla and Bea," she continued, her gaze never leaving his face. "Instead, I'm going to get them out."

His eyes snapped wide, and his lips parted. Eventually, he blinked. "Excuse me?"

"As Captain of the Lord's Watch, you know about *The Passage*, don't you?"

Slowly, he nodded, his expression wary now.

"My grandfather built that escape tunnel under Mir-Brennan Tower for times such as this. My family has been careful to keep its existence a secret … and now is the time to use it. I'm going in through the tunnel to bring them out."

After a long pause, her bodyguard cleared his throat. When he spoke, his voice was a low, incredulous drawl. "Let me get this straight, My Lady … you intend to somehow slip by the Mir-Ferrin blockade and land on Idral … without being caught, before trekking cross-country to Mir-Brennan Tower … avoiding Mir-Ferrin patrols along the way, of course." His mouth twisted. "And then you're going to sneak in, right under Mican Mir-Ferrin's nose, and rescue your brother and his family … and make it out alive?"

Heat prickled across Jenna's skin. In such bald terms, her embryonic plan seemed both foolhardy and flawed. However, she didn't appreciate the patronizing edge to his voice. Captain Malik could mock her, but it wasn't *his* brother whose execution would be broadcast to every corner of the Rith sector.

Someone had to do something.

Ever since she'd seen Mican Mir-Ferrin standing in her brother's solar, ever since the attempt on her life that had killed Mir-Barus and her security team, outrage had been slowly building within her.

She was exhausted, afraid, and overwhelmed—but she wasn't beaten.

Her husband's family wanted to see hers wiped off the galactic map. Once the Mir-Brennan ruling family was gone, her clan's influence would diminish, leaving just two dominant clans in the sector.

I can't let that happen.

A wave of sickly excitement washed over Jenna.

Ever since her eighteenth birthday, she'd worked on her father's team of diplomats, before eventually being promoted to her brother's ambassador.

But now, all of that was gone.

She was in a real battle now. One of survival. She couldn't let herself be cowed by the situation, or by the man sitting across the room. Cathal, Isla, and Bea were relying on her.

Drawing herself up, Jenna favored her bodyguard with an imperious look. "That's *exactly* my plan, Captain … although the finer details will have to be worked out." Glancing down at her tablet, she scrolled once more through the list of departures. "There's a liner leaving for Morith at 0800 tomorrow … it's three systems away from Idral. The moon's in Mir-Brennan territory, which should make it safer for me. It's also a mining colony … and rough enough to draw ex-soldiers and mercenaries." Her chin kicked up, and she met Malik's surprised gaze once more. "I'll pay someone to smuggle me onto Idral."

Captain Malik inclined his head. "Really?"

Jenna pursed her lips. She was seriously tiring of his attitude. Tilting her chin, she favored him with her most aristocratic glare. "As you reminded me earlier, Captain, your role is to protect me on this diplomatic mission. As such, you owe me nothing more once we're safely off Aura Terminal."

Her tone was sharper than she'd intended, yet his incredulous expression didn't change. "I serve the Mir-Brennan ruling family, My Lady. With your brother imprisoned … I take orders from you."

"Well, in that case, once we arrive on Morith, I shall discharge you of duty."

Her bodyguard's large frame stiffened, his condescending air disappearing. "You can't go off on this rescue mission on your own, Lady Jenna," he replied, his tone clipped now. "Especially if you hire mercenaries. Most of them can't be trusted."

Jenna scowled back. "That isn't your concern, Captain."

Her bodyguard rose to his feet and took a step forward, folding his arms over his chest. "Your brother charged me with your safety."

"And as you just pointed out … he's not in a position to hold you to it."

"This plan is suicide."

Jenna's stomach twisted at his harsh reminder, yet she kept her expression shuttered. "No, it isn't … not if it's executed properly."

Muttering a curse, Captain Malik raked a hand through his short black hair, leaving it in spiky disarray. "You've got balls, My Lady, I'll give you that," he growled, "but if you're going back to Idral, I must insist on coming with you."

Jenna eyed him warily, her pulse quickening. "You won't try to stop me?"

He huffed a humorless laugh. "I swore an oath of allegiance to your family when I joined The Watch, Lady Jenna … whatever foolish quest you embark on, I shall stand by it."

Tension rippled between them.

Jenna's gaze narrowed. Rising from the bed, she moved close, stepping right up to him. Malik was much taller than she was, and she had to crane her neck up to hold his gaze. However, she wouldn't let that intimidate her. If she was to succeed at rescuing her family, she wouldn't let herself be bullied by her bodyguard. As such, when she finally answered him, her voice was cold. "I tire of your attitude, Mir-Draven."

9. DIGGING YOUR OWN GRAVE

CAPTAIN MALIK QUIRKED an eyebrow, an arrogant expression that made Jenna itch to slap him. "My Lady?"

"You're here as my protector," Jenna ground out. "Not to sneer at me."

He snorted. "I'm merely pointing out that this plan of yours won't work."

She folded her arms across her chest, mirroring his gesture, even as her heart now thundered in her ears. The truth was that this man *did* intimidate her. It had also been a mistake to stand this close to him. He was so near that she inhaled the musky scent of his skin. The smell did strange things to her breathing.

It made her far too conscious of him.

Swallowing hard, Jenna took a rapid step back. "All right … do you have a better one?"

A silence followed, drawing out, before Captain Malik finally answered. "No, My Lady." His jaw tightened then. "But can you blame me for questioning you? You haven't thought any of this through."

Jenna scowled. "This from a man who wants us to paint our faces green and dress up as Daksari."

"Our disguises are crude, I admit," he replied tersely. "But they're likely to get us off Aura Terminal. Instead, your idea is just going to get us killed."

"You wouldn't question Cathal in this way," she pointed out, her voice hardening.

"That's because your brother thinks before he acts."

"No, it's because you *respect* him … but not me."

Scowling, he withdrew from her then. His gaze cut away, and he began unfastening his body armor, in sharp, angry movements. Heeling off his boots, he stripped down to his underpants, tight-fitting shorts that molded his groin like a second skin.

Jenna moved away. She knew she should avert her eyes, but she couldn't. Instead, she stared at him, drank him in. Clothed, Malik Mir-Draven was an imposing sight—half naked, he was even more impressive. Bronzed skin covered hard, rippling muscle. It was the body of a man who trained rigorously to keep himself fighting fit.

Around his neck, he wore an amulet on a thong: a small silver hammer. Of course, his mother had once been a Jidean priestess. She would have brought up her son to revere the Goddess. Jidea was loved upon Idral. If you visited any of the many towns on the planet's continent, you'd find shrines to the Goddess of Fortune on every street corner.

Panic started to beat in Jenna's chest when he glanced up and caught her watching. Her mouth went dry before she croaked. "What are you doing?"

His mouth twisted. "What does it look like? I'm getting undressed so I can take a shower."

With that, Captain Malik stalked past her and into the bathroom, the narrow door sliding shut behind him.

Alone in the cramped cubicle, Malik switched the shower on full before swearing under his breath.

Jenna Mir-Brennan thought he had no respect for her. It was just as well the woman had no idea where his mind had gone over the years, or she'd have slapped his face.

All the same, she'd caught him off-guard just now. He usually kept his cool better than that.

Muttering another curse, Malik stepped into the shower. The needles of scalding water peppered his flesh, and he stuck his face under it.

He'd scorned Lady Jenna's plan—not *her*. When he'd joined the Lord's Watch, he'd sworn to defend Cathal Mir-Brennan with his life. He liked the clan-lord and served him with pride, but that didn't mean he wished to rush headlong into death.

Squeezing out some liquid soap, Malik washed with deft efficiency, his jaw bunched.

Idiot ... why did you insist on joining her?

Lady Jenna had given him the opportunity to bow out gracefully, but instead, he'd told her she couldn't hire mercenaries without his protection.

It wasn't too late. He could retract his offer; he had his own neck to worry about.

Malik clenched his eyes shut. Damn her. Ever since they'd boarded the shuttle for Aura Terminal, the clan-lord's sister had caused him no end of trouble.

She only had to look his way, fix him with her dark-brown eyes, and he lost his train of thought. Before this trip, the sexual fantasies he'd had about her had been safe—for their paths rarely crossed. He hadn't known her at all, but ever since leaving Idral, that had changed. He'd always thought the clan-lord's sister regal and aloof, yet he'd discovered she was a woman full of contradictions. Vulnerability and grit.

He hadn't expected her to stand up to him as she did—and it had only served to heighten his awareness of her.

When Jenna moved close, and the scent of Desert Rose, and woman, enveloped him, he almost forgot himself. The way she'd stared at him when he'd undressed just now caused lust to flare hot in the pit of his stomach. He'd had to escape to the bathroom before her gaze traveled south and she saw the erection tightening his briefs.

The memory of her wide eyes, her slightly parted lips, made his cock harden painfully now. Malik tried to ignore it.

"Keep it in your pants, Mir-Draven," he muttered, picking up a shampoo bottle. "You're already digging your own grave ... try to do it with dignity."

Malik lathered up his hair and was about to rinse off when the water turned cold.

Seated on the bed, Jenna heard the muffled shout through the wall.

Her mouth thinned, both in sympathy and vindication. *I should have warned him about that.*

But she hadn't.

A short while later, she was scrolling through the Rith sector newsfeed on her tablet, and seeing far too many pictures of herself, when Malik emerged from the bathroom.

Not surprisingly, he looked pissed off.

Without a word to her, he retrieved his body armor—made of form-fitting synthetic material—and hauled it back on.

"So, it's settled then," she said, deciding the best thing was to focus on practicalities. "We have twelve hours until departure. We'll catch the 0800 flight to Morith disguised as Daksari … and from there, we'll hire mercenaries to get us to Idral."

Malik glanced her way, a nerve flickering under one eye. His lips parted as if he might say something before he thought better of it, clamped his mouth shut, and gave a curt nod.

"Good," Jenna replied, careful to keep her voice businesslike. She was still flustered after their exchange earlier. "I need to contact what remains of our space fleet and enlist their help … but I'll wait until we get off this station first."

Her bodyguard's brow furrowed. "Aren't *The Star Tempest* and the *Star Monarch* still in orbit around Staturine II?"

"Yes," she replied, even as her belly twisted. "As far as I know." Before the attack, their space fleet had been split between Idral and Staturine II. The latter had rich mineral reserves that the Mir-Leliths had been demanding access to for years now. As such, Cathal had kept security tight around Staturine II. "And if the Mir-Ferrins hadn't destroyed half our fleet when they struck Idral, I'd order an attack on their blockade right now."

Malik's frown deepened, and Jenna sighed. "However, I realize that wouldn't be wise. Our battleships can assist us in other ways. When we get to Morith, I shall open an encrypted channel to Commander Levi Mir-Brennan on *The Star Tempest* and appraise him of the situation."

"Makes sense," Malik replied, running his hands through his damp hair. The gesture was unconsciously sensual, and Jenna's breathing quickened. She then dropped her gaze to her tablet. *For the love of the Gods, stop it.* "You're going to need all the help you can get."

Malik approached the bed then. "We should try and get some rest." He cleared away the items he'd bought. "Move over, My Lady."

Scrambling over to make room for him, Jenna tried not to let discomfort show on her face.

Of course, there was only one bed in this room. Had she expected him to sleep on the floor? Fortunately, the bed was relatively large. Even so, he was close—too close. The only mercy was that he'd put some clothes on.

Malik stretched out his long body and gave a slow, deep yawn. He rolled over, giving her his back. "Do you mind if I dim the lights?"

"No," Jenna murmured, still clutching her tablet. "Go ahead."

A moment later, only the glow of Jenna's tablet screen illuminated the bed.

Stifling a sigh, she switched on an alarm, so they wouldn't oversleep, and placed the device on the bedside table. Her eyes were gritty, her limbs heavy; she, too, needed to rest.

She slid down flat upon the bed and rolled onto her side so that their backs were facing. Rigid, she lay there, listening to the even whisper of his breathing. To her surprise, it only took a minute or two for it to deepen. Malik had fallen asleep easily, but despite her fatigue, Jenna knew she wouldn't.

She was too keyed up, too nervous.

His unsettling proximity aside, she'd made a decision today that had cast her out of a world she knew and understood, and into the unknown.

10. IN DISGUISE

"TRY TO WALK in long, loping strides," Malik instructed, "and round your shoulders a little."

Jenna frowned. "I thought I was."

"Not enough … you walk like a human, not a Daksari."

Jenna huffed a sigh of frustration. Before leaving their hotel, she'd looked up Daksari mannerisms and body language. Indeed, they had a different gait to humans, with their arms swinging at their sides as if moving through water. She'd believed she'd gotten the hang of it, but Malik thought otherwise. It was early, yet the terminal was as busy as ever this morning, with quite a crowd gathering for the 0800 departure.

Dragging in a lungful of warm, floral-scented air, Jenna followed Malik around the base of the fountain that dominated the terminal. The soft rush of water should have soothed her, but her nerves were stretched taut.

All the way here, she'd been paranoid that the Widow Makers would catch up with her. Her heart had leaped every time the transpod drew into a station, and she'd scanned the platform, looking out for anyone suspicious.

However, since the assassins dressed to blend in with the other inhabitants of Aura Terminal, it was impossible to know who they were.

Jenna's mouth went dry. *They're likely here, right now … looking for me.*

She fought the urge then to survey her surroundings. Moving her head around too much might push the hood of her cloak back and reveal her face. She and Malik had spent over an hour painstakingly applying face clay and paint, to give the illusion of a pronounced brow ridge, gills, and glittery grey-green skin. And once she'd put in her contact lenses, the reflection that stared back at Jenna from the bathroom mirror had surprised her. At first glance she did, indeed, look Daksari.

I hope no one scrutinizes us too closely, she thought, keeping close to Malik's side as he loped across the terminal. *Neither of us is built like Daksari.* The 'water people', as they were often known throughout the galaxy, were slender and long-limbed. Malik was tall yet powerfully built, while Jenna was small with decidedly 'un-Daksari' curves. Fortunately, their cloaks hid their bodies from view. However, she prayed they didn't run into any real Daksari—who'd rumble them in moments.

Heart pounding, Jenna focused on the queue waiting at the security gate. She wanted to voice her worries to Malik, but he'd given her strict instructions to remain silent until they were safely ensconced in their berth aboard the passenger liner. While they could fake their appearance with clothing, body paint, and contact lenses, the moment either of them spoke, the game would be up.

For that reason, they'd waited until the last moment before descending to the spaceport. The less time they spent lingering in the terminal, the better.

Head bowed, Jenna cast a careful glance about her. As expected, there were a number of grey-clad guards around.

Her skin prickled. She didn't want one of the Aura Garrison to recognize her. She couldn't be caught up in days of questions now—or risk Tian catching up with her—not while her brother's life hung in the balance.

Up ahead, two guards stood back from where security-droids were scanning IDs. Their visored gazes watched the line inch past.

Jenna started to sweat under her heavy cloak.

This isn't going to work.

Suddenly, it felt as if she were standing there naked. Her disguise seemed flimsy, ridiculous. Any moment now, someone was going to point at them and start whispering.

Swallowing hard, she shifted nervously.

An instant later, Malik's hand fastened around her arm, squeezing firmly. It was a warning, to keep her nerve. But at the same time, his touch grounded her.

It had every time they'd come in contact.

Not like Tian.

From the first time her husband had ever touched her, Jenna's instincts screamed 'danger'. By the time she heeded them, she was already married to him. She recalled that night, the eve before their wedding, when they'd stood on the balcony outside her quarters. He'd taken hold of her chin, forcing her to raise her gaze to meet his. The gesture had been dominant, controlling.

Sweat now slid between her shoulder blades.

This wasn't the time to relive her mistakes or to think about the man who'd sent assassins after her. Instead, she had to think about her family—the ones who were depending on her.

Drawing in a deep, steadying breath, Jenna tried to master her nerves.

Malik must think I've lost my mind … last night, I announce I'm off to rescue my brother, and this morning, I can barely keep it together.

The thought was a sobering one—and useful. For some reason, it mattered what Malik Mir-Draven thought of her. Jenna's anxiety drew back, and she focused on the looming security gate.

Just three more passengers and it would be their turn.

Minutes later, they moved in front of the security-droid and passed over their IDs. To Jenna's relief, her hand was steady. The shaking that had assailed her in the transpod, while traveling to the spaceport, had calmed.

Breathing slowly and deeply, Jenna waited for the droid to scan their identifications. She hoped Malik had bought them from a reputable source.

"Cleared," the metallic voice announced after a pause. It had only been a few seconds, yet it felt like a lot longer to Jenna. "Have a good journey." With that, the metal claw handed back their IDs.

Giddy with relief, Jenna clutched her ID tightly and followed Malik through the gate and into the clear tunnel leading into the passenger liner. Her bodyguard was doing an admirable job of mimicking a loping Daksari walk, and she did her best to imitate him. Even now, they had to be careful.

Her instincts told her they were still being watched—all the passengers were.

Inside the safety of their berth, Jenna sank down onto the narrow bed and pushed back her hood. "Thank the Gods," she gasped. "That droid seemed to be taking an age to scan our IDs."

"Jidea be praised," her bodyguard replied, before reaching up to touch the amulet around his neck. "I'll admit I got a little nervous." He lowered himself down onto the bed opposite, viewing her with his topaz eyes. "But I paid good money for those IDs … well, actually, you did."

He fell silent then, the only noise in the cramped berth the whirr of the life support. Beneath Jenna's feet, the floor started to vibrate. "They've started the engines," she murmured.

Her belly lurched then, in anticipation of the space sickness that always assailed her during launch.

"We were some of the last to board," Malik replied. "We should be away soon."

Jenna let out a long, slow exhale. Her limbs felt weak in the aftermath of boarding. Nonetheless, she didn't want to show her companion just how anxious she'd been.

Malik already thought she was making a mistake. She didn't want to prove him right. *The Passage* had been built for exactly this purpose—to be used in times of emergency. Once they hired mercenaries, they *could* retrieve her brother and his family safely.

Jenna's stomach tensed then. She wished she didn't need Malik's help, that once they reached Morith they could go their separate ways. But she wasn't a complete fool.

She wouldn't get far without her bodyguard.

Once they arrived on Morith, she'd have to go in search of mercenaries willing to help her—a task that would likely take her into dangerous places. She couldn't do this alone, and Malik knew it.

The oath he'd sworn to her brother obviously meant a lot to him. He might not think much of her, but he thought highly of Cathal. Indeed, Malik's loyalty to the clan-lord was likely the only reason he'd insisted on accompanying her.

"I suggest we don't venture from this berth during the journey," Malik said then, intruding upon her thoughts. "We can order room service … it's safer that way."

Jenna nodded. "Makes sense." They hadn't seen any Daksari while boarding, but that didn't mean there weren't 'water people' aboard the liner. It was wise not to draw attention to themselves.

The journey would be around twenty-one hours—this wasn't a clan-chief's shuttle but a slower craft that would make three scheduled stops en route to Morith.

The passenger liner shuddered then, the engine noise increasing to a whine. Jenna swallowed, tensing as bile stung the back of her throat.

Damn it, nausea was creeping over her.

Delving into her bag, she retrieved the small bottle of tablets Malik had given her during the departure from Idral and a canister of water.

Malik watched her as she swallowed two tablets, and Jenna grimaced. "Space sickness always hits me harder when I'm tired," she admitted. "I didn't sleep that well last night."

"You didn't?" Malik's mouth curved. It felt odd to look at him with his green face and brow ridge. "I slept like the dead."

"I know," she replied dryly, wincing at his turn of phrase. "I heard your breathing change within minutes of you lying down." She paused then, raising an eyebrow. "They say only someone with a clear conscience can go to sleep that fast."

"Or someone who's exhausted." Malik heeled off his boots and stretched out on his bed, rolling over so he was staring up at the ceiling. "I suggest you try to sleep on your back," he said. "We've got more make-up, but it would be best if you don't smear your face … the lighting in here isn't the best. It won't be as easy to reapply."

"I'll do my best," Jenna answered, following suit, and lying on her bed. She'd made sure to book a berth with two separate beds. Her eyes were gritty—from fatigue, not just the contact lenses—and her brain foggy. The assurance that they had twenty-one hours before arrival upon Morith was a relief.

She desperately needed to rest. She wanted to be fresh when they reached their destination, ready to hire a team who'd help her rescue Cathal, Isla, and Bea.

The liner shuddered, and her belly lurched.

And she would get some sleep—once they were on their way.

Malik lay upon his bed, staring up at the dull-silver metal girders that crisscrossed the ceiling of their berth. A few feet away, Ambassador Jenna Mir-Brennan slept deeply. She'd looked peaky during takeoff, but once they'd made the jump into hyperspace, the color had returned to her cheeks.

She'd stretched out on her back, as he'd suggested, the rhythmic whisper of her breathing filling the small berth.

After a good night's sleep, Malik was well-rested. He wanted to get up and do some exercises, some bench presses and chin-ups, to work out some of the tension in his muscles. However, he'd wake Jenna up if he did so. He also could risk sweating off his carefully applied face paint. Exercise would have to wait until they reached their destination.

The faint drone of the engines vibrated through the liner, and he caught snatches of laughter and conversation in the corridor outside their berth. This ship had a lounge and a restaurant, as well as a viewing platform, where passengers could watch the streaks of light flow around them while the liner sped through hyperspace.

But he and Jenna wouldn't be joining them.

He wasn't paranoid, but there was a chance that the Widow Makers weren't just remaining on Aura Terminal. Some of them might have taken passenger liners in case the Mir-Brennan ambassador slipped by.

Turning his head, Malik let his gaze settle upon the woman he'd been charged with protecting.

Damn it, he still didn't like her plan. It was far too risky. However, he'd sworn an oath to Cathal to protect and obey those he served—and he'd uphold it.

That didn't mean he wouldn't question her about it on this trip though. Maybe if he pushed her a little, she'd realize she was making a mistake.

Jenna's face was relaxed in sleep, all the lines of worry and tension from the last two days disappearing. Her full lips were slightly parted, her long eyelashes fluttering against her painted cheeks.

Even covered in face paint, she was lovely.

Malik knew he shouldn't, knew he'd pay for it later, but he drank her in. His attention slid from her face and the halo of brown waves spread out over the pillow, to the rise and fall of her breasts. Her cloak had fallen away to reveal the green tunic he'd bought her. Unlike the ambassadorial robes, which dwarfed her small frame, her new clothes fitted her, emphasizing the ample swell of her breasts, the dip of her waist, and the curve of her hips.

Staring at her, Malik found himself imagining what it would be like to slide his hands over those curves, to push aside the silky fabric and seek out the smooth, soft skin underneath.

His groin started to ache then, his cock pushing against the restrictive, skin-tight body armor.

Enough of this. He gave himself a hard mental slap. *The woman's trouble. Just focus on protecting her. On staying alive.* Jaw clenched, Malik shifted his attention back to the ceiling.

11. HER BIDDING

JENNA DRIFTED INTO wakefulness through the lingering threads of a dream.

She'd been back on Idral, wandering the awning-covered alleys of Melor's markets, sweating in the ferocious heat. The dream had started pleasantly, for she loved the sprawling town. Despite that it was a busy spaceport and could be rough in places, she'd always felt safe in Melor—although her brother always insisted that she took a couple of bodyguards with her whenever she visited.

But in her dream, she'd wandered the stalls alone, inhaling the scents of spices from every corner of the sector. The dream had been a pleasant one until she felt a 'presence' dogging her steps. Her pursuer lay just out of sight, yet as she quickened her stride, she sensed them looming closer. Her pulse sped up, and she'd begun to run.

Blinking, Jenna opened her eyes. Heavy steel girders came into focus above her. She blinked again, and Idral and her stalker disappeared.

For a moment, she struggled to get her bearings—but then she glanced right, at the black-clad figure sprawled on the bed opposite, and everything came back. Suddenly, she wished she was on Idral, trying to outrun her pursuer. The reality she'd awoken to wasn't any less dangerous.

Swallowing, she rolled onto her side before croaking. "How long was I asleep?"

"Nearly ten hours," her bodyguard replied. He glanced her way, just as Jenna raised a hand to scrub at her eyes. "Don't touch your face, My Lady."

Jenna froze, wondering at his command, before she remembered her carefully applied face paint.

"Ten hours." She pushed herself up into a sitting position. "No wonder my head feels foggy."

Reaching for her tablet, she switched it on and brought up the latest newsfeed; it had refreshed when they'd stopped en route to Morith.

"Any updates?" Malik asked as she scrolled.

"No word on how Cathal's trial is proceeding," she replied, gaze tracking down the screen. "And there are still images of me … and you … plastered everywhere." She paused there, her mouth pursing. "The governors of the Mir-Brennan planets are outraged … some of them are calling for our allied clans to stand with them. They want retribution for the attack."

"I'm sure they do," her bodyguard replied, his tone dry. "Their clan-lord has just been imprisoned."

"I hope none of them are going to act rashly," Jenna muttered. "Vigilante justice won't help anyone, right now. Once I get in contact with *The Star Tempest*, I'll instruct the governors to sit tight." Her mind started to churn then. She'd met with several of their clan representatives over the years and recalled a few of them were volatile and ambitious. "I'll also ensure they all know I haven't been kidnapped."

Her pulse accelerated. The last thing they needed was one of the governors attempting to seize power while Cathal was locked up.

Malik nodded. "Are you hungry?" His mouth lifted at the corners. "I ordered food for myself a while back, but I'm ready for another meal."

As if on cue, Jenna's stomach rumbled. "I'm starving," she admitted with a sheepish smile.

Malik swung himself upright. He then rose to his feet and punched the console next to the door. "Can we have two dinners delivered to Berth 82A?"

"Certainly, Sir," a droid's voice responded. "We have two options today … Reldin stew with poached—"

"We'll have that," the bodyguard replied curtly. "Send it up now please."

"Of course, Sir."

When Malik sank back down onto his bed, Jenna favored him with an arch look. "I might have wanted to know what the second option was."

"Believe me, it's all equally bland." He pulled a face. "They use cheap Mir-Lelith food-replicators on most of the passenger liners."

Jenna frowned. "What … they don't have proper kitchens onboard?"

Malik raised an eyebrow. "Of course not." He paused then, inclining his head. "This is the first time you've ever traveled on a commercial liner, isn't it, My Lady?"

Jenna tensed. She didn't appreciate his tone. "You're right," she replied, rising to her feet, and stretching her back and shoulders. "I'm not used to 'roughing it'."

She turned her back on him then. If he thought she was a spoiled, sheltered nob, then let him. She'd soon prove him wrong.

Jenna went to the bathroom, and when she emerged, two trays of food sat on the retractable tables in front of their beds.

A savory, rich scent wafted through the berth.

"Smells good," Jenna admitted, seating herself and peering down at the large bowl of stew. "I thought you said food on these ships was tasteless?"

"It is … try it before you decide."

Jenna picked up a spoon and started to eat. Her first mouthful confirmed that, indeed, the stew smelled better than it tasted. The meat was tough. "Gods," she muttered when she finally managed to swallow. "What did they put in the stew … chelrog hide?"

Across the berth, Malik smiled. "You've eaten the meat of a chasm lizard then?"

Jenna pulled a face. Chelrogs were huge beasts that dwelt in the canyons and ravines upon Idral. "No."

"I grew up eating chelrog … it's delicate and slightly sweet. Nothing like this."

Jenna nodded and took another mouthful of stew. His response was polite enough, yet Malik had just reminded her—once again—of the gulf that separated them.

They'd both been born and raised on Idral, yet they might as well have grown up on planets at opposite ends of the sector.

Pushing aside her irritation, she met his eye. "How old are you, Captain?"

Malik swallowed a mouth of stew. "Thirty-five … why?"

"Members of the Lord's Watch get to retire at forty … you're not far off."

He grimaced. "I was … until this fiasco."

"You'll still get your pension," she assured him.

Malik didn't answer. Instead, he picked up the flatbread sitting next to his stew and tore off a piece.

Jenna took another mouthful of her meal. It was tasteless and tough, but she'd finish it. She had to keep up her strength for what lay ahead. Her throat tightened then, and she swallowed with difficulty—Cathal's life depended on what she did next.

"Forty is young for retirement," she said after a pause. Questioning her bodyguard took her mind off her brother's plight. "What do you plan to do with the rest of your life?"

Malik shrugged. "I haven't given it much thought."

"Will you travel … go see the galaxy?"

"Maybe."

His laconic responses were starting to wear on her, and irritation bubbled up. She should let this subject drop, yet she stubbornly pressed on. "Or perhaps you've got a hankering to be a family man. When you retire, you'll buy yourself a house in Melor and find yourself a wife."

He snorted. "Perhaps."

Jenna's grip tightened on her spoon. She was only trying to make conversation, to ease things between them a little, but she'd have an easier time communicating with this dish of stew.

She wondered then, how far she could trust this man.

Physically, she felt safe with him—he'd recently saved her life, after all, and helped her flee Aura

Terminal. Malik had always been loyal to her brother, but his relationship with Jenna was strained. Perhaps he was trying to undermine her?

We're not friends, she reminded herself. *Maybe you should stop trying to draw him into conversation.*

They finished their meals in silence, and were both sitting on their beds, sipping at the glasses of wine that accompanied the stew, when Malik eventually spoke. "We need to talk about the next step, My Lady."

Jenna took a gulp of wine. *Here we go.* She'd been expecting him to question her at some point during this journey—and she was ready for him.

Giving a brisk nod, she answered, "As soon as we reach our lodgings, I shall contact *The Star Tempest* … then we'll need to get ourselves some mercenaries." She paused. "When I couldn't sleep back on Aura, I did a search on my tablet … it looks like Morith is full of soldiers for hire."

Malik swirled the remnants of his wine about his glass. "Mercs don't come cheap … I didn't check your balance when I used your PCSD earlier. How many credits do you have left?"

"Let me take a look." Jenna set her wine down and picked up her bag, digging around until she found her device. She placed the pad of her thumb on the underside of the PCSD. An instant later, the balance flashed up on the top. "Eleven thousand, four hundred hard credits," she announced.

Her bodyguard gave a low whistle. "You travel light, My Lady."

Jenna stiffened. "You never know when you'll need hard credits," she informed him, her tone cooling. "And it's just as well … since my husband will be tracking my bank accounts … to see where I surface."

"If he hasn't blocked them already," Malik pointed out.

Jenna's mouth thinned. The possibility had also occurred to her. Putting the PCSD back in her bag, she met her bodyguard's eye once more. "So, will it be enough?"

"Eleven thousand credits won't buy you a crew of mercs," he replied finally, "but it might buy us a couple." He paused then before draining the dregs of wine in his glass. "Can I speak frankly, My Lady?"

Jenna resisted the urge to pull a face. "Go ahead … you've never asked my permission before."

Malik's gaze narrowed. "I'm against the idea of you going back to Mir-Brennan Tower … you're too valuable to risk. Best you send me and the mercs to Idral instead."

Jenna's spine stiffened. Her instinct had been right. Her bodyguard sought to undermine her. Like most men, he wanted to take control of the situation, but she wouldn't let him.

"Not a chance," she replied. "This is *my* mission, Captain. I'm allowing you to come along, not the other way around."

Malik's face hardened at her tone. Nonetheless, Jenna held his eye.

She appreciated this man's capability, his protection, but she had to remind him who was in charge here.

He didn't have to like her—he just had to do her bidding.

12. BLACKMAIL

"KEEP SEARCHING FOR her." Tian Mir-Ferrin glared at the man's face hovering above him. "Turn over every inch of Aura Terminal if you have to."

The Master Assassin scowled back. "We spent the last *four days* scouring the station," he replied, his low voice holding an edge of irritation. "The Aura Garrison is hunting those responsible for the attack. We know how to blend in … but they're tightening the noose. I'm not going to compromise my team."

Tian clenched his hands at his sides. For the love of the Gods, the bitch couldn't have gone up in smoke. On her own, Jenna wouldn't have gotten far. The woman was sharp-witted, but she was a soft diplomat and wouldn't be able to defend herself physically.

However, Captain Malik Mir-Draven was with her.

Tian hadn't welcomed the news that the head of the Lord's Watch had led the ambassador's security team to Aura Terminal. The man would be hard to kill—and the fact he'd managed to escape that ambush and get Jenna to safety proved it.

"Are you sure she hasn't managed to get off the station?" Tian asked after a brittle pause. It was hard to keep the frustration out of his voice. He'd hired the Widow Makers to kill the Mir-Brennan delegation before they reached their destination. Their price had been extortionate too—and they'd demanded payment in full before accepting the job.

Tian had been so desperate to see his wife dead, he'd accepted.

The Master Assassin was a sharp-featured man in his mid-thirties with white-blond hair cropped close to his scalp. His silvery gaze remained fastened on Tian.

"We've been patrolling all the gates at the landing bays," the Master replied. "No one fitting their description has passed by." The assassin halted there, his gaze narrowing. "One of your wife's bodyguards was carrying a pyro-grenade," he said, his tone chilling. "He tossed it into the midst of my crew and killed five of them outright … two others were so badly maimed I had to end their lives before the Aura Garrison arrived."

Tian fought a lip curl. He wasn't interested in these details. "And how is that my problem?"

"One hundred thousand credits aren't enough."

Tian went still, his heart suddenly hammering in his ears. He'd paid a small fortune to the Widow Makers. "Excuse me?"

"You didn't warn us they were carrying a pyro-grenade, Mir-Ferrin. You should have."

Tian started to sweat. "I didn't know."

It was the truth. For obvious reasons, he hadn't gone down to the landing bay to see his soon-to-be-ex-wife off. He hadn't realized Cathal had sent Captain Malik with Jenna. Pyro-grenades were expensive, hard to make, and even harder to procure. However, the man leading the Lord's Watch would have them.

"I asked you to provide accurate details about all members of that delegation," the Master went on, his gaze never wavering. "You didn't keep up your end of our … arrangement."

"And you haven't kept up yours." Tian's temper was quickening now. "Jenna Mir-Brennan needs to die … and you're to hunt her down and finish the job you botched."

That was the wrong thing to say. The Master Assassin's face went still.

Tian was no coward, yet he felt a tickle of misgiving all the same.

Nonetheless, he was more concerned about how his father would react.

Mican Mir-Ferrin was a hard man to please at the best of times. Tian had joined space fleet at seventeen and worked his way up through the ranks to become the youngest commanding officer ever. Some had whispered that his meteoric rise was due to the fact he was a clan-lord's son—although no one would have been brave enough to say it to his face—but anyone who knew Tian's father would have laughed at the idea he'd help any of his sons out.

If anything, the clan-lord was harder on his three sons than anyone else.

His expectations of them were virtually unreachable, as Tian had discovered over the years. He'd done as bid, had married Jenna, had bedded the frigid bitch, had established himself at her brother's side and counseled him to take military action against the Mir-Leliths.

And now, thanks to him, they held Idral.

But it wasn't enough for his father. Nothing was.

Mican would be livid about this.

"That'll be another fifty thousand credits," the Master Assassin said, after a long pause. His voice was expressionless now, as was his face.

Tian's breathing choked off. "What?"

The assassin didn't reply. He knew his client had heard him.

"We had an agreement," Tian rasped.

"And now, I'm changing it."

Heat exploded under Tian's ribcage, brushing away the last of his restraint. Taking a menacing step forward, his gaze fused with the assassin's. "I'll make sure you never find work in this sector again."

The Master quirked a silver-blond eyebrow. "I'll take my chances with that."

The man's lazy drawl made Tian want to draw the laser-blade at his hip and stab him through the throat with it. However, striking a holo-image was futile.

"You have twelve hours to transfer fifty thousand credits into the same account as last time," the assassin drawled. "Otherwise, I'm calling my crew off."

And with that, he reached forward and ended the call.

An instant later, the image winked out, leaving Tian standing alone in the clan-lord's solar.

He stood there, merely staring at the empty space above him, where the Master Assassin had been looking down at him just moments earlier.

"I don't fucking believe it," he rasped, hands clenching and unclenching at his sides.

The bastard was blackmailing him.

Fury whipped through him. Breathing hard, Tian stalked to the large floor-to-ceiling windows and placed his palms on the thick glass, trying to regain control. Outside, scorched red earth stretched away for as far as the eye could see, layers of craggy peaks standing out against a pink sky. It was getting late in the day; soon the twin moons would rise.

Bile stung the back of Tian's throat. He'd lived on this rock for over two years now and couldn't understand why his father coveted the planet so. Yes, it had once belonged to his clan, and it sat on the intersection of major trade routes, and for that reason, it was valuable. But the Mir-Ferrin ruling family had been based for the last two generations on Platinum 5, a space station, in the heart of Mir-Ferrin territory.

Tian preferred Platinum 5 and looked forward to one day residing there once more.

He swallowed hard, his fingers digging into the glass. It was cool inside the solar, but outdoors, the heat would be overwhelming. The air had a rank metallic stench from the iron-rich soil, and the valleys and ravines surrounding Mir-Brennan Tower were crawling with creatures that would kill you in a heartbeat.

He can keep this foul place.

His wrist-comm bleeped then, intruding on his rage.

"Tian." His father's voice echoed through the solar. "Have you finished your call yet?"

"Yes," he ground out.

"Good, well, get yourself down here … the court's about to go into session again."

Tian pushed himself off the window. Damn his father. This pantomime was ridiculous.

Cathal Mir-Brennan was on trial for the crimes of his grandfather, the clan-lord who'd warred with Tian's own grandfather. There had once been a bloody conflict that had culminated in the Mir-Ferrins losing their planet.

Tian understood that his father wanted revenge, but he was wasting precious time. Better just to kill Cathal and be done with it—but no, Mican wanted it done formally. He wanted to put the clan-lord on trial, even if the judges had all been bought off by him. That way, when Mir-Brennan was found guilty and sentenced to public execution, his father would feel vindicated.

That way, when Mican broadcast the execution across the sector, he'd stand there, head held high, righteous in his actions.

The Mir-Ferrin clan-lord and his sons had planned this attack meticulously ever since Tian and Jenna's wedding day, biding their time while they rallied their army and resources.

They'd only have the element of surprise once—it had to be done right.

They hadn't been quite ready to strike, but when Jenna had announced she was divorcing Tian, they'd been forced to act.

Nonetheless, they'd never have succeeded if it hadn't been for Tian. He'd laid the groundwork, had sent his father detailed plans of the Mir-Brennan defenses—and had thrown open the doors for their army of battle-droids and cyborgs when they stormed the tower.

His father had yet to acknowledge the part he'd played though.

Tian clenched his hands by his sides. Mican would be furious to learn that Jenna had escaped. However, he wouldn't be blackmailed by the Widow Makers. No, instead, he'd take another approach—he'd put a price on his wife's head. Bounty hunters would be more tenacious, and cheaper, than the assassins. One of them would track her down.

But first, he had a sham trial to attend.

"Yes, father," he replied, heading toward the doors. "I'll be right there."

13. A SOLID PLAN

EMERGING FROM MORHAVEN spaceport, Jenna started to shiver. Even with her thick cloak, the chill, damp air bit into her.

Morith was freezing.

Her breath steamed in front of her as she peered into the murk. It looked as if dusk was settling, but the light levels were always low here, even during daylight hours. The nights were supposed to be long on Morith, fifty-two hours, while daylight lasted just ten.

The moon was a prosperous mining colony. However, its inhospitable climate and lack of sunlight meant it wasn't a tourist hotspot.

Nonetheless, it did have something to recommend it—a stunning view of Triton 4.

Tilting her head up, Jenna's gaze alighted on a massive gas giant that hung in the sky, its surface swirling bands of blue, white, and grey. The huge planet, which was always visible, loomed over the moon.

"Ready?" Malik stepped up to Jenna's elbow, drawing her attention from Triton 4. Other passengers were milling around; it was best to be prudent when conversing until they were away from them.

Jenna nodded. She'd booked them into a room near the central hub. It was a private place, one that she'd paid for in advance, linking her PCSD to her tablet.

"Come on then."

Jenna fell in next to her bodyguard, hurrying out through the spaceport gates into the road beyond.

Clusters of grey-stone warehouses and refineries surrounded Morith's spaceport. Convoys of huge vehicles rumbled past, transporting ore and waste rock from the open-cast mines that pock-marked the moon's surface to the processing plants.

Jenna wrinkled her nose as she inhaled the oily smoke that belched from the vehicles' exhausts. She was surprised they didn't transport the ore about on shunts as they did on Staturine II, which was also a mining planet, where they'd gotten rid of these slow, polluting transporters decades ago.

"It's busier than I expected," she murmured.

Malik grunted. "After the attack on Idral, the Mir-Brennan governors will be readying themselves for more conflict. Prices … and demand … for Crillon are likely to go up all over the sector."

Jenna's brow furrowed. Of course, they mined Crillon on Morith—a valuable mineral that was used to power spacecraft. On their approach to the moon, she'd noted the Mir-Brennan cruisers positioned above it.

Morith was close enough to Idral for the governor here to get nervous. Understandably, they didn't want the Mir-Ferrins stealing their valuable fuel reserves.

Shifting her attention from the vehicles, she took in the surrounding grey hills. They stretched into the distance in every direction and were strangely uniform in shape.

Her gaze narrowed further then. No, they weren't hills, but huge mounds of dirt from the mines.

Ending their brief exchange, Malik and Jenna turned left and headed toward Morhaven township. The land rose before them into a wide, low hill—this one natural rather than made of mining rubble. The top of the hill bristled with antennae, comm dishes, and protruding ventilation shafts, while a great stone arch spanned the base of it: the town's entrance.

Morhaven was the largest of many subterranean settlements that peppered the moon.

It was so cold their breathing steamed in clouds before them as they walked. The damp drilled into Jenna's bones. Pulling her cloak closer still, she marked how Malik scanned his surroundings as he walked. It didn't matter where he went, her bodyguard was constantly alert, on the lookout for threats.

And not for the first time, she was grateful for his vigilance.

She knew he was just doing his job, yet after Aura Terminal, she no longer felt safe. It was an effort not to keep glancing over her shoulder, almost as if she expected to see figures stalking them.

Jenna quickened her step. *I'll be no good to Cathal, Isla, and Bea if the Widow Makers catch up with me.*

The entrance loomed closer, and Jenna spied the Mir-Brennan crest carved into the stone above it: a shooting star above a clenched fist.

Her skin prickled at the sight.

Glory is the reward of valor, Cathal … I'm not giving up on you.

Stepping into the wide entrance tunnel to Morhaven, Jenna and her bodyguard entered another world. A few yards from the archway, warm air feathered over her face. Bright yellow lights, embedded in the rock ceiling, lit their way to a junction where an illuminated map of the town hung.

Pausing, Jenna studied it.

"Gods," she murmured. "You could get lost for days in here."

The network of tunnels curved left and right in a haphazard fashion. It was a real warren.

"The central hub looks as if it lies around half a kilometer in," Malik replied, his gaze narrowed as he mapped their route. "I think we should take the right tunnel."

Jenna didn't argue with him.

They resumed walking, making their way through wide tunnels carved out of the white-grey sandstone. Along the way, they passed shops and dwellings dug out of the rock. Unlike on Idral and Aura Terminal, there weren't many shrines to the Gods here, just the odd neglected alcove to one of the lesser deities, like Bron the Worthy and Eldra the Wise.

There were plenty of residents about, going on errands or lounging on terraces in front of eateries and bars. Vagrants slumped in doorways, and beggars positioned themselves on the busiest tunnels, rattling tins at passersby.

As they approached the central hub, the tunnels grew more crowded. The aroma of roasting meat and the sharp, malty tang of distilling Morith whisky greeted Jenna and Malik as they walked past. The spirit brewed on the moon was almost as prized as the Crillon that was mined here.

The central hub was a wide cavern, festooned with lights, filled with stalls, and edged with a range of shops. A heavy crowd thronged the hub, the excited chatter of voices rising into the air.

"Watch yourself here," Malik warned. "Morith isn't known for attracting the best the sector has to offer."

Jenna didn't answer, although she minded him. She noted he wasn't wrong. Many had made their fortune on this moon, but there was a seedy edge to Morhaven. Despite that she and Malik wore hooded cloaks, they attracted far too much attention from the shadowy figures lurking in doorways.

Jenna quickened her pace to keep close to Malik. She was relieved they'd made it to Morith, but her mind was already racing forward. They had a few vital things to accomplish while they were here.

She was keen to get to their lodgings, but Malik had pointed out that they both needed clean, military-style clothing for the mission once they ridded themselves of their green cloaks and face paint. As such, they stopped off in a store on the fringes of the central hub, where her bodyguard selected items with breathtaking speed and precision: black cargos, t-shirts, and padded jackets for them both. Jenna looked on, bemused, as shop-droids trundled around to retrieve the items he rattled off. Laden down with bags, they then went next door and purchased Jenna a pair of heavy black boots.

Jenna watched the droid pack her new footwear before she cast Malik a sidelong glance. "Are you planning for me to kick someone to death?"

He cocked an eyebrow in response. "If it comes to that … those slippers you're wearing are impractical."

Jenna glanced down at her scuffed golden pumps. Her toes were freezing, and she had blisters forming. He had a point.

Emerging into the cavern outside once more, they made their way past a stall selling barbequed insects and headed toward the far side of the central hub.

Their lodging was in a narrow passageway just behind the cavern. Halting before the plain blue door set into the wall, Jenna punched in the code the host had forwarded her onto the keypad.

The locks released, and Malik pushed the door open.

"This was a good choice," he said casting Jenna a wry smile. "I didn't feel like explaining to hotel reception why we're dressed up as Daksari."

Jenna's mouth quirked. Indeed, it was just as well that droids had served them in the clothing and shoe stores. "No need to look surprised, Captain. I know how to be discreet."

Stepping under the shower, Jenna let out a long sigh of pleasure. She hadn't been able to wash properly in three days; it was a relief to scrub off the face paint. Green water swirled around her feet before spiraling down the plug hole.

The shower in their lodgings was much better than the one in their hotel on Aura Terminal. The room wasn't fancy, but it was central, safe, and clean.

Emerging pink and glowing from the shower, Jenna wrapped herself up in a fluffy towel. She then turned to the clothing she'd brought into the bathroom with her.

She hoped Malik had gotten her size right. She'd suggested she try the garments on in the shop, but he'd brushed the idea aside.

Jenna pulled on the sturdy pair of black cargo pants before she wriggled into her bra and reached for the black t-shirt. Over it, she pulled on a long-sleeved, quilted jacket. To her surprise, all the items fitted.

Catching her reflection in the mirror, Jenna's mouth curved. She'd removed her contact lenses earlier, so her eyes were back to their usual shade. Her brown hair hung around her face, which was flushed from the hot shower, yet her quilted jacket and cargo pants made her look like someone else.

She was no longer the Mir-Brennan ambassador.

Jenna's expression sobered. Her diplomatic skills would still come in useful though. Malik was currently off buying weapons and flak vests for their mission, but it was up to her to secure the support of her brother's military commanders.

Leaving the bathroom, she padded through to the bedroom—a white-washed space dug out of the rock with two single beds and a kitchenette. Sitting down on a bed, she picked up her tablet, switched it on, and deftly opened an encrypted channel to *The Star Tempest*.

She'd been impatient to get in touch with Commander Levi Mir-Brennan since their departure from Aura—but had wanted to think through what she'd say to him first.

"This is Ambassador Jenna Mir-Brennan," she introduced herself crisply when a comms officer upon the flagship answered. "Please patch me through to the commander immediately."

Perhaps it was her tone, but the operator complied with only the briefest of inquiries to confirm her identity. And when Commander Levi Mir-Brennan answered, Jenna switched on the camera.

The commander sat in his office before a wide window of tempered glass, with the curve of Staturine II's tan, grey, and blue surface behind him. What was left of the Mir-Brennan space fleet was now orbiting the planet. His gaze narrowed as he peered out at her. "Lady Jenna?"

Jenna smiled. Of course, the commander had only ever seen her at functions where she was heavily made up, and with her hair elaborately coiffed—not in this flushed, bedraggled state. "Yes, it's me."

Levi Mir-Brennan's features tightened. "It's a relief to see you are safe, My Lady."

"Thank you, Commander."

"We thought you'd been kidnapped … or worse." His features tightened. "Did you know that Tian Mir-Ferrin has put out a bounty on you via the Shadownet? Forty thousand credits. Dead or alive."

Jenna tensed, heat igniting in the pit of her belly. *The shithead.* The Shadownet was a comm-network used by criminals throughout the Rith sector. Of course, the clans monitored it. "No, I didn't," she replied, her tone sharpening. "Although it doesn't surprise me. The assassins he sent after me failed to deliver." She inhaled sharply then. "Apologies for not contacting you sooner … Captain Malik and I wanted to get off Aura Terminal first. I'm safe now though."

The commander nodded, his dark eyes glinting. "Where are you, My Lady? I can send a shuttle to pick you up immediately."

Jenna tensed. Of course, Levi Mir-Brennan would want to take control of the situation, to protect her. He wouldn't like her idea, any more than Malik had.

"It's best you don't know my location," she replied firmly. In truth, there was no reason why she couldn't tell Levi—he was a clansman, after all—other than she was afraid he might try and stop her. "I don't require a shuttle, Commander."

His brow furrowed. "You don't?"

"No … Captain Malik and I will be leading a team to Idral shortly … to free my brother and his family."

Silence followed these words. Jenna watched a myriad of reactions flicker across the commander's face—surprise, incredulity, and concern—before he eventually responded. "But there's a Mir-Ferrin blockade around the planet."

"We'll find a way to slip by."

"And how are you going to get into Mir-Brennan Tower, My Lady?" His tone was respectful, yet brittle.

"There's another way in … one only my family, and the Captain of the Lord's Watch, know about." She flashed him a tight smile. "Rest assured, we wouldn't be going in if we didn't have a solid plan."

Her pulse quickened then, her skin prickling.

A solid plan … is that what you've got?

"Lady Jenna." Commander Levi dragged a hand over his face, letting the strain show for the first time. "Your courage is to be commended, but I really must object. This is far too dangerous. With the clan-lord imprisoned, you are the heir to his seat. We need you here, leading the clan … not putting your life at risk."

Jenna drew in a deep, steadying breath. She'd expected this reaction; even so, it was hard not to let her frustration show.

"This isn't up for discussion, Commander," she replied, injecting steel into her voice. An awkward pause followed before she added, "Don't worry, I don't make this decision lightly. I also have Captain Malik's expertise and protection. I'm not doing this alone."

The commander's mouth thinned. "So, you are resolved, My Lady?"

"I am … but there are a few things I require your assistance with, Commander."

"Very well." Levi's tone was brusque now, although his gaze was resigned. "What do you need me to do?"

14. THE ROGUE CYBORG

JENNA WAS SITTING on the bed, scrolling through a list of Morhaven's taverns and pleasure houses, when the door whispered open.

She glanced up to see Malik, carrying a large backpack over one shoulder, step inside. He'd showered and changed before going out. His hair had now dried into a crown of messy spikes that made her want to smooth it.

Clenching her jaw to quell the unwelcome urge, Jenna lowered her tablet. "Mission accomplished?"

He nodded, his gaze settling upon her. "I managed to get most things we'll need." He paused then. "And I'm pleased to see our earlier shopping trip was successful."

Warmth crept across Jenna's chest at the frankness of his stare. "You picked the right size, at least," she said, keeping her tone light.

"I did," Malik murmured. He'd removed his contact lenses earlier; his eyes were now that startling shade of violet once more. "Were you successful in contacting *The Star Tempest*?"

"Yes … Levi Mir-Brennan will let the governors know I'm alive, and he'll warn them against doing anything reckless, at present. The commander has also agreed to help us get off Idral once we rescue my family. *The Star Tempest* and the *Star Monarch* will be cloaked nearby … waiting to hear from me … as soon as we're ready."

"Glad to hear it." Malik's mouth lifted at the corners. "The Mir-Ferrins will swarm like sand-stingers when we free their prisoners. We won't be leaving the planet without assistance."

Anxiety fluttered up under Jenna's ribs. "Commander Levi let me know that Tian's put out a bounty on me," she murmured.

His brow furrowed. "Really?"

She nodded. "Forty thousand credits."

Malik muttered a curse. "Maybe you should stay in here, where it's safe. I'll find us mercs."

Jenna shook her head before raising her chin in a silent challenge. "They're looking for you too, remember? Both our pictures are all over the newsfeeds." She paused then, holding his eye. "Anyway … this mission was my idea. I'm taking responsibility for whom I hire to help us rescue my family."

Malik's mouth thinned, a muscle in his jaw feathering. However, he held his tongue.

"Don't worry, I'll be careful. I'll keep my hood up … and you should too," she assured him. She then motioned to the tablet on her lap. "I've got a list of places we're likely to find mercenaries. There are quite a few … I suppose we should start our search."

"We should." Malik dumped the heavy backpack at the foot of his bed and turned to face her once more. "Are you ready to go?"

Jenna surveyed the smoky interior of *The Hook and Horn's* common room. Their search for mercenaries who were both available to work, and agreeable to the job, had led them to a host of places.

But so far, they hadn't found anyone suitable.

They'd been trawling taverns and pleasure hours for hours and were getting toward the end of the list she'd compiled.

Stifling a sigh, Jenna inhaled the pungent smell of stale sweat and clove smoke. *Jidea, help us … please let this be it.*

The pleasure house was poorly lit, yet the dimness couldn't disguise that this establishment had seen better days. Faded red drapery and upholstery surrounded Jenna, and the panels that lined the common room were scuffed and dented—revealing that *The Hook and Horn* had witnessed a few brawls over the years.

Dancers, of various galactic races, gyrated upon a podium, while patrons lounged at tables and in darkened booths. Half-naked figures sprawled on the laps of some of the patrons. One of the dancers rose to her feet then, took her Daksari patron by the hand, and guided him toward doors that presumably led to private rooms.

Jenna cast Malik a sidelong look. He still had the hood of his new charcoal-colored cloak up and was surveying the common room, gaze narrowed.

"Does this one look promising?"

"It might be," he murmured.

"It's got to be," Jenna replied. "There's no way we can do this alone … we need mercenaries … and we have to move soon."

Malik glanced her way, brow furrowing. "We'll soon see. Why don't you grab us a booth in the corner and order us a drink?"

Jenna nodded, even as irritation bubbled up. She was getting tired of letting him take the lead when talking to mercenaries. He'd dismissed a couple she had thought might be suitable at the last establishment.

Even so, she let him go without complaint, sliding into a booth a few yards from the door and adjusting her hood to ensure her face was still hidden. Meanwhile, Malik made his way across the floor, weaving between tables.

"What are you after?"

A tall, slender human female, wearing nothing but a tiny, sparkly halter-necked top and brief shorts, stepped in front of the booth, blocking Jenna's view of the floor.

The woman gave Jenna the once over, trying to catch a glimpse of her face in the shadow of her cowl. Jenna stared back, equally fascinated by her glitter-painted eyelids and rouged cheeks and lips. "Sorry?"

"Do want a drink or some fun?"

"A drink will do," Jenna replied. "Ah … two." She inclined her head, indicating behind the server.

The woman turned, her gaze settling on Malik. He'd stopped at a table and was talking to a hulking Vulkar male who was fondling the breasts of the human female squirming on his lap.

There was no mistaking the look of appreciation that flitted across the server's face as she observed Malik. "Is *he* looking for some fun?"

"I wouldn't know … you'd have to ask him."

The server turned back to her, eyes glinting with amusement. "What will it be then?"

Jenna's mind went blank. Malik wasn't wrong about her really. This was the first time she'd had to order her own drink. Brazening it out, she smiled. "Is there a house specialty?"

"There certainly is … The Horn Punch."

"Great, I'll have two, thanks." Jenna withdrew her PCSD and paid for the drinks, sinking back against the upholstered seat to wait for Malik to join her.

Her brief conversation with the server had drawn a few gazes. A group of human males at one of the nearby tables was eying her with far too much interest for her liking. Ignoring them, Jenna glanced over at where Malik had now made his way to the far side of the common room. He was speaking to a human male with an eyepatch, who reclined in a shadowy booth.

Jenna observed them. Malik and his companion were locked in an intense exchange, and the man with the eyepatch didn't look impressed. Meanwhile, her bodyguard folded his arms in a defensive gesture.

Frustration spilled over then, making Jenna swear under her breath. Gods, Malik wasn't going to dismiss yet another candidate, was he?

She needed to find out for herself whether this merc was suitable. Slipping out of the booth, Jenna marched across the floor toward them.

Malik spied her approach first, his broad shoulders tensing.

Jenna merely flashed him a smile and halted at his side. "Are you going to introduce us?"

Mouth thinning, he gave a curt nod. "Jenna ... meet Vic Mir-Riorde, Captain of *The Wayfarer*."

Jenna turned her attention to the mercenary—an instant later, her smile froze.

He wasn't wearing an eyepatch. Instead, the man had a metal plate fixed onto his eye socket.

Her pulse quickened. *Malik was going to hire a cyborg?*

Like most sentients, she wasn't comfortable around bionics. Droids were different; they were machines, built to be soulless. But a cyborg was something unnatural, a reminder that your essence could be stripped from you, and you could still go on existing.

She recalled the cyborgs she'd seen on the newsfeed storming Mir-Brennan Tower then: rows of blank-faced warriors—half man, half machine. The Mir-Ferrins weren't the only ones to use cyborgs in their armies though. Cathal had squads of them too; marines who'd been mortally wounded in the line of duty and then brought back from the edge of death and 'transitioned' so they could serve once more. Every soldier who signed on to space fleet agreed that his body belonged to the Mir-Brennan clan-lord if he fell.

Vic Mir-Riorde stared back at Jenna, his face expressionless. "Good evening."

Shoving aside her discomfort, she nodded back. As her shock faded, she tried to see beyond the metal plate covering his right eye. His left eye was hazel. He wasn't like the cyborgs she'd seen serving in her brother's space fleet. Their eyes usually had a flat, glazed quality to them. But this one was observing Jenna with the same frankness that she was favoring him with. She noted, too, that Vic was attractive—well-built, with short brown hair, and dressed in military-style cargo pants and a fitted t-shirt.

The cyborg leaned forward so he could make out her features inside her shadowy hood. "You're the missing Mir-Brennan ambassador," he murmured after a lengthy pause. "According to the Shadownet, there's a huge bounty out for you."

Jenna tensed, fighting the urge to glance around her. She didn't want her identity announced to the pleasure house. Fortunately, they were talking in a private corner of the common room. "Is that a problem for you?"

Vic held her eye. "Not for me ... but you want to make sure you keep your hood up in case the wrong person recognizes you."

Jenna inclined her head, gaze narrowing. "So, you aren't the 'wrong person'?"

"That's up to you to decide, My Lady."

Inhaling deeply, Jenna wondered if Malik's reserve about this individual hadn't been warranted. Perhaps she shouldn't have interrupted him. They didn't know anything about the cyborg, or whether he was trustworthy.

Damn it, her situation was getting increasingly complex. She already had assassins hunting her; she didn't need bounty hunters on her tail as well. And although this moon was under Mir-Brennan jurisdiction, she didn't want word getting out that she was here. She'd met the Morith governor once, at a clan-gathering, and hadn't been impressed. The woman was an ambitious sycophant, and not someone she wanted to confide in about this rescue mission.

She couldn't afford anyone else recognizing her.

"Vic trades in machinery parts," Malik spoke up then. "And he also runs a smuggling operation. He's got clearance to land on Idral."

"My ship has Mir-Ferrin registration," the cyborg explained. "They're only letting their own people through the blockade at present ... so that should help us."

Jenna inclined her head. "And if they scan your ship?"

"I've got a hidden compartment in the main hold that is lined with Villum ... you two will have to hide in there."

Jenna glanced over at her bodyguard to find him observing her.

He didn't look pleased.

Turning back to Vic, she met his gaze squarely. There was no easy way to say this. "You know there's a price on my head … what's stopping you from turning me in?"

The cyborg stared back at her. His blank expression frustrated her, especially since his remaining eye was veiled. "There's bad blood between me and the Mir-Ferrins," he said after a pause. "They want me for desertion … I'd rather not advertise myself to them."

Jenna considered his answer. Vic Mir-Riorde didn't bandy words. "What's your story then?"

"I used to be a marine in the Mir-Ferrin space fleet, but I took a bolt to the chest during battle and was transitioned. The surgery didn't go as expected. I woke up half man, half machine … but I could still think for myself. I was still me."

Jenna sucked in a breath. That sounded terrifying.

"I deserted shortly afterward," Vic concluded. "Does that satisfy your curiosity?"

There was an edge to his voice, a challenge.

Jenna ignored it. If she was going to put her trust in this individual, she needed to know about his background. "And your crew?" she asked after a pause. "How big is it?"

"There's just the two of us." The cyborg's gaze never wavered. "My fee is ten thousand credits."

Jenna stiffened. "That's expensive … for such a small crew."

"This job comes with a great deal of risk … you could look for a better deal elsewhere, but I doubt you'd find it."

"Nine thousand."

"Ten. It's not up for discussion."

They stared at each other a moment before Jenna let out a slow exhale. She had enough experience with negotiations to know when someone wouldn't budge.

"All right," she agreed warily. "Six before we leave Morith, the rest on completion of the job."

The cyborg nodded. "That's acceptable."

Their gazes met once more. The cyborg's face might have been blank, but Jenna had spent years practicing her best 'diplomat mask' in front of the mirror. It was one her mother had taught her, and it had served her well during tense negotiations.

She couldn't read Vic's face—but he couldn't read hers either.

He had no idea she was worried. Did she want to put her trust in a rogue cyborg?

Jenna's chest tightened then, anxiety twisting within her. They'd spent hours trawling Morhaven's seedy back tunnels. Cyborg or not, Vic Mir-Riorde was the strongest candidate so far, and unlike some of the mercs they'd approached, he was willing to take on the job. Plus, with a price on her head, she needed to avoid further dealings with mercenaries. She couldn't pay as well as Tian and couldn't risk anyone recognizing her.

With each passing hour, Cathal's life was increasingly in peril. They had to get back to Idral—and soon.

"Very well." She stuck out her hand. "You're hired."

Vic's muscular body tensed, his hazel eye shadowing. Her gesture had thrown him, and Jenna wondered why.

Moments passed, and then he nodded stiffly before reaching out and shaking her hand firmly. He then did the same with Malik.

"Your companion tells me we're short on time." Vic drained the dregs of the glass before him and rose to his feet. "However, I'll need to refuel and fill in some paperwork before we can set off. I'll also get us … and your family … fake IDs." He paused then, pulling a small tablet from a pocket on the thigh of his cargo pants. "Can you send me everyone's photos?"

Jenna nodded, pulling out her own tablet and quickly bringing up images. She had numerous pictures of her family stored there, and Malik's photo wasn't hard to locate either. An instant later, she'd shared them all with Vic's device. "Done."

"Good," Vic replied, pocketing his tablet. "We leave in twelve hours … at 0900. Landing Bay 44. Don't be late."

"We won't be," Malik assured him.

15. CONFESSIONS

THE CYBORG DEPARTED, leaving the pleasure house through the sliding doors. Meanwhile, Jenna and Malik returned to their booth on the opposite side of the common room.

They'd only just seated themselves when the server appeared, with two frosted glasses upon a tray. "Here you are," she murmured, viewing Malik under long sparkly eyelashes. "Are you sure there won't be anything else?"

"No, thanks," Malik answered, for it was clear she hadn't been addressing his companion.

Jenna watched the half-clothed woman sashay off. She then glanced her bodyguard's way, expecting to see his gaze tracking the server's backside.

But he wasn't.

Instead, he was viewing Jenna with a narrowed gaze. "I had that conversation with the cyborg under control, you know … you didn't have to interrupt" —he paused then— "and risk drawing attention to yourself."

Jenna pushed back the edge of her hood a fraction and flashed him an arch look. "You were going to turn him down, weren't you?"

Malik's frown deepened.

"I thought so," she huffed.

Mouth compressing, her bodyguard tore his gaze from hers. He then picked up his glass and inspected it. "What's this then?"

Jenna plucked her tablet out of her cloak pocket and made a note of the time and gate number Vic had given them.

"A Horn Punch," she replied, distracted.

Malik nodded before trying it.

Putting away her tablet, Jenna raised her own glass to her lips and took a large gulp. The drink was unusual, both fruity and sharp, and left a tingle upon her tongue. "This is good."

"It is … I've never had anything like it," he replied.

Jenna leaned back in the seat, drumming her fingers on the table. Twelve hours suddenly seemed like forever. She understood that the cyborg would need to make preparations before they departed, but she wished they were leaving now.

"Relax," Malik drawled as her finger tapping increased in tempo. "There isn't anything more we can do for the moment. Once we finish our drinks, we'll head back to the room and get some sleep before our departure."

Jenna heaved a sigh and stilled her finger drumming. He was right: there wasn't any point in getting agitated. There was nothing to do but wait.

She glanced right then at where Malik lounged. They were sitting close, their thighs almost brushing. She was suddenly aware of the heat of him next to her, and the faint hint of spice from the cologne he'd used after shaving earlier.

Blinking, she tried to focus. "So, don't you think I made the right choice … hiring a cyborg?"

He met her eye before his mouth curved into a half-smile. "He'll probably work out. Vic is an ex-marine … he knows what he's doing in a fight."

"Let's hope so." Raising the glass to her lips, Jenna took yet another gulp.

A few yards away, a female human perched astride the lap of a patron. She was grinding her naked breasts in his face as music, a deep bass, thudded through the smoky common room.

Jenna watched them, idly wondering what it would be like to put on such a public display.

"Wow," Malik murmured. Jenna glanced back at her bodyguard to see that he'd drained half his glass and was now peering down at it. "This stuff has a kick … what do they put in it?"

"I have no idea … the server said it was a house specialty," Jenna admitted, before raising her glass again. "But I like it." She let out another long sigh then, sinking into the upholstery. A warm languor spread over her, and before she knew what she was doing, she blurted out, "How old were you when you lost your virginity, Malik?"

Her bodyguard cast her a surprised look, while Jenna favored him with a blithe smile and took another sip of Horn Punch. She was aware she'd just asked something inappropriate, but she wasn't embarrassed. Just curious.

After a moment, he replied, "Sixteen."

"Was it at a pleasure house?"

"It was, actually." Malik leaned back, one hand stretched out on the table between them. Jenna found herself admiring its strength. What would it be like to have his hands on her? "One of the girls my mother worked with offered me her services … as a present when I was accepted into the Melor Guard."

Jenna imagined Malik Mir-Draven at sixteen; certainly, he wouldn't have been as intimidating back then.

Strangely enough, right now his presence didn't put her on edge as it usually did. She felt as if she could have talked to him about anything—that she could tell him her darkest secrets and he wouldn't mind.

"My first time was when I was eighteen," she admitted, taking another sip of her drink. Her glass was almost empty—maybe she should order another one. "He was a Mir-Lelith delegate, and it was my first trip away from Idral."

Malik raised an eyebrow. "What was the experience like?"

Gods, it was as if they were old friends, catching up. An odd sense of liberation flowed over Jenna. She was used to keeping her thoughts and feelings tightly locked away in a cage; being able to set them free was exhilarating.

"A little disappointing if I'm honest." She paused, remembering the fumbling, embarrassing episode. Truthfully, all her sexual experiences had been disappointing—while those in her marriage had left her feeling bitter and used. Usually, thinking of Tian in that way brought up unpleasant memories—more than once he'd called her a cold bitch and accused her of lying there like a corpse while he took her—yet right now, she couldn't bring herself to care. "It was over fast ... he had a good time, at least ... well, I think he did. I've never seen anyone get dressed so quickly afterward though."

Her bodyguard snorted. "He sounds like an idiot."

Jenna let out another deep sigh. "You're right ... he was."

Her bodyguard laughed. The sound was low, yet with a sensual note to it that made her breathing grow shallow. She became conscious then of how alert she was. Despite the long day, every sense was sharp—and her awareness of the man seated next to her in the booth was growing more acute with each passing moment.

She also noted a tightening in her lower belly and a spreading warmth. The sensation was strange and pleasurable while at the same time alarming. It made her want to wriggle in her seat.

However, when she did shift, to ease herself, the warmth deepened, and a gentle pulsing began, an ache that had her arching her back.

Jenna bit down on her lip to prevent herself from groaning.

An instant later, she glanced at Malik to find him watching her under hooded lids.

Their gazes met and held—and suddenly it felt overly hot in their booth.

Jenna was conscious of her breathing, the slow 'thud' of her pulse in her ears, and that throbbing ache in the cradle of her hips that intensified with each passing second.

What was in that drink?

Deep down, Jenna knew she should be concerned, and yet another part of her longed to call the server over and order two more Horn Punches. She was starting to feel as if she could take on the galaxy and win.

Reaching out, she placed a hand over her bodyguard's, trailing the pads of her fingertips up his long, tapering fingers, across the back of his hand, to his wrist.

"I imagine you're a good lover, Malik," she murmured.

He gave her a slow, sensual smile. In the dim lighting inside the booth, his eyes were a deep shade of purple, like the evening sky just before the stars came out. "I haven't had any complaints."

Jenna's breathing caught. His arrogance thrilled her.

He reached up with his free hand then and glided his thumb along her jaw. "You're the sexiest woman I've ever met." His voice roughened. "I've fantasized about having you for years."

"You have?" Jenna was aware her voice had gone high and breathy.

The pulsing ache had spread to between her thighs. She was close to climbing this man like he was her ladder to oblivion.

"You remember that dress you wore for the clan anniversary last year ... the black and gold one?" he continued, leaning closer. His breath feathered her ear, and Jenna shivered, hot and cold bathing her skin.

"Yes," she whispered back.

"I went to bed that night imagining tearing it off you ... I lay there thinking about taking you up against the wall, fucking you slowly until you screamed my name."

Jenna swallowed hard. She was sweating now. Their surroundings—the coarse laughter of patrons, the giggle of the females working here, and the rhythmic thud of deliberately sensual music—all faded.

All Jenna could think about was that if Malik kept talking, she was going to straddle him here and now.

As if reading her mind, her bodyguard leaned in closer still. He drew back the edge of her hood, his lips grazing the shell of her ear before trailing down her jaw. "I want you, Jenna … tonight."

"Can I get you two anything else?" An amused female voice interrupted them.

Drawing back from Malik, Jenna slowly turned her head and focused on the server from earlier. The woman was smirking as she watched them. "We have private rooms out back … ten credits for an hour."

"No, thanks," Malik replied, a rasp to his voice now as his fingers entwined through Jenna's and squeezed. "We're leaving."

16. WILD

THE WOMAN WATCHED the couple depart the pleasure house.

Keisha scowled. After downing those Horn Punches so fast, she was sure they'd take her up on her offer of a room hire.

"Cheap bastards," she muttered under her breath, returning behind the bar.

Irritated, she stabbed at her tablet on the countertop, bringing up the Shadownet. It was a slow night, and boredom was setting in. Maybe there would be something on there that would distract her from her worries.

Keisha had owned *The Hook and Horn* for a few years now, but with the opening of three new pleasure houses locally, business had been tough. Maybe she needed to find some new dancers—some prettier human females like the brunette who'd just departed on the arm of her handsome companion.

Yes, Keisha had noticed the looks the woman had received from many of the patrons when she'd crossed the floor earlier.

Even cloaked and hooded, she had an unconscious sensuality men noticed.

Scrolling through the Shadownet newsfeed, with one eye on the floor, where a dancer wearing nothing but a glittery gold thong was wrapping herself around a pole, Keisha read the latest stories and notices.

Halfway down the page, she froze.

The brunette who'd just left her pleasure house stared back at her. The woman had tried to hide her face, but the Horn Punch had made her careless; her hood had slipped back when Keisha approached their booth just before.

It was definitely her.

Keisha breathed a curse.

She'd heard about the attack on the Mir-Brennan ambassador on Aura Terminal a few days earlier—but she hadn't seen a picture of Jenna Mir-Brennan herself until now.

The Mir-Ferrins had put a bounty for forty thousand credits on her.

Keisha's mouth curved then, excitement fluttering under her ribcage.

Her money worries could be over.

Pushing herself off away from the counter, she sashayed her way back out onto the common room floor. A punter beckoned to her, holding up an empty glass.

Keisha ignored him.

Instead, she made for a table at the back where four human males lounged. One of them had a woman perched on his lap. His hand thrust roughly between her thighs as the dancer squirmed, trying to free herself of his hold.

"Stop it, Merv," Keisha snapped. "You know you pay extra for that."

The man sneered, even as he obeyed her.

Keisha stepped closer to the table, lowering her voice. "Listen up … I've got a job for you boys."

The tunnel outside the pleasure house was dimly lit, the air cold and musty. Ropes of lights stretched overhead, casting an orange hue over the pitted rock, although some of them flickered. There was no heating in the outer tunnels, for they were far from the central hub.

Jenna thought the cool air might clear her head, might ease the tingling in her limbs, the ache deep within her womb—but it didn't.

Still grasping her hand, Malik led her away from the gaudily lit façade of *The Hook and Horn*. The tunnel was empty, although, in the distance, the sound of drunken laughter echoed against stone.

However, they'd only gone around two hundred meters when Malik stepped into a side passage, pulling Jenna with him.

The next thing she knew, he'd pushed her up against the wall, and his mouth was on hers.

Malik's kiss was hot, hungry, and demanding, and she gasped, her lips parting. Jenna writhed against him, desperate to taste him, touch him.

Groaning low in his throat, Malik pressed his hips against hers, and she felt him—rock-hard against her lower belly; his erection was painfully evident, even through the material of his cargos.

Unable to stop herself, Jenna let out a needy whimper.

Whispering a curse against her mouth, Malik gripped her by the hips and lifted her up, sliding a leg between her thighs to spread them.

An instant later, he was grinding himself into her.

Jenna arched against him, yearning for more. She didn't care that they were standing in a dark passage, that the rock was cold against her back, or that they were still fully clothed.

She wanted him. Here. Now.

Malik let her slide down the long, thick length of his erection, in a slow, sensual movement, and she shuddered, the pulsing ache in her womb almost unbearable now.

She pushed her hands under his cloak and dug around under his padded jacket and t-shirt, her fingers exploring the hot skin underneath.

All the while, he devoured her, his tongue tangling with hers.

Jenna went wild, biting down on his lower lip as she plucked at the waistband of his cargo pants.

And then, an amused snort reverberated across the passageway.

Malik froze. And although she was close to drowning in lust, Jenna did the same.

"Sorry to interrupt," a voice drawled. "But your night is about to take a disappointing turn."

Dazed and breathing hard, Jenna leaned back against the wall, her gaze flicking right to the tunnel they'd just stepped out of. Four broad-shouldered human males stood there, their faces shadowed by deep hoods. One of them had a laser-pistol pointed at Malik's head.

Observing the men, Jenna wondered why she wasn't scared. They were clearly in trouble, yet her reaction was more one of mild concern.

Time seemed to slow as Malik leaned into her once more.

"I don't believe it," one of the others sniggered. "He's gonna keep going."

"Just kill him then," the man who'd spoken first replied. "It's her we want, anyway."

"Get down," Malik whispered in Jenna's ear.

A heartbeat later, he whirled away from her, drawing his own laser-pistol from where it hung at his side, under his cloak.

Jenna dove for the ground.

White light flashed across the tunnel and the passage beyond.

Rolling onto her side, she glimpsed the shocked faces of their attackers—three of them now, for their leader was down.

Surprise jolted through her. She recognized them.

Malik moved fast, closing in on the thugs as they raised their weapons to shoot him. He kicked the pistol out of one man's hand and punched him in the throat, sending him flying back into his companion. While the two men reeled backward, Malik then dodged a laser bolt from the third attacker.

Jenna shielded her eyes as the bolt detonated on the wall behind Malik.

Holstering his pistol, her bodyguard kept moving— and an instant later, the hum of an igniting laser-blade echoed off the surrounding stone. The longsword blade swept in a silvery arc, decapitating the shooter. Bright-white light illuminated the dingy tunnel once more. Laser-blades had three settings: blue for sparring, orange for stun, and white for kill.

But their attackers weren't cowed by the weapon. The two Malik had dealt with earlier came back for a second go, their curses echoing down the tunnel. Moments later, both lay sprawled at his feet.

Out of breath, Malik shut off the weapon and hooked it back onto his belt.

Gingerly, Jenna rose to her feet. Her body felt loose and fluid, and despite the dangerous situation Malik had just dealt with, her mind was oddly calm and focused. She was also impressed—she'd known her bodyguard could handle himself in a fight, but she'd never seen anyone move with such brutal precision.

"Are you all right?" she asked, stepping close to him.

Malik's face was all hollows in the dim light. "Yes … are you?"

Jenna nodded. "Those men were drinking at *The Hook and Horn* … at a table near us."

"I recognized their faces too," Malik said roughly. "They were after you."

Jenna looked down at the four bodies that littered the ground around them. And despite the warm glow that still enveloped her, she shivered.

Gods, had the news of the bounty traveled that fast?

Raising her gaze once more, Jenna met Malik's eye. She reached out then, slipping her hand into his and squeezing tight. "Let's get out of here," she murmured.

Ensuring their hoods were pulled up, Malik and Jenna left the bodies of their attackers sprawled in the tunnel—their blood pooling across the pale stone—and headed toward the central hub.

Despite his close brush with death, Malik felt strangely relaxed. His limbs were light, his body energized. The feel of Jenna's hand in his caused a tingling sensation to run up his arm to his chest—and his groin started to throb once more, as it had before they'd been interrupted in the passageway.

If those thugs hadn't attacked them, he'd have taken her there, damn the consequences.

In the back of his mind, beneath the hunger that made it nearly impossible to focus on anything else, Malik was aware he shouldn't be doing this.

You're going to get yourself fired, the voice of reason whispered.

That was all true. Lady Jenna was his employer, and he was stepping over an invisible line tonight—yet right now, he couldn't bring himself to care.

Turning left into a wide tunnel that led directly to the central hub, they walked past a line of clubs. Music throbbed from the doorways, and brawny bouncers eyed the couple as they walked by.

Malik squeezed Jenna's hand, and she returned the gesture. His breathing quickened, in anticipation of what would happen when they got back to their room.

The moment they were inside their lodgings, the door hissing shut behind them, Malik pushed Jenna up against the wall, his mouth slanting over hers. Unlike the kiss in the passage, which had been brutal and urgent, Malik slowed this one down. He explored her mouth gently, his teeth grazing her lips.

Jenna groaned and arched up against him, her arms linking around his neck.

Malik drew back, his breathing labored now, before he slammed his palm against the panel next to the door, ensuring they were locked inside.

He didn't want anyone else interrupting them.

Jenna threw herself at him, all restraint gone now. Their mouths collided, tongues tangling as they fell against the wall. The scent of Desert Rose drifted up between them, and Malik's gut twisted. Ever since they'd left the pleasure house, his need for this woman had grown, to the point where it was becoming unbearable.

Fortunately, Jenna appeared to want him as much as he did her.

She clawed at Malik, shoving off his cloak, her fingers fumbling with the quilted jacket underneath. "Gods, you're wearing too many clothes," she muttered. "Get them off!"

Malik didn't need to be told twice. Stepping away from her, he shed his cloak before he started tearing off his clothing. He'd never undressed so fast.

Likewise, Jenna wriggled out of her cargo pants and jacket. Seconds later, she stood before him, naked.

The sight made his chest ache. She was all soft pale skin and lush curves. Her breasts, heavy and rose-tipped, begged to be sucked.

Groaning low in his throat, Malik reached for her, but Jenna launched herself at him first, literally climbing him now. Her hot mouth grazed his chest, throat, and jaw before she found his mouth once more.

Dizziness slammed into Malik. Jidea preserve him, he could hardly bear it.

His hands were everywhere, squeezing, rubbing, stroking her soft curves, her satiny skin. They kissed again, devouring each other, while he teased her swollen nipples with his fingers.

Jenna took him in hand then, her fingers curling around his erection that thrust up between them. His member jerked at her touch, and a groan dragged up from his throat.

Their mouths met once more, hot and hungry, while she stroked his length.

Malik glanced down to see the swollen head of his cock was wet with need.

If she kept touching him like this, he was going to explode.

"Malik," Jenna gasped. She leaned back against the wall, spreading her legs and guiding his shaft between them. She then stroked its wet tip against her sex. "I can't bear it ... I need you ... now!"

Malik's breath caught in his throat. She wouldn't have to ask him twice.

Catching hold of Jenna's hips, he turned her around, so she was facing the wall. He then guided her hips back so that she was forced to brace herself against it with her hands.

"I'm going to fuck you now," he ground out.

Jenna gave a needy, desperate sigh, spreading her legs for him, exposing herself to him. "Please," she whimpered.

Malik pushed into her, sliding in slowly, inch by inch, stretching her as he went.

Jenna gave her hips a long, sensual roll, and he made a choking sound in the back of his throat.

Gods, this woman was going to kill him. He gripped her hips, preventing her from repeating the move. His fingers dug into the soft flesh as he seated himself fully inside her.

Jenna gave a long, trembling sigh. "This is perfect," she whispered. "*You're* perfect, Malik." She wriggled against him, although he still held her fast, hampering her movements.

He started to thrust then, deep and slow, withdrawing almost to the tip before plunging deep once more. "I've dreamed of fucking you like this," he admitted roughly. "The clan-lord's haughty sister. You're even hotter than I imagined."

Jenna gave a guttural groan in response, and he increased his rhythm to match the rasp of their breathing.

Jenna hung her head between her braced arms. He could feel the way her body quivered with each thrust, the way her core fluttered against his cock. She was drawing close. He wanted to push her over the brink.

Malik let go of her hips then, and one hand slid down between her shoulder blades as fingers traced the indentation of her spine, before both his hands splayed out across her backside. He spread her wider still then, lifting her up to change the angle of his penetration.

"Malik!" Jenna's voice turned high, raw.

He thrust into her again and felt a rush of wet heat. Growling her name, he increased the speed and force of his thrusts.

Jenna writhed against him, impaling herself on his length, and bringing him deeper still.

Malik took her wildly now, vaguely aware that Jenna was crying out, gasping words, pleas.

She still needed more. And when he reached between her thighs, his fingers sliding through her wetness to the sensitive nub there, Jenna's raw cry filled the room.

Arching hard against him, she shattered.

And at that moment, all Malik's fantasies came true—for Jenna Mir-Brennan screamed his name.

17. EVERYTHING

AN INSISTENT 'BLEEPING' roused Jenna from a deep sleep.

Stretching upon the bed, she came awake slowly, as if rising from a deep, warm pool. Sleep tugged at her, beckoning her back. However, that annoying sound wouldn't let her be.

Jenna's eyes flickered open, and she groaned as pain lanced through her temples.

She was aware then that she lay stretched out across a naked male body.

Malik lay upon his back, cradling her against his broad chest—and the bleeping was coming from the device strapped to his wrist.

Pain lanced across Jenna's temples, and she stifled another groan. Her mouth was dry and her mind foggy.

Dragging her gaze down Malik's nakedness, and then realizing that she, too, was unclothed, Jenna tried to make sense of the situation.

An instant later, it all came back, barreling into her with such clarity that she gasped.

Their search for a mercenary. Hiring Vic the cyborg at *The Hook and Horn*. The cocktails they'd drunk together. The attack outside the pleasure house. The wild sex she and Malik had once they got back to the room.

Every detail was etched in her mind, and yet at the same time, it was as if she was remembering someone else's memory.

Pulse fluttering at the base of her throat, Jenna gently shook her lover awake.

"Malik."

His eyelids fluttered, and then his eyes opened, their violet depths unfocused for a few moments before they sharpened.

For a heartbeat, he stared up at Jenna. "What?" he croaked.

"Your wrist-comm."

Blearily, he brought his wrist close to his face and squinted at it. He then swore. "We need to be at the spaceport in an hour."

An instant later, her bodyguard rolled off the bed and to his feet before striding naked into the bathroom.

The moment the door shut behind him, Jenna buried her face in her hands.

The Gods strike her down—what had they done?

Her heart started to pound then, sweat beading on her top lip. They hadn't even used any protection last night. She was on birth control—something she'd deliberately hidden from Tian over the past two years—but there were other consequences to not taking precautions with sex.

Shit.

The sound of water rushing reached her, rousing her from her panic and mortification. Jumping up from the bed, she retrieved her clothing from where it lay scattered across the floor and hurriedly dressed. Her shower would wait until later.

They couldn't afford to arrive late at the spaceport. What if Vic got jumpy and left? She'd already paid him a hefty deposit after all.

Her carelessness could cost Cathal his life.

She was sitting on the edge of the bed, and had just finished lacing her boots, when the bathroom door slid open.

Jenna automatically looked up to see Malik stride out, still gloriously naked. Glancing hurriedly away—which felt like a ridiculous move, especially after last night— Jenna rose to her feet.

"Are you okay?" Malik asked. His voice held a rasp, betraying the fact he, like her, was badly dehydrated. They'd both need to down some water before they set out for the spaceport.

Jenna drew in a slow breath and raised her chin once more, carefully avoiding looking anywhere except his face. "I think so." She exhaled sharply then. "Although I can't believe what an idiot I am."

Malik raked a hand through his dark hair. "None of what happened was your fault."

"It wasn't?" Her voice sounded brittle. "I'm the one who ordered those drinks."

A groove appeared between his brows. "The server didn't tell you what you were ordering?"

Jenna winced. "No."

"I'd say she was hoping we'd make use of one of their rooms." He reached for his pants before glancing up at her. "How much of last night do you remember, Jenna?"

Not 'My Lady' or 'Lady Jenna'. They'd gone way past formalities.

Swallowing, Jenna held his eye. "Everything."

Her breathing caught then, for he was looking at her with such disarming intensity, it was impossible to break his stare.

"So do I," he admitted softly.

Long moments stretched out, and then Jenna cleared her throat. "Yes, well … neither of us were ourselves." She strode to the kitchenette in the corner of the room. "Water?"

"Yes, thanks."

Pouring them tall glasses, Jenna turned back to find Malik dressed in yesterday's clothing, like she was. Their fingers brushed as he took the glass from her, and Jenna tried to ignore the way her pulse leaped in response.

Get a grip, Mir-Brennan.

Last night had been delicious, sexy, and forbidden. But it had also been a mistake.

If they hadn't been influenced by that cocktail, neither of them would have transgressed.

Heat washed over her then as images from the night before resurfaced. The things they'd done, the way he'd taken her against the wall—and the way she screamed his name. She had no idea she could let go like that, or that she could experience such pleasure. A small shiver passed through her as her body responded to the memories, to the things he'd said. She tensed then, embarrassment prickling her skin.

He thinks I'm haughty?

Jenna shut her reaction down and took a few gulps of water. She drained her glass and turned to put it on the counter.

However, when she turned back, she found Malik standing close, towering over her.

Wordlessly, he hooked his fingers under her chin, gently raising her face so she met his eye. Her bodyguard's expression was shuttered, yet his gaze seemed to see right into her soul. "I repeat … you're not to blame," he murmured. "The fault is mine. I should have checked out what we were drinking before we touched them." His features tightened then. "And I shouldn't have behaved as I did once we left the pleasure house … especially now there's a bounty out on you."

Heat washed across Jenna at the memory of their savage kiss in that passageway. If those thugs hadn't interrupted them, they'd have had sex there, heedless that they were in a public place.

Jenna bit down on her lower lip—a mistake, for the act made his gaze drop to her mouth. Suddenly, the air between them was charged, dangerous.

Her breathing grew shallow, in anticipation, but Malik let go of her chin and stepped back. Looking away, he drained his glass of water.

Jenna dragged in a deep breath, relief warring with disappointment. Clamping down on her reaction, she moved toward the bed and retrieved her bag, stuffing her tablet inside. "There isn't any point in regretting what happened," she said then, more to herself than to him. "What's done is done."

"I don't." She turned to find Malik watching her. "I just wish neither of us had been drugged last night." His gaze glinted. "You deserve better than that, Jenna."

Closing the door behind her, Jenna followed Malik out into the narrow tunnel. She carried her bag slung across her back, while he'd shouldered his heavy backpack. They exited the passage, and were about to head back into the central hub beyond, when Malik halted, causing Jenna to run into him.

She opened her mouth to protest, but he raised a hand in warning.

Peering over his shoulder into the cavern they were about to enter, Jenna's gaze alighted on a knot of black and grey uniformed officers with laser-rifles slung over their shoulders.

Her pulse accelerated. *The Morith Guard.*

The officers had just stopped a human couple and were questioning them. "The shooting took place around ten hours ago, near one of the pleasure houses in the nor-west tunnels," one of the officers intoned, his voice carrying across the cavern. "The owner of the pleasure house reported it. There were four fatalities … and a couple was seen fleeing the scene. We believe they were Ambassador Jenna Mir-Brennan and her bodyguard, Malik Mir-Draven." The officer held up a tablet. "Have you seen either of these people?"

"No," the woman replied, her tone cowed.

"Neither have I," her companion muttered.

Jenna hurriedly backed up, and Malik followed her.

He turned, meeting her gaze briefly before he gestured for them to retrace their steps down the narrow tunnel. Fortunately, it wasn't a dead end. "Come on," he grunted. "We'll have to find another way out of here."

Malik and Jenna managed to avoid the patrols that roamed the network of damp tunnels of Morhaven in search of those responsible for the murder of four of its citizens.

As they slipped through the shadows, Malik silently cursed.

Someone at the pleasure house had told the Morith Guard that Jenna was here; it wouldn't be long before every mercenary on this rock would be hunting her.

Forty thousand credits wasn't a small sum.

Malik scanned his surroundings constantly while he navigated the tunnels, senses sharp.

Jenna wasn't safe on this moon any longer—he had to get her out.

By the time they emerged into the murky light beyond the underground city, he was sweating, and he welcomed the slap of icy air on his face. It was still dark outdoors, for Morith's night would last a while yet, and the air was so cold it hurt to breathe in too deeply.

By the time they reached the spaceport, Malik noted that Jenna was starting to shiver, despite that she'd wrapped her cloak tightly around her. It wasn't any wonder the inhabitants of this cold moon had built their settlements underground.

They entered the terminal—a low-slung utilitarian building built out of grey mud-brick—and headed left. Despite that it was still night, the port was busy. Cloaked figures towing cases hurried past heading toward the gates.

Jenna and Malik weren't leaving from here, but from one of the small, privately owned bays on the outskirts of the port. Unlike the covered terminal, the bays were outdoors and little more than craters carved out of the rocky soil.

Landing Bay 44 lay in shadow as they approached. Slowing his stride, Malik glanced down at the glowing dial upon his wrist-com. "We're a few minutes early," he murmured, his breath steaming in the frigid air. "But I expected him to be here already."

"It's definitely Bay 44," Jenna assured him. "I wrote it down on my tablet after he left."

Malik studied the freighter parked in front of him.

The ship was a sleek gun-metal-grey vessel shaped like an arrowhead. Malik had seen this style of freighter before; it was an older-class Mir-Ferrin vessel, with physical shields rather than the transparent deflectors the new ships used.

And as he continued to observe the freighter, lights winked on under the hull, and a ramp lowered with the hiss of hydraulics.

Malik slowly released the breath he hadn't even realized he'd been holding. He then moved off toward the vessel, glancing behind him at Jenna. "Let me lead … just in case you hired the wrong man."

Jenna pulled a face. "I really hope I didn't."

Malik did too. And after his own lack of care a few hours earlier, he wasn't taking any unnecessary risks.

His jaw tightened then. He was angry with himself for being so reckless, but he'd told Jenna the truth earlier. He didn't regret what had happened between them, only that the Horn Punch had altered their senses. They'd both consented to sex, but the drink had blurred things. It had robbed them both of inhibitions and torn down the walls of position and class that divided them, revealing red-hot lust.

And now, she knew about the dirty thoughts he'd entertained about her over the years.

Upon waking earlier—to find Jenna's supple body pressed against his, her dark-brown eyes filled with alarm—he'd virtually fled to the bathroom. He'd needed to ready himself to leave, but he'd also required a minute or two to pull himself together.

Malik's gut coiled then, heat igniting across his lower spine.

Even now, he was acutely aware of Jenna. She was a well-brought-up lady, the clan-lord's sister and ambassador, but underneath that buttoned-up reserve, she was fire.

Pushing the heated images aside, Malik's gaze swept the shadowed bay.

Enough. You need to focus.

He couldn't let Jenna's presence distract him. He couldn't do his job properly otherwise.

Approaching the ramp, he peered into the belly of the freighter.

An instant later, Malik spied a tall, broad-shouldered figure, dressed in slate-grey cargo pants and a padded jacket, emerge from the hull and descend the ramp.

18. ABOARD THE WAYFARER

VIC NODDED TO them. His expression was inscrutable, but as a cyborg, that was to be expected. Nevertheless, Malik found his lack of emotion unsettling, as he had back at *The Hook and Horn*.

He'd never had dealings with cyborgs before, having only ever seen them from a distance when he'd accompanied Cathal on his visits to space fleet. He remembered their blank faces, frozen stares, and rigid postures.

Vic was different to those soldiers. He had free will and was a deserter—but he was also an unknown quantity and had once served the Mir-Ferrins.

Vic also knew about the bounty on Jenna. Could they trust him?

"Good to see you're on time," Vic greeted them smoothly. "You might as well board. We're about to start the engines."

They followed the cyborg onto the freighter, stepping into a paneled entranceway. The ramp rose behind Malik and Jenna, sealing them in. The overhead light flickered then, and Vic squinted up at it with his good eye. "I thought I'd fixed that," he muttered. He then glanced over at Malik, noting that he carried a heavy rucksack. "You came prepared?"

Malik nodded. "I've got pistols and protective gear." He then patted the utility belt at his waist, "… and two pyro-grenades."

It was just as well he'd strapped three of the devices onto his belt before departing Mir-Brennan Tower. They wouldn't have escaped the Widow Makers without them.

"I got those IDs and gathered some weapons as well," the cyborg replied. "Although nothing as useful as a pyro-grenade." He then moved ahead up the passage. "This way."

Malik glanced behind him at where Jenna stood silently. He could see the strain on her face, the veiled anxiety in her eyes. However, he also recognized the determined set of her jaw. She was both braver and tougher than he'd initially taken her for.

All the same, Jenna wasn't a trained soldier like he was.

Did she realize exactly what they were up against? Her brother, sister-in-law, and niece would be heavily guarded. Getting in and out unscathed and uncaptured was going to be hard, even using *The Passage*.

Jenna caught him watching her then. Gaze narrowing, she raised her chin. "Before you ask … yes, I'm fine," she said crisply. "I'm just worried about Cathal … I hope we manage to reach him in time."

Malik was about to answer, but she was already moving past him, following Vic forward.

Wordlessly, he joined her, stepping out into a wide grey-paneled cabin, lined with seats and a table on one side, and a stack of bunks on the opposite one. An open door and a set of steps led up to the cockpit.

Jenna halted abruptly in front of him, her sharp inhale a warning.

Malik stopped, his attention snapping to the large, bipedal droid that stood in the center of the space. Gleaming black plate armor covered its lanky form, and glowing red eyes stared at the passengers. Long arms hung at its sides, and the droid's knees were bent slightly, as if it was preparing to pounce.

Malik's skin prickled. He glanced Vic's way. "Please tell me this isn't your crew member?"

Vic inclined his head. "He is … meet my first mate, Obsidian."

"Your first mate?" Malik looked at the towering black battle-droid once more, unease rippling through him. These droids were exclusively used by the Mir-Ferrin clan-lord, warding his flagship and marching into battle alongside his cyborgs. Malik had heard enough about them over the years to know you didn't want to mess with a battle-droid; just one look and you could see it was lethal. "Where did you get one of these?"

"When I deserted from the Mir-Ferrin space fleet, I took him with me." Vic paused there, noting Malik and Jenna's tension. "Don't worry, he's been reprogrammed … Obsidian no longer takes orders from Mican Mir-Ferrin."

"That's a relief," Jenna muttered.

"Greetings," Obsidian spoke then. The low, rasping drone of the droid's voice made the fine hair on the back of Malik's neck bristle. "Welcome aboard *The Wayfarer*."

"At least it's got manners," Jenna murmured.

Malik's gaze narrowed. He'd watched the newsreels of the attack on Idral, had seen these killing machines cutting down the House Guard and his own men. Vic should have told him his first mate was a battle-droid.

Malik didn't trust droids; unlike Jenna, who'd had a utility-droid at her side since childhood, his experience with non-sentients in childhood—the police-droids that patrolled the streets of Melor—had imprinted unpleasant memories.

You couldn't reason with a droid or plead with one.

Mir-Ferrin battle-droids were built with just one purpose: to kill.

Ignoring Malik's frown, Vic glanced back at his first mate. "Go ahead and start the engines … I'll get our passengers settled in."

"Yes, Captain." Obsidian turned, moving with almost sentient suppleness as it mounted the stairs to the cockpit. Only the low whir and rattle of its metal parts belied it.

Meanwhile, Vic turned back to Malik and Jenna. He then gestured to the seats behind them. "Strap yourselves in … we'll be off now."

"How long until we reach Idral?" Jenna asked.

"Just over five hours."

"And you're sure you can get us through the blockade?"

Vic nodded. "As sure as I can be. I'm flying a Mir-Ferrin ship … and I'll be using a fake ID. Vic Mir-Riorde is wanted for desertion by the Mir-Ferrins, so I'd rather not advertise myself to them." He paused then, folding his muscular arms across his chest. "I've got a hold full of machine parts to off-load in Melor if they start asking any questions."

Jenna held his gaze for a moment before nodding. She then moved over to the row of seats, lowering herself into the one nearest.

Malik divested himself of his heavy rucksack, which he secured to the cabin wall, and sat down next to Jenna. She'd opened her bag, retrieving her space-sickness tablets and a bottle of water. Swallowing the tablets, she then clipped on her harness.

The woman wore a determined, grim look upon her face, as if she were going in for a tooth extraction without anesthetic.

She hadn't suffered too badly when they'd departed Aura Terminal—yet they'd been traveling upon a passenger liner, and the departure had been smoother than this one would be.

Malik focused then on strapping himself in as the deck beneath his feet started to vibrate.

Vic strolled past, moving with the loose-limbed agility of one used to living in cramped quarters, and threw himself into the pilot's seat. Obsidian crouched next to him, clawed hands roaming over the console.

The cyborg then hit a button on the console and leaned forward. "Tower, this is *The Wayfarer*. We're ready for our 0900 slot. Do we have clearance for takeoff?"

"Affirmative, *Wayfarer*, you're cleared," a slightly bored voice drawled back.

The vibrations beneath Malik's feet reached a crescendo, a high-pitched whine echoing through the cabin.

He glanced over at where Jenna sat, rigid in her seat, her fingers clenched around her harness straps. Her face had gone bloodless—not a good sign.

"Hang on," he murmured. "These small ships make a lot of noise on takeoff and landing, but things will be smooth once we get in the air."

Jenna gave a jerky nod. Nonetheless, her pinched expression didn't ease. "I'll be all right," she ground out.

The freighter shuddered then, lifting off the landing pad. Peering forward, Malik watched the lights of the spaceport recede as the ship gained height. His stomach then dropped as the ship turned and accelerated up out of the moon's atmosphere.

Merciful Syr, it was a blessed relief when they'd finally made the jump into hyperspace.

Jenna sat there, heart pounding, belly roiling, and cold sweat bathing her skin. And when the freighter lurched forward, bile stung the back of her throat.

She swallowed it down, focusing instead on Cathal, Isla, and Bea—the reasons she was sitting in this cargo ship. The reasons she'd hired a questionable individual and his even more dubious sidekick to help rescue her family.

Vic concerned her—after all, he hadn't told them he worked with a battle-droid—but at least he was confident he could get them through the blockade.

She hoped it wasn't just bravado, although they'd find out soon enough.

A moment later, the vibrations beneath her feet changed to a deep purr, and the sickly waves of nausea receded.

Exhausted, she sank back against her seat. After a few moments, she cast Malik a sidelong glance.

He was observing her. His violet eyes drew her in, and his mouth lifted at the corners in a half-smile that made warmth ignite under Jenna's breastbone.

Their stare drew out, and the heat spread across her chest. No words had passed between them since takeoff, yet there was no denying the intimacy of the look they now shared. It was a reminder of a different kind of intimacy—a carnal one.

"You can take off your harnesses," Vic interrupted them. The cyborg had left his first mate at the controls while he entered the cabin once more.

Jenna dragged her gaze from Malik's, grateful for the distraction. Unclipping herself, she rose to her feet and unsteadily moved past her bodyguard. Her knee brushed his thigh as she did so, and her pulse quickened in response.

Damn it, the man had a primal effect on her. She needed to get ahold of herself.

Turning to Vic, she shifted her attention back to their mission. "Where's the smuggler's hold we'll be hiding in?"

"Right here." He tapped the heel of his booted foot on the metal deck. "They'll do a full scan of the ship … but as I told you, it's lined, so they won't find you."

Jenna glanced down at the metal deck, her belly clenching. It was getting real now, and she felt underprepared for what lay ahead. Her diplomatic skills likely wouldn't be of much use to her when they reached Mir-Brennan Tower. Instead, she needed to be able to defend herself at least.

Glancing back at Malik, she flashed him a tight smile. "In the meantime, we need to start preparing for our rescue." Their gazes held. "And I should learn how to handle myself with a laser-pistol."

19. DISTANT PLANETS

"WHICH HAND DO you favor?"

"My left … why?"

"You need to grip the pistol in your dominant hand."

Malik's expression was all business as he passed her the weapon, butt pointed downward. It was a small handgun, far less cumbersome than the ones he'd brought for him, Vic, and Obsidian.

"Whenever you're practicing, make sure the energy output is set at zero. Fifty percent will stun … while anything over eighty percent is lethal," Malik explained. "And always hold the pistol with the barrel facing down and away from you when you're adjusting the output."

Jenna nodded, mouth thinning. She would have thought some things didn't need explaining. Nevertheless, she'd asked for this lesson. Once they landed on Idral, they'd be able to start planning the rescue mission in detail. Right now though, she needed to know how to shoot straight.

"Steady it with your free hand." Malik moved behind her. "That's good." They stood at the cockpit end of the cabin. Vic had switched on a target screen at the opposite end, up against the wall. The screen was equipped with a laser sensor. Fortunately, as an ex-marine, Vic had one; he liked to keep his shooting sharp. "Now place your feet shoulder-width apart, and step forward with your right foot."

Jenna obeyed. She then squinted at the target. Its various rings glowed yellow and blue on the screen. "So, I just point and shoot then?"

Vic gave a soft snort. The cyborg lounged on a nearby bunk, watching the lesson unfold. Jenna wished she didn't have an audience, but since this was Vic's ship, she could hardly banish him from her presence.

She just needed to focus, to forget everything except that target on the far wall.

"Open your left hand … like this." Stepping up behind her, Malik took hold of Jenna's hand and spread her index finger and thumb. He then pushed the grip of the pistol into the web of skin between them. "Keep your thumb on the grip, and the rest of your fingers curled securely around the other side of the trigger guard," he continued. "Relax your grip a little, Jenna … it should be firm, not tight. If you grip the gun too tightly, it'll shake … and you won't be able to accurately control your aim."

Unclenching her jaw, for the feel of his hand on hers was doing wild things to her pulse, Jenna nodded.

"Now, keep the pistol steady with your other hand … hold it underneath, supporting the weight of the weapon."

Jenna did as bid, trying to ignore the way his fingertips trailed down from the back of her hand to her wrist as he guided her.

Despite that the life-support inside the cabin was on the cool side—cyborgs and droids clearly didn't feel the cold—she was sweating.

"Okay … now place your index finger on the bottom of the trigger guard … or in front of it, if you prefer."

"Right," Jenna murmured.

"Your firing stance is important," Malik continued. "Bring your left hand forward, about a step past your right foot … that's good. Lean forward slightly with your knees bent, making sure you're balanced properly." His hand splayed across her back, in between her shoulder blades, pushing her forward into the correct position.

Jenna sucked in a breath; his palm felt like a brand, even through her clothing.

And then to make matters worse, Malik's fingers curled around the crook of her left elbow. "This needs to be almost straight," he murmured, "while the arm steadying the gun should be bent … like this."

"I had no idea I had to contort myself," Jenna muttered, trying to dredge up irritation to mask the fact she was now flustered. She wished he'd step back and give her some space.

Concentrate. Don't think about him … think of the host of Mir-Ferrin soldiers standing between you and your brother.

The reminder galvanized her, and Jenna focused on what she was doing.

"Okay, now we're ready to aim," Malik continued. "Align the front sight with the rear sight … it's easier if you close your right eye so you can focus with your left."

"All right," Jenna replied, doing as bid. "What now?"

"Level the pistol at the center of the target … take a deep breath and hold it. Let your body relax." His tone was soothing now. "You'll see the laser sight is moving … tracing a figure of eight … that's your heartbeat."

Indeed, Jenna had marked the movement, and had thought it was due to nervousness. It was a relief to know it was normal.

"When the sight comes to the bottom of the figure eight, pull the trigger … slowly, in a smooth, controlled motion."

He released her arm then, and she felt him step away. "Ready?"

Jenna squeezed hard, and a stream of laser hit the top edge of the target screen, causing a red splotch to flower across it. The screen emitted a dull bleep.

"Shit," she muttered. "That wasn't great."

"Maybe you should let the rest of us do the shooting on this mission," Vic quipped.

Jenna cast him a quelling look.

"You're holding the pistol too tight." Malik stepped close once more—and she felt the heat of his body burning into her back, even though they weren't even touching. Then he reached forward, his hands lightly gripping her arms. "You're pointing it too high … here, that's better. Squeeze the trigger more gently this time."

Jenna drew in a slow breath and held it.

Pushing aside her awareness of the man who was still holding her arms in place, she gently pulled the trigger.

The laser hit the second ring of the target—and this time the screen gave a much brighter chirp.

A grin spread across Jenna's face. "I hit it."

"Well done," Malik murmured in her ear. "Now, let's try that again."

Leaning against the archway, Malik folded his arms across his chest and watched the distorted streaks of light that flew toward him through the cockpit window. Obsidian was still seated in the co-pilot's seat, its claw-like hands moving across the console.

Malik's mouth thinned as his gaze slid over the battle-droid's gleaming black carapace. "Aren't Mir-Ferrin battle-droids bronze?" he asked, without thinking.

"We usually are," Obsidian rumbled. "But after Vic and I deserted, he decided bronze would draw too much attention."

Malik cocked an eyebrow. The droid's conversational style of speech was disconcerting, and not what he'd have expected from it.

Turning from the window, his gaze traveled to where Jenna was showing Vic a rough plan of Mir-Brennan Tower she'd just drawn on her tablet. Like Jenna, Malik knew the layout of the tower well. However, Vic didn't yet.

The drone of the engines filled the cabin, although Malik made out their conversation clearly.

"The building is long and rectangular … with a cavernous landing bay on the bottom level," she explained, tapping her fingertip on the screen.

"We'll be entering from there?" Vic asked.

"Yes … *The Passage* leads into a service corridor near the main doors."

"Is that the only way in and out of the landing bay?"

"Yes ... apart from ventilation and service shafts. There's an entrance hall on the other side of the doors with a row of elevators. We won't take them though ... it's too risky. The service elevators are in a narrow passage on the far side of the entrance hall."

Vic nodded. "Where's the detention block?"

"Underground ... the service elevators will take you there too."

Malik continued to listen to them. However, his attention settled upon Jenna; it was difficult not to look her way whenever she was present. For years now, she'd drawn his eye whenever she entered a room.

Malik's mouth curved then. She'd surprised him at firing practice. After a rocky start, Jenna had proved she had a steady hand and was an accurate shot. Even Vic, who'd been making cynical quips from the sidelines, fell silent as she hit the bullseye three times in a row.

After he was content that she knew how to handle a pistol, Malik had shown her a couple of self-defense moves, just in case anyone grabbed her. She'd proven a quick study at that too. His shin still ached from where she'd kicked it to release herself from his hold.

Malik had enjoyed being her teacher for an hour or two, had enjoyed the physical closeness to the woman who managed to confuse, frustrate, and excite him, all at the same time.

His smile faded then as the reality of the situation crept in. *Don't forget your place, Mir-Draven. You're her bodyguard.*

He needed to keep things professional. The truth was that Jenna Mir-Brennan was out of bounds. If this mission was successful, and if they managed to escape Idral with their lives, things would go back to how they'd been before.

They'd return to being distant planets orbiting the same sun.

Malik's jaw tensed. It was better that way too. Over the years, he'd had women—a few of them—although all his relationships had been casual, and none of them lasted longer than a week or two. He always cited his job as the reason, but it was an excuse.

Truth was, Malik didn't want entanglements. He wanted to remain in control—and he had until this fateful trip.

He'd let his proximity to Jenna, his desire for her, cloud his judgment. He was in serious danger of getting himself burned.

A buzzing sound intruded then, jerking him out of his brooding.

Vic glanced up. "That's our signal," he announced. "We're about to come out of hyperspace." His gaze flicked from Jenna to Malik. "Time to get you two hidden."

20. A TEMPTING OFFER

IT WAS DARK inside the smuggler's hold. Dark and overly warm.

"Does this hold actually have ventilation?" Jenna murmured, pulling her knees into her chest, and trying to breathe properly. It felt airless in here; the darkness was suffocating.

"Vic assured me it does," Malik replied, his tone dry. "He won't get the rest of his payment if he kills us before we land, will he?"

Knowing Malik couldn't see her, Jenna pulled a face. "I know he deserted from Mir-Ferrin space fleet, but a forty-thousand credit bounty might make him rethink our agreement." A sickly sensation washed over her as she considered the possibility. "Tian is paying four times what we are … and he won't care if I'm delivered dead or alive."

"You have a point," Malik replied quietly.

Dragging in a deep breath, Jenna tried not to think about the risk Vic would betray them. She held her breath in for a moment or two before exhaling slowly. It was a trick she employed before tense negotiations, one that kept her centered and calm. "So, you're happy to let me carry a laser-pistol?" she asked after a few moments. Best not to focus on the claustrophobic darkness or the cyborg who held their lives in his hands.

"I am … you handle yourself well, for a novice."

"Thank you," Jenna replied, her mouth curving. "That's praise indeed from the Captain of the Lord's Watch."

She placed her palms on the cool floor on either side of her body. The steady thrum of the engines changed then, and *The Wayfarer* shuddered. They were coming out of hyperspace.

Idral—and the Mir-Ferrin blockade—would be looming before them.

"Do you want me to kill your husband?"

The question, uttered in barely more than a whisper, caught Jenna off-guard.

She went rigid, her pulse accelerating.

"Gods, you don't know how tempting that is," she replied. "However, I think it's best we concentrate on getting Cathal, Isla, and Bea freed."

"I want to save your brother and his family too … but Tian deserves to die." Malik's voice was still quiet, yet there was no mistaking the steel just underneath. "What kind of man sends assassins after his wife?"

Jenna's mouth twisted. "One who doesn't like being bested by her … one who wants the last word."

Silence fell once more, and when Malik finally broke it, there was an edge to his voice. "That was quite a sacrifice you made … binding yourself to him."

"It was," Jenna agreed softly. Her throat tightened then. "I should never have let my father promise me to him."

"So why did you?"

"It's the way things are in the ruling class, I suppose … duty is everything." She paused then, sliding her palms across the cool metal floor, and trying not to think about the fact the Mir-Ferrins were likely scanning this freighter right now. Nonetheless, her pulse started to race. She hoped Vic was right about this hold. "It didn't occur to me to say no."

A pause followed this revelation. "So, there was never any affection between you?"

"No." A weight settled on Jenna's chest then, as memories of the first days of their marriage returned. She hadn't gone into the union determined to hate Tian—the opposite, in fact. A part of her, the romantic dreamer, had hoped that once they got to know each other, she'd discover a different man beneath the arrogant façade.

But their wedding night had extinguished that hope.

"Tian wasn't easy to warm to." She reached up and rubbed her temples. Talking about Tian gave her a headache, yet at the same time, it was strangely cathartic, and a welcome distraction from their currently tense situation. It had been a strain, not saying anything to Cathal or Isla. "Believe me … I tried." She drew in a deep breath then. "But behind closed doors, he was a bully."

Silence fell once more, and when Malik broke it, his voice roughened. "Are you sure you don't want me to kill that piece of shit? I'd be happy to."

Jenna let out a shaky laugh. She didn't need to tell Malik the details about her marriage; she'd said enough, and he'd guessed the rest.

Shuffling closer to her bodyguard, she reached out in the darkness, her hand closing over his knee. She then squeezed. "I want you to know, I don't regret what happened between us back on Morith either," she murmured, shocked by her own admission. Hadn't she promised herself she'd locked that episode away? "I might have been under the influence, but I knew what I was doing … I wanted it."

She felt his body stiffen under her hand.

Heat washed over her then. Damn it, she'd let her mouth run away from her. The forced intimacy, the darkness, had lowered her barriers.

She was about to remove her hand when Malik's hand closed over hers.

Wordlessly, he squeezed back.

It seemed an eternity before Vic finally yanked open the hold doors.

Bright artificial light flooded in, causing Jenna to blink rapidly.

"Sorry about the wait," the cyborg greeted them.

"What kept you?" Malik asked, his tone hard-edged.

They'd both started to get suspicious as time had drawn out inside the hold. Jenna had begun to worry her earlier comment might have been prophetic.

"Border security was more stringent than I thought," Vic replied. "They accepted my fake ID but interrogated me for a while and then asked to see my logbook. After that, they had even more questions."

Jenna's breathing quickened at this news. "We're through?"

The cyborg nodded. Reaching down, Vic caught her by the hand and hauled her out of the hold. He then helped Malik climb out before he turned and made his way toward the cockpit. "We're beginning our approach … you both need to get strapped in."

The Wayfarer bounced then as the freighter entered the planet's atmosphere.

Both Jenna and Malik stumbled—straight into each other's arms.

Her bodyguard's arms went about her waist, steadying her, before he steered them across the cabin.

The freighter started to buck and shudder, pitching them both into their seats.

Jenna sucked in a relieved breath when her harness clicked into place, pinning her securely to the spot.

"Re-entry into Idral is never this rough," she muttered, casting Malik a sidelong look.

He pulled a face. "That's because you're used to your brother's shuttles. These craft aren't as smooth."

"She'll get us there, all the same," Vic called back.

Evidently, their pilot had overheard him.

"If Jidea permits," Malik muttered. He reached up then, his fingers enclosing the small hammer he wore around his neck.

Jenna shifted her attention forward, watching Vic's hands move expertly over the controls. Beyond the cockpit window, she spied the surface of her home planet; the swirl of rust, cream, and white.

She hadn't been away from Idral that long, and yet it felt like a lifetime.

So much had happened in the interim; she didn't feel the same person who'd nearly face-planted in the doorway of that shuttle.

The freighter started to shudder, so violently that Jenna's teeth rattled. Gripping the hand rests to her seat, she focused on keeping her breathing slow and even. At least she wasn't feeling sick. Usually, the nausea only visited her during takeoff and the jump into hyperspace. Even so, she couldn't wait until they landed on terra firma.

And as they descended through the atmosphere, Jenna kept her gaze firmly on the cockpit window. They flew through clouds, and Idral itself hove into view.

They roared over the glittering sea and jagged coastline, before reaching the rocky, sun-burned mountains beyond. It was a brutal, but beautiful, sight, and Jenna's breathing grew shallow.

She hated knowing that this planet was lost to her clan—for the moment, at least. It wasn't a matter of territory or ownership, but heart. Idral was her home.

Jenna's jaw tightened. *One day, we'll get it back*, she vowed silently. She'd never thought herself one to nurse revenge, but the Mir-Ferrin treachery cut deep. It felt personal. It *was* personal. She'd sacrificed herself for peace only to discover everything her father and brother had worked for had been based on a lie.

The Mir-Ferrins had never wanted peace. Tian had married her knowing that.

Jenna's fingernails dug into the armrests. Not from nerves now, but from anger.

Do you want me to kill your husband?

Malik's offer whispered to her once more. Oh yes, it was tempting indeed. There were few people she truly wished ill, but Tian deserved a slow, painful end.

Maybe she could be the one to give it to him.

21. FOUND GUILTY

A WAVE OF dry heat hit Jenna in the face the moment she disembarked the freighter. An instant later, she inhaled the tang of iron, and a smile curved her lips.

The smell of home.

Behind her, Vic coughed. "I never get used to the air here."

"You do … eventually," Malik replied. "If you grow up in Melor as I did."

"I've always liked the smell," Jenna admitted, pulling up the hood of her cloak. Melor would be full of Mir-Ferrin soldiers; it was best to be careful. "It goes with the red earth and the heat."

They climbed the steps out of the landing crater and stepped out onto a covered walkway that led between terminals. There were freighters everywhere, most of them Mir-Ferrin these days, docked in the surrounding craters.

Melor spaceport was huge—a sprawling collection of low-slung, circular buildings made of dusty red stone. It took them a while to navigate their way, under covered walkways, from the private landing bays to the arrivals terminal.

They'd all donned cloaks, and Vic had draped Obsidian in a dark blue cloak that matched his own, disguising the droid a little. That was a wise idea, for if a Mir-Ferrin soldier spotted the gleaming black battle-droid, suspicions would be aroused.

As they entered the bustling terminal, Jenna surveyed her surroundings. She'd never actually been inside Melor's spaceport before, having always traveled off-planet on one of her family's private shuttles. Polished wine-colored pavers stretched across the wide floor. The musky odor of sweat mingled with the scent of expensive spices and perfumes, and the chatter of many galactic tongues rose high into the steel girders that formed the ceiling inside the terminal.

Various races crowded the space, yet several of the humans inside the terminal were bronze-skinned and dark-haired with violet gazes. Malik indeed blended in here.

Jenna continued to scan the crowd, noting the large groups purchasing tickets or lining up at security. Quite a few citizens appeared to be leaving Idral—and she guessed that many of them would be Mir-Brennans intent on escaping Mir-Ferrin rule.

As they headed for the exit, Jenna spied figures clad in gleaming bronze and black, weaving through the crowd.

Mir-Ferrin soldiers.

A banner hung from the rafters at the far end of the terminal. It bore the Mir-Ferrin clan insignia: a crescent moon and twin crossed blades.

Heat ignited in the pit of Jenna's belly, outrage flooding through her.

They don't belong here.

Her clan had ruled Idral peacefully for the last fifty years. The planet's inhabitants had welcomed the Mir-Brennans, after the brutal Mir-Ferrin regime, and had prospered under their influence. This planet was part of the Mir-Brennan free market collective these days, and its location on a busy trade route had helped it thrive. Hundreds of thousands of colonists from Staturine II had settled on the planet over the decades. They'd brought business and expertise with them and had integrated swiftly with the local population.

Despite that they always took bodyguards with them whenever they left the tower, Jenna and her family had always been able to wander the labyrinthine streets of Idral's towns without fear for their safety.

Until the attack, Idral had been the Mir-Brennan clan seat. Her grandfather had built the tower as a symbol of his clan's strength and influence.

It seemed unthinkable that the Mir-Ferrins had seized it.

Jaw clenched, Jenna followed her companions out of Melor spaceport and stepped once more into the baking heat of an Idralian afternoon.

It was blindingly hot, so much so that she found herself gasping for breath as her body adjusted to it. She'd just spent the last week in space, with a brief sojourn upon a bitterly cold moon; Idral's heat came as a shock in comparison. Underneath her cloak, Jenna had donned a tank top and cargo pants, and like her male companions, she wore heavy combat boots. Sweat was already starting to trickle between her shoulder blades, although the cloak protected her from the biting sunlight.

They were on the outskirts of town here, and there was little in the way of shade. The sun shone so brightly upon the squat sandstone buildings and hard-packed earth that they seemed to glow red. Jenna's eyes started to water.

She lifted her chin, her gaze alighting on a collection of intricately carved rust-colored spires that rose above the rooftops, piercing the pale pink sky. The Temple to Jidea sat at the heart of Melor and was visible from every corner of the town. As a gesture of goodwill, the first colonists from Staturine II had financed the building of this temple soon after settling here.

"I know a quiet hotel in the center," Vic announced, slowing his stride so that he walked alongside Jenna. Like Malik, he carried a rucksack hung over one shoulder. "I don't usually bother to book ahead when I stay there … shall we see if they've got a suite available?"

"Sounds good," Jenna replied. "Let's see if we can reserve one for a few days, at least."

"We'll also need to hire a couple of hoppers for the ride out to the tower," Malik added. He walked a few strides ahead of them, his hooded gaze sweeping the street, while Obsidian brought up the rear. "There's a place in the northern ward that'll hire them out without any questions."

"Do we need ones with side-cars to carry passengers on the way back?" Vic asked.

Jenna shook her head. "There are hoppers parked in a bay at the outer door of *The Passage*." Although she'd never been inside the escape tunnel, her father had described it to her. "Cathal, Isla, and Bea will be able to take one."

Vic nodded, apparently satisfied by her answer.

Jenna cast him a sidelong look, taking in his profile, shadowed by the cowl of his cloak. So far, she'd been wary of the cyborg—had braced herself to be double-crossed by him—but he'd gotten them safely to Idral and was asking all the right questions.

Maybe he and Obsidian were trustworthy after all.

They walked through the sprawling suburb, past warehouses and spaceship yards, before reaching the main road into the center.

It would take nearly an hour to walk the distance, unpleasant in the heat, and so they took a shunt. The air-conditioning dried the sweat on their bodies as the gilded caterpillar wound its way through gradually narrowing streets toward the heart of Melor. And when they alighted, the buildings huddled closer together, creating much-needed shade, while the scent of spices lay heavy in the sweltering air.

The party of four kept walking, passing a roadside shrine to Jidea. A clay figurine of the Goddess wielding her great hammer towered above a bank of candles. There were plenty of these in every town across this great continent, despite the plethora of temples to the Goddess.

"Jidea be praised," Malik murmured as he walked by.

Jenna also whispered a prayer to the Goddess of Fortune. So far, their mission was going smoothly, but she hoped Jidea would continue to watch over them.

They kept moving, and Jenna tried to ignore the sweat that now bathed her body. It was so hot that the air shimmered. Eventually, as they reached the most crowded part of the center, they walked under awnings stretched out over the streets.

A group of human children ran shrieking past them, chasing a rock-bounder—the long-tailed leporid bounced past on large, clawed feet, its eyes wild.

Jenna watched the rock-bounder dive for an alleyway, her mouth curving. You didn't usually see one of those in populated areas.

They walked by market stalls selling spices, expensive cloth, and fresh and dried fruit. Jenna's gaze slid over the familiar sights. They passed by one of her favorite stalls, which sold musk-melons. The heavily scented fruit bobbed in a barrel of iced water, keeping it cool until the vendor cut the melon into chunks for you to consume immediately.

Jenna might have relaxed even now, might have stopped to buy some melon—if figures clad in gleaming bronze didn't patrol the streets of Melor. The Mir-Ferrin soldiers were vigilant—their visored gazes scanning their surroundings.

And despite that the center was as busy as ever, Jenna noted the tension in the air, the scowls on many of the faces she passed. After decades of Mir-Brennan rule, the natives of Melor didn't welcome the Mir-Ferrin occupation.

Jenna pulled at her hood, ensuring her face remained shadowed, even as her lips thinned.

With any luck, the locals would rise up against them.

Their hotel was hard to find—indeed, Jenna would have walked right by if Vic hadn't stopped. It lay in a nondescript sandstone block, and there was no sign above the door, nothing to suggest it provided lodgings at all.

It was a good choice considering that Mir-Ferrin troops roamed Melor, and no doubt undertook random raids on guest houses and hotels, to ensure no Mir-Brennan soldiers had taken refuge there after the attack.

And, fortunately, the droid that greeted them at the door assured them there were rooms available.

Stepping into a cool, shadowy lounge in their suite, which had three rooms off it, Jenna pushed back her hood and wiped the sweat off her forehead. It was still oppressively warm in here, for the accommodation wasn't climate controlled. However, it was a relief to exit the searing heat outdoors.

Like her companions, she stripped off her cloak and hung it up behind the door. She then kicked off her heavy boots, wishing she could strip down to her underwear as well.

She wouldn't though.

A fridge hummed in the corner of the lounge, and she opened it, smiling when she spied a large jug of pori-pori. Turning to her companions, she held the jug of juice up. "Thirsty?"

Both men nodded.

Pouring them all drinks, Jenna took a seat upon one of the long sofas that furnished the lounge and pulled out her tablet. While they'd been in hyperspace, she hadn't been able to check the news, and there hadn't been time to connect to the public Sectornet during landing, yet she was anxious to do so now.

Her brother's trial would be over. His execution would likely be scheduled.

Bringing up the newsfeed, she started to scroll, freezing when the headline she'd been dreading flashed up.

Mir-Brennan clan-lord found guilty of crimes against the Mir-Ferrins.

And despite the stifling heat, goose bumps shivered across her skin. "What day is it?" she asked.

Malik glanced down at his wrist-comm. "Day 84, S.I.T ... why?"

Jenna met his eye. "Cathal's been found guilty. They've scheduled a public execution on the covered terrace in front of Mir-Brennan Tower ... at 1200, Day 85, Standard Idralian Time."

Her pulse quickened then, her mouth going dry. *Tomorrow ... at noon.*

"It looks like we'll be going in at dawn then," Vic murmured.

"That was my thinking," Malik agreed.

Jenna's brow furrowed. "Do we have enough time to prepare?"

Malik nodded, although his expression had hardened. "We'd better get those hoppers now." He retrieved his cloak and shrugged it on. A moment later, Vic did the same.

"I'll just stay here and hang out with Obsidian then," she said, gesturing to where the battle-droid had perched on the edge of one of the sofas, red eyes glowing. In truth, she wasn't sure how she felt about being left alone with it. However, pride prevented her from admitting such.

"Jenna ... could you also show me the plan you drew of Mir-Brennan Tower?" the droid rasped. "I would like to study it, while our companions are occupied elsewhere."

"All right," she replied, taken aback. She hadn't expected Obsidian to be proactive. She'd always thought of battle-droids as drones. They followed orders; they didn't think independently.

But this one was different.

As soon as she and Obsidian were alone in the lounge, she picked up her glass of juice and took a large gulp, sighing as the cool, sweet liquid ran down her throat. She then withdrew her tablet from her bag, sat down next to the battle-droid, and brought up the outline she'd drawn earlier.

She knew Mir-Brennan Tower intimately, having grown up there. She and Cathal had spent hours as children playing hide-and-seek in its secret corners. They'd even ventured down to the detention block once—much to their father's fury.

Thinking of her brother made Jenna's stomach clench.

His execution was scheduled; there was no time to waste. Things were moving fast now, faster than she'd anticipated. But they'd get there in time. The Mir-Ferrin clan-lord wouldn't get the public spectacle he wanted.

We're coming, Cathal.

Tian stood outside the cell and observed the man inside.

The Mir-Brennan clan-lord couldn't see him. Cathal sat upon the sleeping pallet, his back against the wall, staring sightlessly at the featureless wall opposite. The man's face was desolate, his brown eyes glazed.

Tian's mouth curved, a shaft of vindictive pleasure arrowing through him. No longer the supremely confident clan-lord, but a broken man—Cathal had lost hope.

Next to Tian was a comm, through which he'd informed the Mir-Brennan clan-lord that he'd been found guilty by a jury of his peers. The following day at noon, he would be escorted onto the terrace in front of the tower, where an executioner would take his head off with a laser-blade—for the whole sector to see.

"You've delivered the news then."

Tian turned to see a tall, spare figure dressed in flowing bronze striding down the corridor of the detention block toward him. The harsh overhead lighting highlighted the ruthless lines on the Mir-Ferrin clan-lord's face. Two battle-droids marched at his heels, the rattle of their armor and whirr of metallic joints echoing off the featureless walls.

Tian tensed at the sight of his father. He should have known the old man would come down here to check he'd done the job properly. Hiding his irritation, he nodded. "Mir-Brennan asked to see his wife and daughter."

Mican drew to a halt, glancing through the one-way glass at his prisoner. "And what did you tell him?"

"I denied his request."

A smile slashed across his father's face. "Good lad."

"What are we going to do with Isla and Beatrix?" Tian asked. He was mildly curious as to his father's plans for the last two members of the Mir-Brennan ruling family.

Don't forget about Jenna, he reminded himself then, his gut hardening.

The Widow Makers had let him down—but surely the price he'd put on his wife's head would get her dealt to. A bounty hunter would find her.

"The girl will be sent to the Sisters of Awe," Mican replied. His lack of hesitation revealed that he'd given this some thought already.

Tian nodded, impressed by his father's choice. The convent—which was located on Pillarus One, a barren planet on the outer reaches of the sector—was the ideal place to send Beatrix. Many ruling-class families sent unwanted daughters there to watch over the eternal flame that burned in honor of the Gods.

"And her mother?"

His father quirked a greying eyebrow. "Well ... her fate depends on you, my son."

Tian stiffened. "What do you mean?"

Mican's mouth pursed. "Once Jenna Mir-Brennan is dead, you're going to marry Isla."

Tian jolted as if his father had just slugged him in the stomach. "What?"

"Don't look so surprised," his father snapped. "Isla's a Mir-Galbreth ... an influential clan I intend to seek an alliance with."

Tian clenched his jaw, folding his arms across his chest. Ignoring his glare, the clan-lord continued. "The Mir-Brennans are dealt with, and the Mir-Leliths must be treated with care ... it's time for us to look beyond the ruling clans. We'll only prevail if we get the sector behind us."

"I've done my duty, father," Tian choked out. "Get Elijah or Lucas to marry the bitch." Of course, Elijah was engaged to the Mir-Starne clan-lord's daughter, a long-standing arrangement he needed to make good on, but Lucas was available.

His father's dark gaze narrowed, and Tian tried to ignore the lump of ice that slid down his spine. Mican had a stare that could freeze this furnace of a planet.

"Your duty is what *I* deem it to be, Tian," the clan-lord replied, his tone as cold as his glare. "If I say you shall marry the Mir-Brennan widow, then you will."

Tian stared back at his father, bitterness flooding his mouth.

Growing up, this man had dominated Tian and his two elder brothers to the point where all three of them were terrified of displeasing him. They were all adults now, yet they still danced to their father's drum.

For a few years, Tian had thought he'd escaped his father's influence. He'd thrived in the Mir-Ferrin space fleet, had risen through the ranks to commander in record time. He'd thought his father might be impressed—he hadn't dared entertain the thought he'd actually be *proud*—but Mican hadn't seemed to notice.

He'd ignored his youngest son until the day the Mir-Brennan clan-lord—Cathal's father—had contacted him, offering his daughter's hand in marriage in a peace alliance.

Tian had never understood why Mican chose him and not Elijah or Lucas. Their father had been equally hard on them all—but it appeared he did play favorites, after all.

A heavy silence fell in the hallway as father and son stared at each other.

Suddenly, Tian was five years old again, cowering before the clan-lord.

"Is that clear?" Mican asked finally, his voice gravel on steel.

Gods, Tian wanted to plant his fist into the old man's face, to shatter his nose and send him sprawling across the cold metal floor.

But instead, he let hardwired fear get the best of him. His father had to be obeyed, in all things.

And so, slowly, his movements jerky, Tian nodded.

22. DAWN IT IS

"THE CLAN-LORD IS LIKELY to be held in a separate location from his wife and daughter," Malik pointed out. He leaned back in his seat and crossed an ankle over his knee. "Cathal will be detained in a high-security area."

Seated on a sofa opposite, Vic nodded. "I suggest we split into two groups. You and I go after the clan-lord… while Obsidian and Jenna free the other two. I imagine the girl will be kept with her mother."

Malik's mouth compressed. "I'd prefer not to let Jenna out of my sight."

Vic held his eye. "You can rely on Obsidian to protect her."

Malik's brow furrowed, clearly not impressed by the idea.

"It's a sound plan," Jenna spoke up then before he could voice any objection. "It'll be faster if we split into groups."

Malik's frown deepened. "The detention block's underground," he said after a pause. "But we can't go in blind; we'll need to know exactly which cells they're holding the prisoners in."

"Obsidian will take care of that," Vic assured him. "Find him an outlet somewhere once we emerge from *The Passage*, and he'll plug himself in and locate them for us."

"There will be one in the service corridor outside the tunnel," Jenna assured him, impressed that Vic appeared to have a solution for most things so far.

Likewise, Malik's grim expression had eased a little.

"Since we'll be exiting through the landing bay, have you considered stealing a Mir-Ferrin shuttle once we collect the clan-lord and his family?" Vic asked then. "It'll be faster than the tunnel."

"And riskier," Malik replied. "The Mir-Ferrin clan-lord wants the Mir-Brennan ruling family exterminated. He'll have us shot out of the sky."

Vic gave a slow nod, while Jenna suppressed a shiver.

Indeed, Mican Mir-Ferrin wouldn't think twice about destroying one of his shuttles, if it could rid him of Cathal and his family.

She exhaled sharply then. "So, dawn it is?"

Malik nodded, his gaze finding hers. "I'd suggest we went at night, but even with the fast hoppers we've hired, it's too risky … most of the things that'll eat you on this planet are nocturnal. We don't want to cross paths with a felda or a chelrog before reaching the tower."

Jenna tensed. No, she wasn't keen on an encounter with a giant desert crab or a chasm lizard either. She then rose to her feet. "We should all get some rest."

Vic sank back in his seat and raked a hand through his short brown hair. "I suggest you do … we'll leave here at 0600."

"The trip to the tower shouldn't take longer than an hour," Malik replied. "*The Passage* exit lies a klick south of it."

"Will the Mir-Ferrins have seen the exit?" Vic asked.

"Both the entrance and exit are disguised," Jenna assured him, before adding, "it's at the end of a ravine. The door looks like a sheer wall of rock … there's no way the Mir-Ferrins will know about it … unless Cathal has told them."

Vic leveled a look at her. "Would he have told your husband?"

She shook her head, surprised at how sure she was. Cathal might have discussed military strategy with Tian, but there were some things he would never reveal.

An ache rose under her breastbone. It would be strange sneaking back into a place that had once been her home. The Mir-Ferrins would have killed or imprisoned the Lord's Watch and the House Guard, but what about the other staff who resided within the tower? She imagined they'd been 'replaced' with droids.

Swallowing a sigh, Jenna glanced over at the lounge's single window. The shutters were open, revealing a strip of pink sky. The light was just starting to fade. The twilights were long on Idral—darkness wouldn't settle for another couple of hours—but she needed a shower and some sleep. Her eyes were gritty, and tiredness dragged down at her. "Right … I'm off to bed then," she announced. "See you both at dawn."

"You might want to set an alarm," Malik reminded her. "I'm going to."

"I will."

Leaving the lounge, Jenna stepped inside her small bedroom and pulled the door closed behind her. She then glanced around, taking in the plain sandstone walls and the tiny shower cubicle just off it. Her bag—her only luggage now—sat on the narrow bed.

It felt strange to be alone after spending the last few days with Malik.

Despite that he was only next door, she found herself missing his presence—a realization that disquieted her. In such a short space of time, her bodyguard had become important to her.

Trying to push aside the unsettling sensations, Jenna stripped off her clothes and stepped into the shower cubicle. She switched it on, gasping as cool water peppered her skin. Water was precious on Idral—and although she'd been able to shower for as long as she wished back at Mir-Brennan Tower, most people who lived here didn't enjoy such luxuries.

As soon as she turned the water on, Jenna noted there was a timer on the shower, which gave her three minutes to hurriedly soap down and wash her hair. She'd just rinsed the last of the soap suds off her roots when the water clicked off.

Grabbing a towel, she wrung out her hair and stepped out of the shower, walking naked across to the bed. The moment she left the cubicle, the warm air dried her. By the time she stretched out on the bed, her skin was barely damp.

Next door, she could hear the rumble of Malik and Vic's conversation in the lounge. Listening to the rise and fall of their low voices, Jenna yawned and dug into her bag. Retrieving her tablet, she turned an alarm on for 5:30. Half an hour would be plenty for her to ready herself to depart. If she got up any earlier, nerves would just get to her.

She'd be nervous now if she wasn't so exhausted.

Rolling over onto her stomach, she closed her eyes.

"Do you want a drink?" Vic retrieved a can of local brew from the fridge and held it up.

Malik nodded. He then stretched back on the sofa and placed his bare feet up on the low table. His limbs felt heavy, and he had a slight headache. He'd need to retire soon as well. However, he'd enjoy a cool drink first.

Beyond the open window, the sky was turning mauve, and now that the fiery sun was setting, the heat had started to wane. This had always been his favorite time of day on Idral: the long evenings when the town's streets came to life, when you could finally breathe again.

The can opened with a hiss, and the first mouthful of brew bit at the back of Malik's throat.

Vic seated himself on the sofa opposite. "This place is a furnace ... did you really enjoy living here?"

Malik's mouth quirked before he nodded. "Where's home for you?"

"Platinum 5."

Malik arched an eyebrow. "Under the clan-lord's eye."

"My father was a space fleet pilot ... and as soon as I was old enough, I enlisted."

Malik observed the cyborg intently for a few moments. The brutal silver and black plate protruding from his right eye socket dominated his face; it was difficult not to stare at it. "So, you no longer have any loyalty to the Mir-Ferrins?"

Vic lifted the can of brew to his lips and took a sip. He then shook his head.

"None at all?"

"I deserted and stole one of their battle-droids … I'd say that speaks for itself."

Malik continued to survey his companion. He'd worked alongside soldiers his whole life, had led them, and considered himself a half-decent judge of character. The cyborg had a direct communication style that Malik appreciated. It made it easier to take him at his word.

"How much of you is actually machine?" he asked after a pause.

Vic took another gulp of brew before replying, "My right eye, most of the frontal lobe of my brain … and my right lung." He lifted his left hand and rapped something hard on his chest with his knuckles. "I also have a central processor, attached to my heart … to keep it beating." Vic's left eye glinted then, and when he continued, bitterness tinged his voice. "I always dreaded being badly injured in the line of duty … better to die than be transitioned."

"But you agreed to it when you signed up, didn't you?"

"I was seventeen and trigger-happy … I'd have signed away a kidney and a lung just to follow in my father's footsteps."

A hollow sensation settled deep in Malik's chest at this admission. Vic had known his father, had looked up to him.

What must that feel like?

Malik had never known his own father—had no idea who the man was. His mother had refused to talk about him.

"So, what did go wrong?" he asked, pushing his own, unpleasant, memories away.

"No idea. I woke up in a hospital ward and was told I'd been transitioned. They observe you for a while, to make sure there aren't any issues … but right from those first hours, I knew something was off. I never said anything because I knew they'd put me under again … and do the job properly this time … but I still felt like me." He paused then, draining the last of his can of brew. "I'm different to before though. I'm stronger … my resting pulse rate is slower, and my body's temperature runs hotter."

Malik considered his words, trying to imagine—and failing—what it would have felt like to wake up from transitioning with your self-awareness intact.

Vic leaned forward, placing the empty can on the table. "Cyborgs are expendable. We sleep in stacks of cells, like a mortuary." Resentment crept into his voice once more. "There's no heating, and they feed you nothing but tasteless nutri-bars. Two weeks after going back to work, I deserted."

Malik's gaze flicked to where Obsidian was now plugged into the wall. Its head was bowed as it recharged. "Why steal a battle-droid?"

Vic glanced Obsidian's way, his lips twitching into something that was the shadow of a half-smile. It was the first time he'd seen the cyborg show a facial expression of any kind. "Being part machine changes how you see everything," he murmured. "Obsidian was assigned to me … before I was injured. After my transitioning, I discovered that we have a bond of sorts."

Malik cocked an eyebrow. He had to be joking; no one formed an attachment to battle-droids.

Noting Malik's expression, Vic's hazel eye narrowed. "Obsidian and I understand each other," he said, his tone cooling. "We have a partnership … and our freedom. We were both slaves once, but now we serve no one but ourselves."

23. MY RUIN

JENNA ROLLED ONTO her back, rising from a deep sleep. Opening her eyes, she stared up at the darkness. It was deathly quiet, a sign dawn was still some way off. She was surprised she'd awoken—for she'd thought she'd sleep deeply until her alarm went off.

Fumbling for her tablet, she checked the time. There were still five hours to go.

I need to go back to sleep.

She closed her eyes, waiting for sleep to pull her down into its clutches once more.

But it didn't.

She was now wide awake—her mind jumping forward to what lay ahead.

In just a few hours, they'd steal into Mir-Brennan Tower and free her family. Adrenaline spiked then, and her heart started to race.

Nothing could go wrong.

Jenna swallowed then and realized she was thirsty, almost painfully so. Her mouth felt like Idral's sunbaked earth.

She lay there for a while, debating whether just to ignore her thirst, but she couldn't. Eventually, she pushed herself up and switched on a globe-lamp on her bedside table, blinking as soft light flooded her room.

Pulling on a tank top, Jenna stood up and padded barefoot across to the door. She was reaching for the door when she hesitated and glanced down at herself. She was half-naked; underwear wasn't the right attire to venture out of her room.

However, at this hour, there wouldn't be anyone around.

She'd risk it.

Letting herself out into the lounge, she peeked around, just to be sure.

As expected, the space was empty, except for the battle-droid; Obsidian was plugged into the wall, recharging. Someone had left one of the wall lamps on, probably in case any of them needed to get up in the night and didn't want to fumble around in the darkness.

Satisfied she was, indeed, alone, Jenna walked across to where the fridge hummed. A water dispenser sat on top of it. Grabbing a glass, she filled it and drank deeply. She then refilled it.

"Thirsty too?"

Jenna's breathing caught as she swiveled around—and came face-to-face with Malik.

"Gods." She brought a hand to her chest, over her wildly kicking heart. "Don't sneak up on people like that."

His mouth curved. "I thought you heard my door open."

"I didn't." Jenna clenched her fingers around her glass before she thrust it at him. "Here."

Her manner was abrupt, yet her heart was still hammering.

She'd just realized her bodyguard was wearing even less than she was.

Malik was clad in nothing but a pair of black shorts—the kind that molded to him. It was impossible not to admire his bronzed skin and the muscle that rippled just under it. And it was difficult not to let her gaze drift lower.

Those shorts left nothing to the imagination, and without even meaning to, Jenna's gaze dipped south, before she snapped it back up to meet his eye.

Curse him, he'd seen. Was that a smirk she'd noted curving his lips?

Malik took the glass, his fingers brushing hers, and drained it in two gulps, passing it back to her. "Neither of us drank enough water yesterday," he said. "We're both dehydrated."

He was looking at her with that expression she recalled from Morith—when they'd been in that booth in the pleasure house. His gaze was hooded; it smoldered, making something low in her belly catch fire.

Her breathing quickened, and she abruptly turned away and refilled the glass. "Do you want any more?"

"Yes, thanks … but you drink first."

Jenna took a few gulps from the glass before setting it under the water dispenser and topping it up.

The skin on the back of her neck prickled; she could feel his hot gaze on her. Part of Jenna wished he'd back off—but another part of her craved his attention.

She was suddenly hyper-aware of Malik, as she had been that night.

Only this time, she couldn't blame the Horn Punch.

Marshaling her thoughts, Jenna turned and handed Malik the glass once more.

He drained it and then set the glass down on the bench before meeting her eye. "We should both try and get some more sleep … it's still early."

"I don't think I'll be able to sleep anymore tonight," Jenna replied, pulling a face. "I'm wide awake now … I can't stop thinking about the mission, about everything that's at stake."

"We might fail," he said softly, his gaze never leaving hers. "You do realize that?"

She swallowed. Her first instinct was to disagree with him, but there was little point in arguing against what they both knew to be true.

"I do," she whispered. "But I have to believe we'll succeed."

His mouth curved. "Nothing defeats you … does it, Jenna?"

Her pulse started to flutter in the base of her throat. Gods, she loved hearing him say her name.

"Not while you're with me," she replied huskily.

Their gazes fused then, the moment drawing out.

Jenna's heart started to buck against her ribs, sweat beading on her upper lip. Wis, Seer of Truth, give her strength, it was no good. She couldn't hide from this any longer.

She wanted this man, body and soul.

She didn't want boundaries between them any longer. She wanted to wake up to his voice in the mornings, and to feel his arms around her as she drifted off to sleep at night. She wanted his hands on her. She wanted him buried deep inside her. She wanted to lose herself in him.

Without being able to stop herself, Jenna reached out, placing the palm of her hand upon his chest.

Time stood still.

The heat of his skin seared her palm, and the intensity of those violet eyes engulfed her.

"I don't want to be alone tonight, Malik," she whispered.

The beat of his heart quickened under her hand, and when he answered, his voice held a rasp. "Neither do I." He raised a hand, placing it over hers. He then stepped close, bringing up his free hand to brush his knuckles across her cheek. "I've always been alone, Jen," he murmured, "But it never really bothered me until a few days ago … until fate threw you and me together." His throat bobbed then. "When we're apart, I feel your loss."

Jenna's throat started to ache. "You do?"

He nodded. The pad of his thumb swept across her lower lip, and the sensual gesture made her shiver, heat pooling between her thighs. She drew in a deep, shaky breath. It was difficult to concentrate with him standing so close, with him touching her like this—but his words emboldened her.

"I know what it's like … to feel lonely," she said, her voice turning husky. "I've spent my life surrounded by people, but no one's ever *seen* me … not like you do."

Malik's gaze held her fast. "There was a day, nearly a decade ago now, when I was patrolling one of the recreation decks in the tower … and I saw you standing on a viewing platform, looking south," he admitted, his thumb brushing across her lower lip once more. "The sun created a halo behind you, making you look like a handmaiden to the Gods. You were so regal, untouchable … and I just stood there, watching you, when I should have been working."

"You did?" Jenna inclined her head. She'd had no idea the Captain of the Lord's Watch had noticed her all those years ago, wanted her. Malik had always seemed as untouchable as the stars.

His expression turned wry. "You've been my obsession for far too long. I should have known you'd one day be my ruin."

Jenna sucked in a deep breath, her heart hammering in her ears. "I don't want to be your ruin," she whispered. "I just want to be yours."

Malik's breathing hitched. A second later, he drew her to him, his mouth claiming hers. The kiss consumed her. The taste of him, the feel of his tongue sliding against hers, and the rasp of his stubbled chin against her cheek ignited a hunger inside her that couldn't be denied.

No, her senses weren't impaired this time. She'd thought the Horn Punch had addled both their wits, but instead, all it had done was tear down the reserve between them.

The honesty between them was raw. Need scorched the air.

Jenna stepped into him, her hands coming up to link around his neck. The next thing she knew, he'd walked her back against the wall, and their bodies were pressed flush.

Jenna writhed against his hard, muscular body, her legs parting to wrap around his, to draw him closer. She felt his erection, straining through the material of his shorts, pressing urgently against her core. She wanted to tear the two layers of fabric that separated them apart so he could plunge into her, so she could lose herself. She forgot where they were, or that Vic could walk in on them at any moment.

But fortunately, Malik still had his wits about him.

Tearing his mouth off hers, he pushed himself off the wall, stepped back from Jenna, and then took her hand, entwining his fingers with hers. "Let's take this somewhere more private," he rasped.

24. OUT OF BOUNDS

INSIDE JENNA'S ROOM, they fell on each other, all restraint gone.

Breathing hard, Jenna clutched at Malik as he stripped her naked and pushed her back on the bed. Looming above her, he then pushed down his shorts, kicking them free of his ankles.

Gaze riveted upon his cock, which thrust toward her, its swollen tip beckoning, Jenna reached for him again.

But Malik's mouth curved into a sensual, purely-male smile that made her blood heat and her belly flip-flop. Climbing onto the bed, he brushed her clutching hands aside and spread her thighs wide.

He gazed down at her sex. The hunger on his face made heat pulse in the cradle of her hips.

Jenna's breathing hitched, excitement arrowing through her. He lowered himself between her parted thighs then.

He's going to—

A deep groan ripped from his chest when he tasted her, and his reaction made her roll her hips against him. His tongue began a wicked dance, and Jenna bit down on her bottom lip to choke the high, keening cry that clawed at her chest. She dug her fingers into Malik's short hair, urging him on as he pleasured her, pushing her hips against his face, grinding herself against him.

Malik responded by devouring her.

It was too much, too intense. Moments later, Jenna climaxed against his mouth. Her thighs started to tremble. If he hadn't been holding her up to him, she'd have collapsed on the bed.

Boneless and gasping for breath, she lay there when he released her.

Gods, the room was spinning.

Malik then crawled up over her, his lips and tongue tracing over her belly and ribcage to her breasts. There, he lavished them with attention, drawing each aching tip into his mouth and suckling hard until she had to bite her lip again.

"You're delicious, Jen," he growled, moving up so they were eye-to-eye. "I've been aching to taste you properly."

Her breathing quickened, heat flooding through her. His frankness drove her wild. Reaching down, her fingers wrapped around his rigid cock.

It jerked her grip, and he gasped at her touch.

"On your back, Malik," she whispered huskily. "It's my turn to taste you."

An instant later, he'd rolled beneath her, and Jenna was kissing and licking her way down his chest— exploring each ridged muscle, each hard plane, and the dip of his navel—before she focused on his groin once more.

Malik groaned low in his throat when she tasted him there too. He was big, so she worked the tip of him with her mouth, while her hand fisted the root of his shaft. She pumped slowly, enjoying each groan, each choked gasp.

She'd have continued, would have brought him to climax in her mouth, if he hadn't eventually yanked her up, pulling her astride him.

There, he lifted her and slid the head of his cock against her slickness. He then pulled her down, impaling her on him.

Jenna threw back her head, groaning at the feel of him filling her. This position was so intense—for the tip of him was pressing against her womb—and when he gripped her hips, moving them in a slow circle, the pleasure that rippled through her lower belly made her forget herself.

She cried out before slapping a hand over her mouth. "Shit," she mumbled through her fingers. "We don't want to wake up Vic."

"Who cares about him," Malik growled, guiding her hips in a slow roll once more. He then gave a low, sensual groan that made her forget about everything else.

Everything except Malik.

She felt as if she were teetering on the brink of something—something that both exhilarated and terrified her. Before sex with Malik, she hadn't known she could feel like this. He dredged up a primal need within her, one that made her feel like a goddess, like she was capable of anything.

Rocking forward, she let him slide out of her, almost to the tip, before she sank down on him once more.

Gods, the sensation was incredible. The head of his cock was stroking a sensitive spot, deep inside her, and every time he hit it, she felt a wet rush of heat. She was so wet, he risked sliding out of her.

Shuddering, Jenna looked at Malik squarely then, their gazes fusing. It was intense to watch his face, as she rocked back and forth in a steady rhythm, and she had to fight the urge to close her eyes, to let herself be carried away by the moment.

But she didn't.

"Ride me, Jen." His voice was rough, urgent. "Harder!"

His words caused what little was left of her restraint to shatter. Biting down hard on her bottom lip, Jenna increased the tempo of her rocking. The rasp of their breathing, the wet sound of sex, filled the room—and then when Malik reached between her thighs, the pad of his thumb stroking her, she went wild, bucking against him as hot, rippling waves of ecstasy pounded through her loins.

She couldn't help it—her choked cry echoed through the room.

The next thing she knew, Malik had flipped her onto her back and slung her legs over his shoulders before driving into her in deep, savage thrusts.

Jenna arched back against the bed, her limbs trembling uncontrollably now. And when she felt him come—felt the hot rush of him empty inside her—a sense of completeness that had eluded Jenna her whole life filled her.

"I'm sure Vic must have heard us," Jenna murmured. She lay sprawled against Malik's sweat-slicked chest. "I made a lot of noise."

Malik huffed a laugh, his fingertips stroking a lazy, sensual line down her spine. "You did … but who cares?"

Jenna sighed, sliding her hand over his chest. "I could never get enough of you," she murmured. "We'd better both live through tomorrow … just so I can have you again."

"Well, if that isn't enough motivation to survive … I don't know what is." He caught her hand then, their fingers entwining. Yet when he continued, there was an edge to his voice. "It's official … you are my ruin."

Jenna lifted her head, her gaze seeking his. "Why do you call it that? Is wanting me wrong?"

He gave a wry smile. "It *is* when you want the married sister of the man you serve."

"Tian and I are estranged … soon to be divorced," Jenna reminded him, pulling a face. "The asshole wants me dead, remember?"

"You're still out of bounds."

Jenna snorted. "Says who? My brother?"

"Will the clan-lord want the Captain of the Lord's Watch consorting with his sister?"

Jenna tensed. He wasn't wrong. Cathal likely wouldn't be impressed; her class had unspoken rules about such things. Nonetheless, she wouldn't bow to social pressure. She'd already set a precedent when she'd told her brother she was divorcing Tian—her relationship with Malik was just one step further. "I'll deal with him," she murmured.

Silence fell between them. Jenna's gaze roamed over Malik's proud features, curiosity wreathing up. Their forced proximity over the past few days had broken down a lot of barriers between them, but the man was still an enigma in many ways.

He wasn't someone who let down his defenses easily—but then neither was she.

Malik's hand squeezed hers then. "I've fought this, you know."

"We both have," she replied softly, "but some things are too powerful … you can only resist them for so long."

25. THE PASSAGE

HOT, DUSTY AIR peppered Jenna's face, making her grateful for the goggles she wore. Arms wrapped around Malik's waist, she leaned into him as they raced out of Melor.

The sun was rising, a bloody orb breaking the edge of the craggy mountains to the east. Its arrival painted the sky vermillion. An Idral sunrise was always a thing of beauty, but Jenna was too tense to admire it.

They'd set off now—there was no turning back.

Twisting her head left, her gaze caught Vic crouched low over the handlebars of his needle-nosed hopper. Like her and Malik, he wore heavy googles, while Obsidian perched on the seat behind him. Malik, who knew this landscape better than any of them, led the way through Melor's empty backstreets, taking a circuitous route out of town.

Mir-Ferrin troops would be patrolling the most frequently traveled route north to the tower, and so Malik would take them in a loop, east for a spell, before heading toward the canyon where the escape tunnel entrance awaited.

Leaving the outskirts of Melor behind them—the last of the low-slung sandstone houses surrounded by high walls to keep insects and desert creatures out—the two hoppers headed through a shadowed ravine. Red dust boiled in their wake, for even though the craft sped around three feet above the ground, their passing disturbed the earth and the creatures that inhabited it.

Jenna spied a sand-scarab scuttling out of their way—a huge black beetle that was the symbol of Idral for many. Indeed, her family used it on their banners, and Malik had worn an embossed design of a sand-scarab upon the breastplate of his armor.

Back when he was Captain of the Lord's Watch.

Back when there *was* a Lord's Watch.

Despite the warm air that rushed over her skin, goosebumps rose on Jenna's arms. She hated to imagine the slaughter that occurred as Mir-Ferrin troops and their battle-droids stormed Mir-Brennan Tower, but she forced herself to dwell on it now.

It helped to remind herself what was at risk.

Not just her life, or the lives of those she loved, but the future of her clan.

Would her family ever get back what it had lost?

The ravine gradually deepened, and Malik angled his hopper up one side. It was best not to travel along the floor of the steep-sided valley, for these places were home to chelrogs.

And as they headed east, Jenna caught a glimpse of one of the chasm lizards. A chelrog was crawling up the opposite side of the ravine, its claws digging into rough sandstone. Spines bristling, its huge bulk rippled with muscle and fat, the beast's expanse of silver scales glinted in the dawn light.

Jenna stared at its great maw and the row of dark eyes that gleamed like wet pebbles. The lizard's jaws were powerful enough to crush bone like chalk. As the two hoppers rocketed by, the chelrog turned its large head, observing them with a heavy-lidded, hungry stare.

It took them just under an hour to reach the gorge. They saw no one on the way, for Malik had, indeed, taken them on a roundabout route, ensuring they wouldn't cross paths with Mir-Ferrin patrols.

By the time they entered the narrow-sided valley, the sun was rising into the sky, turning it from a deep red to a dark rose. The heat had risen too, and soon sweat trickled down Jenna's back, making her tank top stick to it. Even the air that rushed by them was no longer cooling.

A sheer wall reared up at the end of the gorge—red sandstone studded with protruding growths of spiky succulents and cacti. Malik and Vic drew up their hoppers. Dust billowed out from under the sleek craft as they lowered to the valley floor.

Jenna dismounted, her boots scuffing on the dusty ground. She glanced around, half-expecting to see a chelrog lumbering toward her, for this was exactly the sort of place the chasm lizards dwelled. Fortunately though, the gorge was deserted, for the time being at least.

Malik and Vic were heaving the rucksacks they'd brought strapped to the back of the hoppers onto their backs. Meanwhile, Jenna turned from them and walked up to the sandstone wall, her gaze moving along its pitted surface.

Both her father and Cathal had told her what to look for—a few times over the years, just in case this day should ever come. At the time, she'd humored them, never believing it ever would.

But it had—and here she was.

And there it was, an oval-shaped hollow, with a long fissure at the top. The space was just big enough for her to insert her hand, which she did—stretching her fingertips in.

Her breath caught when she touched cold steel.

She pressed hard and the metal shifted beneath her fingertips.

For a few seconds, there was nothing, and then a rumble from deep within the wall began. Exhaling sharply, Jenna withdrew her hand.

A grinding noise started then, and the wall rolled sideways, revealing a small bay within.

A row of neatly parked hoppers sat inside, ready for a quick getaway. A small utility-droid sat in an alcove, kept here to service the hoppers. Its amber lights flickered as they entered. A circular passageway led into the cliff.

Malik and Vic walked past Jenna into the bay, with Obsidian close at their heels. The battle-droid took long, loping strides, its blood-red gaze sweeping the space, on the alert for any danger.

"Come on," Malik said, catching her eye. "We have to move fast now … Cathal's only got until noon."

Jenna nodded, although she didn't need reminding of her brother's impending execution.

She followed the two men into *The Passage*, their heavy boots clanging on metal, while Obsidian brought up the rear, its wide, rubber-soled feet thudding behind her.

Unspeaking, the party of four marched forward, their footfalls ringing in the circular tunnel. Dim panel lighting illuminated the pewter-colored metal panels surrounding them. It was a featureless, depressing space—but then it had been built as an escape route, not as lodgings.

Time drew out—although none of them spoke—and eventually, the far end of the tunnel appeared. A heavy metal lever protruded from the wall.

Moving toward the lever, Jenna reached for it.

"Wait." Malik's hand caught her arm. "We need to ready ourselves before we set foot out there."

Chagrined, Jenna dropped her hand. Of course, they did.

He and Vic dumped their rucksacks onto the ground and pulled out weapons.

Malik then passed Jenna a laser-pistol, and his fingers brushed hers as she took it.

Their gazes met and fused for an instant before his mouth lifted at the corners. Even though Malik was serious and focused now, he was still letting her know things had changed between them.

He hadn't forgotten the things they'd said to each other the night before.

And neither had she.

Wordlessly, Jenna holstered the pistol. All three of them wore flak vests they'd donned before leaving the hotel.

Meanwhile, her male companions were arming themselves as if they were preparing to take on the whole Mir-Ferrin space fleet single-handedly. Malik clipped two laser-blades to his belt, as well as his two-remaining pyro-grenades. He carried a laser-rifle over his shoulder and a laser-pistol at his hip.

They armed Obsidian heavily as well. The battle-droid carried two rifles and two laser-pistols.

"We'll likely meet other battle-droids on this trip," Vic said, drawing Jenna's attention. "If that happens, get behind Obsidian and let him deal with them."

Jenna eyed the gleaming black carapace that covered the droid. "And what if they bring Obsidian down?"

Vic moved behind the battle-droid. "Your laser-pistol won't do anything against their armor," he replied before slapping his hand at where the back of Obsidian's neck met its shoulders. "But the droids have a weak spot … here."

Jenna nodded, paying close attention. Nonetheless, she did wonder how easy it would be to get behind a rampaging battle-droid.

"The outlet Obsidian can plug into is just a few yards away," she reminded Vic.

"They'll have guards patrolling the landing bay though," Malik murmured. "The droid will need to work quickly."

The cyborg nodded. "He will."

Jenna's belly clenched. Once they knew Cathal, Isla, and Bea's exact locations, they'd need to deal with the guards—without alerting the whole tower to their presence.

Sucking in a deep breath, she stepped up to the door. "Ready?"

"Go on then," Malik replied.

Grabbing hold of the lever, Jenna twisted it.

The circular door opened with a soft hiss.

Vic went first, followed by Obsidian, and then Malik and Jenna.

They stepped out into a narrow passageway covered in embossed gold paneling.

The rumble of engines coming from the landing bay vibrated the floor beneath them and covered up any noise their feet made as they traveled the passage, halting before the outlet.

Sticking out a metal hand, Obsidian plunged a finger into the central portal.

As the droid worked, it emitted a low hum.

Moments ticked by, and Jenna started to sweat. Thanks to the climate control, it was cool in here; however, the fact they were all gathered before the outlet, exposed for anyone passing by to see, put her nerves on edge.

She hoped the droid wouldn't take much longer.

Minutes passed before Obsidian finally spoke, its rasping voice carrying in the passageway. "Isla and Beatrix Mir-Brennan are being kept under guard on Level 12, Chamber 23F … while Cathal Mir-Brennan is in the detention block, Level 3, Cell 771. He's scheduled to be collected for his execution in three and a half hours."

26. TRY NOT TO GET YOURSELF KILLED

JENNA'S PULSE ACCELERATED. Those two locations were at opposite ends of the tower. The detention block lay underground, whereas her sister-in-law and niece were being housed in one of the guest suites on an upper level.

"Okay, synchronize wrist-comms," Malik whispered. "Are you ready … one, two, three, set."

Jenna tapped the device Malik had strapped onto her wrist before they departed Melor earlier that morning, her pulse leaping as the screen started its countdown.

"Aim to be back here within thirty minutes," Malik continued, his gaze meeting hers.

"And if I'm not?"

His gaze didn't waver. "Then I'll come looking for you."

"What if you're held up?"

"Stay in the tunnel and wait for us." He paused then, his gaze narrowing. "Don't venture down into the detention block … it's too risky."

Jenna swallowed once more, to ease the tightness in her throat. Thirty minutes didn't seem like a long time.

Obsidian detached itself from the wall then, while Malik and Vic crept up to the end of the passageway. Carefully, the cyborg ducked his head out before yanking it in again.

Turning to Malik, Vic gave him the thumbs up, held up four fingers, and then pointed left.

Jenna slowly let out the breath she hadn't even realized she'd been holding. The thumbs up meant the way was clear—for the moment at least. She presumed four fingers meant there were four soldiers nearby.

Malik nodded, and then both men drew laser-blades. They'd discussed earlier that going in firing pistols would only draw attention to them. You had to get up close to someone with a laser-blade, but they were fast, quick—and quiet.

Malik then gestured for her and Obsidian to follow.

Whispering a silent prayer to the gods, Jidea especially, Jenna moved.

They emerged from the safety of the service passage onto the walkway that lined the back of the landing bay. The vast gilded hangar opened before them.

Jenna glanced right at the armored doorway that led into a wide entrance hall and the bank of elevators. It was unguarded, although when she swept her gaze left, she spied four bronze-clad figures patrolling the bay below.

A shuttle was leaving, providing a welcome distraction. One of the huge hangar doors rolled open, bringing with it a blast of hot, dusty air. The guards were all watching the shuttle as it nosed forward.

Jenna's heart lurched, hope surging within her.

They'd stumbled upon a small window of opportunity; they had to seize it and move now.

Malik reached the exit first, slamming his hand down on the panel next to it. The door slid open silently, and they hurried through.

Two soldiers stood in the hallway beyond—but neither had time to reach for their weapons or to raise the alarm.

The hum of laser-blades igniting cut through the air as the door slid shut behind them, a flash of white light following. Jenna raised a hand to protect her eyes, and when she lowered it, the two Mir-Ferrins were on the ground, their armor smoking.

Vic then gestured to Obsidian, who marched forward, leaned down, and grabbed the fallen soldiers by the ankles. The droid then dragged the bodies into an alcove, leaving a wet streak on the polished black floor.

The party of four moved past the bank of elevators, into a narrow passageway where two service elevators awaited.

Malik punched the button of one, while Obsidian called the elevator opposite.

Heart beating in her throat, Jenna swept her gaze over Vic and Malik. They both were so calm—although they were trained for this, and she wasn't.

Her and Malik's gazes fused then, and her breathing hitched. "Be careful," she whispered. "Try not to get yourself killed, Mir-Draven."

His mouth quirked. "I won't." Malik then glanced over at Obsidian. "Look after her."

The battle-droid's head jerked, in a facsimile of a nod. "I shall."

An instant later, the elevator doors behind Malik and Vic slid open. The men stepped inside, just as Jenna and Obsidian's elevator arrived.

Turning from her bodyguard—her lover—Jenna followed the droid inside. Obsidian reached out a clawed hand and punched Level 12. It was almost a relief when the doors closed. The anticipation of being on her own was worse than the reality.

The elevator shot upward, making Jenna reach out to steady herself against the wall.

"It's just you and me now, Obsidian," she murmured.

The droid inclined its head, those disquieting crimson eyes fixing upon her. "I suggest you stay close to me, Jenna ... and let me take the lead."

She nodded. "Don't worry, I will."

The elevator jerked to a halt, and the doors opened. Hanging back, her hand upon the grip of her laser-pistol, Jenna allowed Obsidian to exit first. She then cautiously ventured out.

However, the service passage beyond was clear.

Leaving the elevator behind, which would be their escape route back down to the landing bay, the pair traveled along the passage, halting at the end of it.

Jenna's pulse started to race, her breathing quickening.

Here we go.

As soon as they stepped out into the gilded corridor beyond, they'd be in the open. Speed was what mattered now.

Drawing her pistol, Jenna turned its energy output up to 'lethal'. Fortunately, her hands were steady. Her heart slammed against her ribcage with each frenzied beat, yet her mind was oddly clear and calm—each nerve on edge and ready to act.

Obsidian strode out into the corridor first, laser-rifle unslung, domed head tilting left and right, while Jenna darted out behind him.

This hallway—painted soft gold and lined with desert succulents on pedestals—was empty, and as they passed guest suites, Jenna silently counted the numbers on the doors. *Eighteen F … Nineteen F.* They were in the right place—and their destination was just around the corner.

And so would Mir-Ferrin guards be.

Obsidian quickened its pace, the creak and squeak of the droid's robotic joints echoing high into the spider-vaulted ceiling. Along the way, they passed a statue of Raul the Destroyer, the God of War. The hulking figure, carved from Idralian sandstone, carried a sword in his left hand, and an axe in the other.

Jenna's mouth thinned as her gaze slid over the god's grim face and blood-red eyes—twin rubies the sculptor had set into the stone.

She had her own reaper with her today, one that would show no mercy.

They rounded the corner, and Jenna spied two guards stationed outside a door halfway down the corridor.

There was no time for stealth or laser-blades.

Blinding-white bolts detonated, the sound ricocheting down the corridor—and the guards, who'd just raised their own rifles and were about to fire upon the battle-droid, crumpled.

Jenna's jaw clenched hard.

They'd just shouted their presence.

Reaching the door, Obsidian stuck a metal finger into the socket beneath the keypad, overriding the lock.

The door whispered open, and Jenna lurched past the droid and dove inside.

Isla Mir-Brennan, who'd been seated on the recliner in the living area, jumped to her feet, while her daughter scrambled off her lap. "Jenna!"

Clad in flowing white, both Isla and Bea's faces were pale and strained. Of course, Cathal's execution was looming—noon was barely more than three hours away—and soon they'd likely be escorted out to the terrace to witness the event.

Isla's lips parted once more, yet Jenna held up a hand to silence her. No doubt her sister-in-law had an avalanche of questions, as she would have too, in the same situation, but they had to wait.

"There's no time to explain anything right now," she said, once again surprised at how calm her voice sounded. "We have to leave."

Not needing to be instructed twice, Isla nodded. She then gripped Bea by the hand and hurried toward her. "Cathal?" she asked.

"He's being freed," Jenna replied. "We're meeting him and the others downstairs ... come on."

They emerged into the corridor, where Isla let out a startled cry and shoved Bea behind her, shrinking back at the sight of the hulking battle-droid.

"It's all right," Jenna gasped, making a grab for her sister-in-law. Of course, Isla would have already had a few encounters with some of these droids since the tower had been stormed. It wasn't any wonder that the sight of another one terrified her. "This is Obsidian ... and it's going to ensure we get out of here."

"What?" Isla croaked.

"Questions later, remember?" Jenna replied, shoving her ahead of her. The thunder of running feet, and shouting to their right, warned her they'd soon have company. "This way!"

The four of them made it halfway up the first corridor when Mir-Ferrin soldiers caught up with them.

"Behind me," Obsidian ordered.

Its three companions obeyed, shielding themselves as laser bolts scorched the wall. Their protector whipped around and returned fire.

When she peered around Obsidian, Jenna's heart lurched in her throat.

The Mir-Ferrin soldiers weren't alone—tall battle-droids, their bronze carapaces glinting, flanked them.

The wail of claxons began then, vibrating through the tower.

Jenna's gut clenched. If Mican Mir-Ferrin didn't know there were intruders before, he would now.

Another laser bolt detonated overhead, and she ducked, yanking Isla with her. "The service elevator that'll take us back down to the landing bay isn't far away," she told her sister-in-law. "When I say so, run!"

Malik drew to an abrupt halt at the high-pitched alarm that shattered the dull silence in the underground detention block. Like his companion, he was wearing earplugs, yet even they couldn't block out the noise.

Next to him, Vic sheathed his laser-blade and unslung a rifle. He then pointed forward.

Nodding, Malik followed suit, even as his pulse kicked up a notch.

He and Vic hadn't set the alarms off—which meant Jenna and Obsidian had. Not for the first time, he doubted his decision to send Jenna with the battle-droid. His instinct was to always keep her close, yet Vic's plan made sense.

The detention block was the most dangerous of the two destinations; Malik knew that. In truth, he was letting his feelings for the woman he'd been charged to protect cloud his judgment.

Now that he'd admitted to himself he wanted Jenna, that he'd longed for her for years, it felt as if he'd just let himself out of a self-imposed prison. But emotions were dangerous, especially at times like these.

He had to stay focused and trust that Obsidian would keep Jenna safe.

At present, he and Vic still hadn't located the clan-lord's cell.

Nonetheless, things had gone smoothly enough so far. They'd killed the four guards they'd encountered in the security entrance to Level 3 of the detention block, bringing down one of them, a woman who'd moved laser-fast, an instant before she reached the alarm.

They'd just jogged past Cell 750, but with the blaring claxons, there wasn't any time to lose. Both men broke into a run.

Rounding the corner, Malik saw two battle-droids standing guard before a large window.

His pulse accelerated further, adrenaline spiking.

He'd hoped they wouldn't have posted droids in front of the cell. However, both he and Vic had readied themselves for the eventuality. It was why they'd put in earplugs.

Vic dropped low onto one knee, firing on the battle-droids.

The guards raised their own weapons, advancing on them—and the moment they'd moved away from the front of the cell, Malik withdrew a pyro-grenade from his belt, pulled out the pin, and tossed it at them.

Both he and Vic hit the ground, covering their heads with their arms as the floor buckled and shuddered underneath them. Even with the earplugs in, the explosion vibrated through Malik and made his ears ring.

Clenching his jaw, he rode it out, pushing himself up onto his haunches as acrid smoke filled the corridor and the crackling of fried circuits joined the siren's pulse.

Vic was up too, shaking his head to clear it, and then the pair of them cautiously ventured forward, stepping over chunks of masonry.

One of the battle-droids had been blown to bits, while its companion dragged itself through the rubble toward them, red eyes focused on them with eerie intensity.

Vic didn't waste any time. Dodging its grasping hand, he drew the laser-pistol at his hip and shot the droid at the spot at the base of its neck, as he'd shown them before exiting the tunnel earlier.

Malik stepped around the inert droid, removing his earplugs as he went. The window the battle-droids had been standing before was cracked from the blast, yet he could still see through it.

A tall, dark-haired man clad in a flowing white tunic and pants stood within.

27. NECESSITY

CATHAL MIR-BRENNAN'S GAZE fixed upon the window, his face taut.

For a moment, Malik thought the man was looking straight at him, but then he realized the door was one-way glass.

The clan-lord knew there had been an explosion outside his cell. But he had no idea who was out there.

Glancing down at the keypad, Malik frowned. There wasn't any point in trying that—he'd never guess the pin. Instead, they'd have to enter the cell using brute force.

He shifted forward and pressed the comm next to the door. "My Lord, it's Captain Malik ... stand back and protect your face. We're coming in."

Cathal's eyes snapped wide. He then obeyed, moving to stand against the far wall, raising an arm to shield his face.

Satisfied, Malik shifted back a few paces, took aim at the glass with his rifle, and fired.

The panel jolted, a spiderweb of fine cracks splintering across its surface.

Together, Malik and Vic kicked it in.

Around them, the alarm had increased in pitch; there was a hysterical edge to it now.

They'd know the detention block had been breached. Reinforcements would be arriving.

"Captain!" Cathal pushed himself off the wall and approached. "How did you—"

"No time to explain, My Lord," Malik cut in. Usually, he'd never dare interrupt the man he served, but he did so now. "Lady Jenna is freeing your wife and daughter as we speak ... we're meeting them in the landing bay."

"Let's go," Vic growled. "Time's short."

The three men crunched over the rubble, skirting the remains of the two battle-droids. The shoulder and arm of one of them—the one Vic had finished off—was still twitching, despite that it had been blown to pieces.

The sight made Malik's skin crawl; those things were virtually indestructible.

Leaving behind the chaos they'd created in order to free the clan-lord, they hurried back toward the entrance to Level 3.

They were halfway there when the thunder of booted feet approaching made all three men skid to a halt.

"It looks like we won't be getting out this way," Malik announced.

The first of the Mir-Ferrins—a squad of armored cyborgs—rounded the corner, only to be cut down by Malik and Vic. As soon as they'd caused the oncoming unit to pause for a moment, Malik jerked his head to his companions. "This way."

Vic offered no complaint. They'd already discussed the possibility that they'd have to take the service conduit up to the landing bay. Detention blocks were constructed to be difficult to get out of, and the Mir-Ferrins would have both the main elevators and the service lifts guarded now.

Likewise, Cathal held his tongue. His face was set in grim lines, and he nodded his thanks when Malik passed him a pistol.

All of them needed to be armed.

Another squad of cyborgs tried to intercept them two corridors on.

Laser bolts illuminated the dimly lit space as Malik, Vic, and Cathal returned fire.

Malik activated the cyan-shield on his wrist. The blue sphere appeared before him with a low hiss, giving Malik and his companions protection as they dove for the safety of the next passageway.

They continued on their way, sprinting now, while Malik swept his gaze left and right, counting the doorways.

Luckily, he knew the detention block well. He just never thought he'd one day be trying to escape from it.

"Faster!" Vic grunted, lengthening his stride. "They're too close behind us … we'll never get into the conduit in time."

Malik clenched his jaw, pushing himself faster. Sweat trickled down between his shoulder blades. Beside him, Cathal easily kept pace. Fortunately, the clan-lord took pride in keeping himself fit; before taking his father's place at the head of his clan, Cathal had served in the Mir-Brennan space fleet.

It was just one of the reasons Malik respected the man, and just as well—for Cathal would have slowed them down otherwise.

The circular metal door that led into the service conduit loomed ahead. Reaching it, Malik wrenched the wheel-lock left, spinning it to release the door.

And all the while, the blare of claxons pulsed through him. The floor beneath his booted feet shuddered from the advancing troops.

Malik threw the door open, and Cathal dove in, followed by Vic.

He raised his cyan-shield once more as armored figures appeared at the end of the corridor, the tall outline of a battle-droid among them. The shield was designed to hold off a rapid burst of laser, but not a sustained hammering.

It started to crackle ominously, and Malik heeded the warning.

Lowering the shield, he opened fire on the ceiling between them, bringing down a cascade of wires and chunks of rock—and filling the corridor with smoke.

He'd bought himself a few seconds, and he wouldn't waste them.

Clambering into the conduit, he hauled the door shut after him.

"I don't believe it." Mican Mir-Ferrin stared down at the screen upon the tablet the battle-droid held out to him. "Isn't that your wife?"

Tian, who'd just finished buckling a laser-pistol holster around his hips, froze. "What?"

"Jenna," Mican answered, slowing his speech as if speaking to a half-wit. "She's here." He stabbed a finger at the screen, his expression stony, before grabbing it from the utility-droid and thrusting it at his son. "See for yourself."

Pulse pounding in his ears, Tian grabbed the tablet and stared down at it.

The security camera images were grainy, but he could easily make out the small woman huddled behind a battle-droid. Dressed in black cargo pants and a tank top, her brown hair pulled back in a tight braid, Jenna looked nothing like the elegant ambassador who'd departed days earlier—yet her face was unmistakable. Isla and Beatrix crouched a few yards back from their rescuer.

And as Tian stared down at the screen, Jenna ducked out from behind the droid and fired a round of laser bolts haphazardly down the corridor. An instant later, she shouted something to her companions, and they ran, with the battle-droid loping behind them.

Tian's gut clenched. What was a battle-droid doing helping her?

"Fuck," he growled.

"Your wife should be dead," the clan-lord replied, ice in his voice now.

Tian knew that tone well.

He'd pay for his mistake later.

"Well, she isn't," Tian replied, thrusting the tablet back at his father and striding toward the doorway of his solar. "But she soon will be."

The clan-lord didn't answer. However, there was a menace in his silence, one that made the skin between Tian's shoulder blades crawl.

Bitterness filled his mouth.

Why couldn't Elijah or Lucas be down here, dealing with the poisonous bastard? Instead, they were commanding *Defiance* and *Dominion,* the two Mir-Ferrin flagships holding the blockade.

No doubt, Mican would be opening a channel to Elijah right now, informing his eldest son of Tian's blunder.

Outside the solar, five members of Tian's security team awaited him, flanked by two hulking battle-droids.

"Status?" Tian barked at the team's commander.

"The breaches on Level 12 and Detention Block, Level 3, have been now confirmed, Sir," Commander Anik replied, his visored face impassive.

"I know that," Tian snapped. "But how did the intruders get in here?"

"We haven't yet ascertained how they got access, Sir. No breaches have been located."

"And the prisoners?"

"All of them have been released from their cells. Three individuals and a battle-droid on Level 12 have reached a service elevator and are traveling down to the ground floor ... while three human males in the detention block are climbing out of it via a service conduit."

Tian listened, his mouth twisting. "They're all heading to the landing bay."

They didn't know how Jenna and her friends had gained access to the tower, but he guessed they intended to steal a shuttle to make their escape.

Tian swiveled on his heel and strode toward the banks of elevators. Wordlessly, his team fell in behind him. "And so are we."

"They're going to be waiting for us once these doors open," Jenna informed Isla and Bea. Her niece clung to her mother's leg, gaze wide and frightened. Bea hadn't spoken since they'd left the relative safety of their quarters. Fear had rendered her mute. Meanwhile, Isla's face was taut, and a nerve flickered upon her cheek; yet she remained calm.

They were traveling down in the service elevator. Someone had tried to override it, to prevent their descent, but the battle-droid had dug a finger into the control panel and reversed the command. "Obsidian will exit first and clear a path … so stay back and don't move until I say so." Jenna halted then, realizing she hadn't yet told Isla where they were headed. "We're meeting the others at *The Passage*."

Isla nodded. Of course, being Cathal's wife, she knew about the secret way in and out of the tower. However, her gaze remained riveted upon Jenna's face. "What happened to you?"

Jenna's mouth quirked. "What do you mean?"

Isla gestured to Jenna's attire and the pistol she still gripped at her side. "This."

Jenna snorted a laugh. "Necessity."

She glanced down at her wrist-comm, her already racing pulse jumping up a notch.

Twenty-five minutes had passed—although it didn't seem that long.

In that time, they'd managed to alert the entire tower to their presence.

Her skin prickled then. Malik and the others should have already reached the landing bay by now.

If they hadn't, things were about to go seriously awry.

Her gun-toting might have impressed Isla, but it was easier to be brave when a seven-foot-tall battle-droid was covering you.

Two of them against an unending supply of Mir-Ferrin troops and droids wasn't going to end well.

As if reading her thoughts—which was impossible, of course—Obsidian swiveled around to face its human companions. It fixed Isla with its eerie blood-red stare and then unslung a laser-pistol from around its metal waist. "You will require this." It then handed the weapon to the clan-lord's wife.

"Do you know how to use one of those?" Jenna asked.

Isla nodded. She took the gun from Obsidian, buckled the holster around her hips, and then drew the weapon, turning its output up to 'lethal'. Jenna felt a little envious of the ease with which she handled the pistol.

Of course, Isla was born a Mir-Galbreth—a warrior clan. She would have learned how to fire a laser-pistol as a child. There was a steely glint in her blue eyes that told Jenna she was ready for whatever they faced when the elevator doors opened.

Isla met her gaze then, her jaw firming. "Aim for the neck, armpits, or groin," her sister-in-law instructed. "It's where their armor will be weakest."

Jenna nodded. Despite her unskilled shooting, she'd already managed to bring down at least half a dozen soldiers. If she survived this, the reality of it would likely sicken her.

But for now, she didn't let herself go there.

Isla didn't look concerned about killing any Mir-Ferrin who blocked her path.

The elevator slid to a halt, the doors flew open—and Obsidian launched itself into the entrance hall beyond.

28. KILL OR BE KILLED

JENNA HAD BEEN correct about the welcoming committee.

Around ten soldiers guarded the entrance hall.

But, even so, the suddenness of Obsidian's attack threw them.

Toting two laser-rifles, the battle-droid swept its fire in a wide arc, mowing down the bronze-clad figures as they charged it.

Isla was right behind, shooting in Obsidian's wake, while Jenna and Bea brought up the rear.

Pulse roaring in her ears, Jenna looked left to the armored doors leading out to the landing bay beyond.

They were open—although one of the soldiers was moving toward the control panel next to the doors.

Jenna's heart lurched, panic clawing up her throat. He was going to seal them in. They needed to reach the escape tunnel fast.

She fired on him, hitting the man in the throat. He went down, and Isla took out the next soldier who moved in the direction of the doors.

Laser bolts scored the gilded wall next to the women, so close that the heat from one scorched the skin of Jenna's shoulder.

Ducking, she moved in closer to Obsidian, inching forward as the droid continued its deadly sweep.

More laser bolts slid by the battle-droid's guard, setting fire to the wall this time. Thick black smoke poured into the entrance hall. It stung the back of Jenna's throat, and she coughed.

Behind her, Bea whimpered. Jenna shuffled back, putting an arm around her niece's shoulder. Gods, she wished she could spare the girl this.

Meanwhile, she didn't dare shift her attention from the rapidly dwindling numbers of Mir-Ferrin soldiers, and the doorway, which still seemed yards away.

Choking, toxic smoke filled the entrance hall, and anxiety started to beat its fists against Jenna's breastbone. They had to get out of here.

Obsidian moved left, lurching toward the door—and the two women and child behind the droid shadowed it.

An instant later, they were through, and as soon as Bea was clear, Obsidian jammed a fist into the control panel.

The door closed, just as armored bodies slammed up against it.

The crackle of frying circuitry followed, and smoke curled out from the control panel.

"How long will that keep them at bay?" Jenna panted.

"I estimate around twenty minutes," Obsidian replied. "That door has three layers of Lazda steel. It will take them a while to burn a hole in it."

"Good," Isla replied, her tone clipped. She then turned to Jenna, her gaze glinting. "Now, where—"

The rapid tattoo of detonating laser bolts cut Isla off, and she whirled around, pistol raised. Jenna followed suit, while Obsidian stalked forward to shield them.

Peering around her protector, Jenna looked across the vast gilded space, past the central core, to where a squad of Mir-Ferrin marines had bailed someone up. The huddle was in the far corner of the landing bay, at the end of a row of shiny bronze shuttles.

Her breathing hitched when she saw a dark-haired man lurch out from behind one of the parked shuttles and fire upon them with a laser-rifle.

Malik.

And as they watched, two more human males emerged from behind a stack of pallets.

Vic and Cathal.

"Dad!" Bea squealed, finally finding her tongue.

"Hush, love," Isla hissed back. "Don't distract him."

Jenna's mouth thinned. Indeed. Although Malik, Vic, and Cathal were all armed, they were outnumbered by the troops who now had them surrounded. There were over a dozen of them, although she sucked in a relieved breath to see there were no battle-droids there.

The tattoo of detonating laser bolts echoed through the cavernous space.

Obsidian turned to Jenna then. "Get to safety. I will assist the others." Turning from her, the battle-droid raised its two laser-rifles and began firing upon the Mir-Ferrin soldiers.

"I don't think so," Isla snapped. "Not while my husband is fighting for his life, and I've got a weapon in my hand."

Jenna flashed her a thin smile. She liked Isla's ballsy attitude. "Exactly."

Shouts and thuds drew her attention then, and she glanced over her shoulder at the door Obsidian had locked.

The droid had done a good job, and the door was sturdy, although they'd get through eventually.

Turning back to Isla, she nodded. "Let's make sure Bea is out of harm's way first though."

They stepped out onto the walkway that ran along one side of the landing bay and ducked left into the first service corridor—the one that led to *The Passage*.

Trying not to focus on the pitched battle that was going on at the other end of the space, and the wail of agony that had just reverberated high into the rafters, Jenna hunkered down in front of her niece and met her eye.

"Your Ma and I are going to help the others, Bea ... but I need you to hide somewhere safe, okay?"

The child nodded, her throat bobbing as she struggled to remain brave. "I lost Daisy, Auntie Jen." Her voice quavered. "I'm sorry."

The anguish in the girl's eyes made Jenna's chest constrict. "Don't worry about that, sweetheart," she murmured. "Now ... see these panels?" She touched the circular gold disc with a sand-scarab embossed upon it behind Bea. "The third one from the end of the corridor is a secret door. Move the disc to one side and you'll find a button underneath. Press it hard and the door will open. I want you to climb inside … and wait. We'll be there soon."

Bea glanced over at her mother, eyes glittering with tears. "Come with me, Ma."

"I'll be there as soon as I can, love," Isla murmured before she stepped close and gave her daughter a quick hug. "Go on!"

Watching her niece trot off down the passageway, her slippers whispering on the metal grating beneath her feet, Jenna then turned back to Isla. "Let's go."

As soon as they exited the corridor, Jenna could see Obsidian had been busy. Below the walkway, bronze-armored bodies lay scattered around the central core, their blood glinting on the polished black floor.

The battle-droid had done a lot of damage, although some of the Mir-Ferrins were now attempting to bail Obsidian up against one of the hangar doors. There were still far too many marines firing on the three men cornered at the far end.

"Shit," Jenna muttered, anxiety clutching her by the throat once more. "We aren't going to be able to do much."

"No, but we can draw their fire and let Cathal and the others get into a stronger position," Isla replied.

Jenna nodded, even as her pulse started thundering in her ears.

Crouched low, the two women edged along the walkway, getting as close to the fray as they dared.

And then they opened fire.

Malik rolled across the floor, feeling the heat of a laser bolt skim overhead, and took refuge behind a trolley used by the mechanics for bringing parts out to the shuttles.

Finally, he'd managed to get out of the corner they'd been trapped in.

Upon emerging from the service conduit, he'd thrown the metal hatch shut and melted the lock with his laser-blade.

Yet Malik and his companions hadn't gone more than a couple of steps before a squad of soldiers stormed into the landing bay, boxing them in.

He'd seen Obsidian and its companions gain entry a short time later, had witnessed the battle-droid jam the door to the landing bay.

Jenna should have made her way to *The Passage*, as agreed, but instead, she and Isla had provided a distraction.

Damn it, that wasn't the plan.

Malik put his earplugs back in. He then reached down, his fingers closing over the last of his pyro-grenades. He hadn't wasted the previous grenade, but this one really had to count.

He peered around the edge of the trolley, to see Jenna duck out from behind a column and fire upon the troops once more. She only just moved away in time to avoid a volley of laser bolts that tore into the panel behind her.

Malik's pulse shot up. Gods, she was going to get herself killed.

Gaze sweeping left, he saw that Obsidian was still defending itself against a posse of soldiers who'd bailed it up against one of the hangar doors. Malik's gaze narrowed. If he tossed his grenade just behind the soldiers, he'd likely cause enough damage to bring down a few Mir-Ferrins without harming anyone on the periphery—or without damaging the central core and potentially bringing the roof down on them.

Malik was sweating heavily now. He'd be taking a chance, but since they were still dramatically outnumbered, and that armored door wouldn't hold forever, he had few other options.

Drawing in a deep breath, Malik waited until Vic had just launched a volley of shots at the soldiers and ducked back under cover as they returned fire.

He then pulled the pin on the grenade, launched himself to his feet, and tossed it over the heads of the soldiers.

He hit the concrete once more as an explosion rocked the landing bay.

A wave of heat barreled into him, so intense his breathing caught, yet Malik kept his head down, holding his breath through it. Then, as dust and mortar rained down on him, he scrambled to his feet and hoisted his laser-pistol high.

It was time to ensure any surviving Mir-Ferrin soldiers were dealt with.

Jenna peeled herself off the walkway. Her ears were ringing, and nausea rolled over her. She and Isla had been a decent distance from the blast, but even so, the heat and power of it had knocked them both off their feet.

It was a pyro-grenade, the same weapon that Malik had used to save their lives in that plaza on Aura Terminal.

Staggering to her feet, and bracing herself against the column to steady herself, she glanced down at where Isla sat on her backside rubbing her ears. Relieved her sister-in-law seemed unharmed, Jenna glanced down at the wreckage below.

Her breathing caught as she watched Malik, Vic, her brother, and Obsidian move through the rubble.

One wounded marine tried to rise from where he'd been thrown against a pallet. The soldier's helmet had come off, revealing a young man with white-blond hair and pale skin. His face was set in a grimace as he reached for his weapon.

However, Cathal found him first. Her brother didn't hesitate. Raising his pistol, he shot the man in the head.

Jenna looked away, bile stinging her throat.

She knew it was necessary—it was 'kill or be killed'—but it was also brutal. Of course, her brother was a trained soldier. She'd forgotten that.

All the same, she hadn't imagined he could act so ruthlessly.

Turning away once more, Jenna focused on helping Isla to her feet. And when she and her sister-in-law viewed the floor once more, all the Mir-Ferrin soldiers were dead.

29. EXTREME MEASURES

BREATHING HARD, MALIK looked up at the walkway, his gaze fusing with Jenna's.

Her face was pale and tense, yet the resolved set of her jaw, the way she still gripped the laser-pistol at her side, told him she had it together.

Jenna was a warrior, but then she always had been. Beside her, the clan-lord's wife looked equally fierce.

Satisfied both women were unharmed, Malik turned away, his gaze sweeping over Vic and Cathal. They were covered in dust and grime, but neither of them had been injured in the blast. Likewise, Obsidian still had all its limbs intact.

A hissing sound filled the landing bay then.

All gazes swiveled to the armored door: the center of it glowed red-hot. They hadn't been able to breach the locks, but they were going to burn through it.

"Time to go," Malik announced.

He set off toward the stairs leading up to the walkway, but his step faltered when Cathal called out behind him, "Wait!"

Swiveling around, Malik saw the clan-lord striding toward the central core. The wide golden column dominated the landing bay. "My Lord," he called out. "We have to go ... now."

The entrance door was starting to smoke; time was running out.

The clan-lord ignored him. Instead, Cathal ripped off the covering of one of the panels and plunged his hand into the core.

Pain rippled across his face, yet he held tight.

"Cathal! What are you doing?" Isla rushed down from the walkway and clambered over the rubble to reach her husband. Jenna followed close at her heels.

"We don't have time for this," Vic muttered, stepping up next to Malik.

Malik's pulse quickened. He didn't know what the clan-lord was up to—but he was close to wrecking this rescue attempt.

"My Lord," he barked, moving close. Cathal had just punched something into a digital display. "You can't—"

His voice cut off as his gaze alighted upon the panel. The numbers '15:00' glowed up at him.

The fine hair on the back of Malik's neck prickled.

"It's all right," Cathal replied, pressing a button. The display started to count down. "I'm done here."

The clan-lord stepped back then and tried to pull his hand from the opening.

He grunted, pain rippling over his face. He then cursed.

Isla's brow furrowed. "What's happening?"

"Have you just activated a DNA lock?" Jenna demanded, her tone brittle.

He nodded.

"On what exactly?"

Cathal's jaw bunched as he struggled to pull his hand free. "I set a pyro-detonator to go off in fifteen minutes," he muttered. "Why the fuck won't this thing release me?"

Jenna gasped. "Why would you put a bomb in the central core?"

Cathal met her gaze, his dark eyes wild, sweat beading on his brow. "I didn't ... this was our grandfather's idea." His throat bobbed then. "Father told you about *The Passage* ... but he didn't tell *either* of us about the detonator. He left instructions behind that I could only read after his death. No one but the incumbent ruler of our clan can know about it." He tore his gaze from hers and looked at where his hand had been swallowed up by the column. "It's driven three spikes into my palm ... but they're supposed to retract once the timer's been set."

Silence fell in the landing bay, broken only by muffled, angry shouts and the hiss of blowtorches behind the armored door.

Cathal's face had drained of blood as his gaze swept over the small crowd that had gathered about him. When he spoke, his voice came out in a rasp. "Any ideas?"

Malik glanced over at where the battle-droid observed the unfolding scene. "Obsidian … can you take a look? Be careful though."

With a nod, the droid moved up to the central core. Gently, it inserted a finger into the console next to the display. Obsidian emitted a low hum while it ran diagnostics.

Moments slid past, and sweat trickled down Malik's neck. He glanced over at the door. Lazda steel was hard to breach, although the red center was spreading now.

"The trigger mechanism has corroded," the battle-droid announced, shattering the brittle hush around the central core. "It has now fused. If you remove your hand, or if we tamper with it, the detonator will explode."

Cathal made a choking sound. "Of course, it's been sitting in there for fifty years … and never been serviced. I can't believe I kept that escape tunnel maintained but forgot about the fucking detonator."

"Cathal," Isla whispered, taking a cautious step toward her husband. "What have you done?"

A nerve jumped in the clan-lord's jaw, and he held up his free hand. "Stop, Isla … best you don't touch me." His gaze fused with hers then. "I'm sorry, my love … it looks like I've just made a huge mistake." He broke off there, swallowing once more. "Since we were escaping, I intended to set the timer on the detonator first … to prevent the Mir-Ferrins from enjoying the prize they'd stolen."

"Why?" Jenna gasped, her eyes wide with horror. "Wasn't escaping enough?"

Her brother's expression turned grim. "I had to do it. This tower is swarming with Mir-Ferrin troops. The moment we left *The Passage*, they'd be hunting us. We'd never have gotten off the planet."

"We'd have had to lie low for a bit," Malik admitted, focusing once more on the counter. *Ten minutes.* "But we'd have managed it. There was no need for extreme measures."

Cathal shook his head. Sweat gleamed off his bloodless face now. "In a few minutes, this core is going to explode and blow this building sky-high … you all must leave before it does."

Isla let out a wail and rushed forward. However, Vic caught her, holding her fast as she struggled.

"No, Cathal!" Jenna choked out. Her face was stricken. "We're not leaving you here!"

"You have to, Jen," he ground out. "There's no stopping this."

"No!"

Brother and sister stared at each other. "You lead our clan now," Cathal rasped. "The fight against the Mir-Ferrins has only just begun. You can still lead our people to victory, you can still take back what was lost."

She shook her head, her eyes filling with tears.

The clan-lord inhaled sharply. "Listen to me, Jen … during my interrogation, Tian revealed that the attempt on my life at your wedding was *his* doing. The Mir-Lelith ambassador was a Mir-Ferrin sleeper agent. You need to let the Mir-Leliths know … it will help rebuild our relationship with them."

Jenna swallowed a sob. "I don't care about that."

"You must … I'm passing the torch to you now." There was steel in that look, a determination that would not be argued with. Cathal was afraid, but he'd mastered it. He glanced over at Malik once more. "Take her and the others to safety, Captain."

"No!" Isla sobbed, still fighting Vic's iron grip.

Cathal shook his head. His gaze seized hers. "I love you, Isla."

"And I love you!" Isla cried, hysterical now, tears pouring down her face. "Don't sacrifice yourself like this!"

"I've been left with little choice." Cathal's features tightened before he shifted his attention to Malik. "Do it."

"Don't you dare." Jenna shot Malik a warning look. "There must be a way to stop this thing!"

"Captain," Cathal growled. "Do your duty."

"Don't listen to him," Jenna countered, her voice hardening.

Malik hesitated.

"Sorry to interrupt," Vic growled, "but we *really* don't have time for this."

Malik ignored the cyborg, his gaze riveted upon Jenna.

"Captain." Cathal's voice turned to steel. "You knelt before me and swore an oath … to obey your clan-lord in all things."

Gut clenching, Malik shifted his attention back to Cathal.

The clan-lord stared him down. "Was that an empty promise?"

"No," Malik whispered.

"Take my sister then … ensure she gets to safety. Protect her with your life."

Malik's pulse thundered in his ears. His gaze flicked between Cathal and Jenna's faces, and for a few instants, he was torn. Jenna's gaze was desperate. He didn't want to let her down, but he also didn't want to break the oath he'd sworn.

The oath he'd lived by for over a decade and a half.

"Malik." It was the first time Cathal Mir-Brennan had ever used his name without his rank. There was a rawness to the clan-lord's voice. Despair.

Malik moved to Jenna. Before she could evade him, he took hold of her arm and hauled her away with him, heading toward the steps leading up to the walkway.

Sparks were now coming from the armored door, and the metal was turning molten.

They'd be through in a couple of minutes.

"Let me go, you bastard!" Jenna fought him hard, kicking and clawing at him, wriggling to get free. She was a small woman, yet strong. Likewise, Vic was having difficulty maneuvering Isla up the stairs. The woman's screams echoed through the landing bay.

Reaching the walkway, Malik threw Jenna over his shoulder. He glanced then, back at the central core—and at the man he served.

Cathal stared back at him, his face set.

Alone in the landing bay, Cathal heaved in a slow, deep breath—and then another.

They'd all gone, but they hadn't done so quietly.

Captain Malik and his cyborg companion had struggled to hold his wife and sister, but they'd done as he'd commanded.

Isla and Jenna were being carried to safety.

Cathal's eyes closed then, and he listened to the faint sound of footfalls on the metal grating of the service corridor, and the rhythmic clank of the battle-droid's loping stride.

The last minutes stretched out, and when Cathal finally opened his eyes and looked down at the counter, his pulse leaped to see that only three minutes remained.

Fear cramped his bowels then, a cold sweat coating his skin.

It had been easy to be brave earlier—in front of the others.

But the truth of it was that he was terrified.

He didn't want to die, but the Gods had turned against him.

He would never see Isla or his sweet Bea again.

Cathal had no one to blame but himself—like a blundering fool, he'd rushed in and set the detonator, and it couldn't be stopped.

The groan of wrenching metal made him look away from the counter. His gaze went to the landing bay entrance to see the glowing red fragments of the door tossed aside. Soldiers, cyborgs, and battle-droids swarmed inside the wide gilded space, and as they fanned out before the door, weapons raised, a tall, dark-haired figure followed close behind.

"Tian," Cathal called out. "You're just in time."

His brother-in-law, the man he'd trusted as a military adviser, had been surveying the wrecked landing bay. But his attention now snapped to the clan-lord.

And when their gazes met, Cathal's gut twisted, fury pulsing through him.

In that instant, he forgot about his fear, his fury at his reckless stupidity, and his sorrow to be leaving those he loved behind.

This man had lied to him, plotted against him, and betrayed him. He'd taken the bastard into his household in good faith after their clans had finally made peace.

But Tian betrayed him right from the start. He'd tried to have Cathal assassinated two years earlier, while placing the blame on the Mir-Leliths—an act that had sparked conflict between the two clans, propelling them into open war.

Hate was too mild a word for what he felt for this traitor. It was right that in their final moments they'd face each other again.

Tian's gaze narrowed then. "Where are the others?"

Cathal ignored him. Instead, he glanced down at the counter. *Twenty seconds.*

And when he looked up once more, Tian raised his pistol, aiming it at his head.

Laughter bubbled up within Cathal. It was too late. There was no stopping this.

Tian's mouth twisted. Of course, from this angle, he couldn't see that his hand was buried inside the central core, for the clan-lord had leaned up against it, adopting an indolent pose. "Just in time for what?"

Cathal smiled back as the last seconds of his life ran out. "For this."

30. ALL GONE

THE EXPLOSION HIT when they were deep in *The Passage*. Even so, it threw Malik against the wall. He loosened his grip on Jenna, and she slid to the ground.

He reached for her again, but she pushed herself away from him. "I can walk," she croaked. "Let me go."

The tunnel shuddered, the metal panels around them groaning in protest.

Jenna tried not to think about what had just happened behind them—about her brother's tragic mistake.

Grief would flatten her later—yet she had no time for it now. Instead, she stumbled onward, ignoring Malik.

Asshole. She'd pleaded with him to help her, but he'd denied her. Instead, he'd obeyed Cathal.

Ahead, Isla's raw sobs echoed through the tunnel. Vic now carried the struggling woman over his shoulder. They'd found Bea waiting for them inside *The Passage*, but the moment the girl saw her hysterical mother, she'd burst into tears. Obsidian had swept Bea up in its metal arms and entered the escape tunnel first.

Her wails echoed down the tunnel now, blending with her mother's sobs.

Grief did barrel into Jenna then; it gripped her around the throat and squeezed tight. She hated to see Isla and Bea so distraught.

Cathal. Her brother was gone.

Tears stung her eyelids, yet Jenna staggered on.

Smoke drifted through *The Passage* as the aftershocks of the explosion died away.

Bile surged into Jenna's throat. She couldn't believe her grandfather had built a detonator into the core of Mir-Brennan Tower. She barely remembered Nial Mir-Brennan, for he'd died when she was five. He'd become a father late in life, and so Jenna's father took his seat at the age of twenty-five. Her shadowy memories of her grandfather were of a quiet man with an intense gaze. His victory against the Mir-Ferrins had been hard-won, and when he'd built his fortress upon this planet, he'd clearly been paranoid that it might fall into enemy hands.

However, he'd never intended to sacrifice his life.

Neither had Cathal.

Jenna continued up the tunnel, her gaze focused on where Isla hung over Vic's back, sobbing gently now as exhaustion claimed her. Around them, metal panels creaked and rumbled ominously in the aftermath of the explosion.

As soon as Jenna stepped out of the tunnel, the heat hit her. The late morning sun burned onto their exposed skin.

Vic and Obsidian set their charges down, and Jenna hurried across to them, scooping a trembling Bea against her with one arm, while she embraced Isla with the other.

The three of them clung together for a few moments, a silent knot of grief.

Someone cleared their throat nearby, and Jenna glanced up to see Malik standing before them. His face was taut, his gaze shadowed. "I'm sorry, Jenna … but we need to go. It's not safe here."

For a few moments, Jenna merely stared back at him, fury pulsing in her belly.

"Malik's right," Vic agreed. "There are still plenty of Mir-Ferrin soldiers about … we need to avoid them."

Jaw clenching, Jenna nodded. As much as it galled her, she knew they had to leave. Lingering near the tower, or what was left of it, was dangerous. Despite that the explosion would have taken out most of the Mir-Ferrin force, there would still be patrols nearby.

Malik moved back inside to where his own hopper was parked, ready for departure, and retrieved hooded cloaks for them all. He then handed them out to his human companions as they followed him back into the tunnel. At his hour, they had to wear them. If they didn't, the ride back to Melor would blister their skin.

Malik's hand brushed Jenna's as he passed her a cloak, and she jerked back from him as if she'd just stuck her hand into a live socket.

Her bodyguard's mouth compressed at her reaction, his gaze narrowing.

Nonetheless, he knew better than to say anything.

Jenna was a primed pyro-grenade right now. One word would set her off.

Malik and Vic started their hoppers, while Obsidian took one from the neat row in the corner of the bay.

Wordlessly, Jenna threw on a cloak and pulled up her hood. She then retrieved her own hopper. Kicking the engine into life, she felt Malik's gaze upon her but ignored him. Her needle-nosed craft lifted off the ground before she angled it toward the exit and opened the throttle.

The four hoppers roared out into the gorge. Isla and Bea sat on the back of Malik's hopper, while Vic, Jenna, and the battle-droid traveled alone.

They barreled down the narrow space, red dust boiling in their wake, and when they finally emerged onto the sun-scorched hills beyond, Jenna glanced over her shoulder in the direction of Mir-Brennan Tower.

Part of her didn't want to, and yet she couldn't help herself. They were too distant from the tower to see the rubble—but the sky told the grim story of what had transpired behind them.

Indeed, a purple-black cloud billowed high into the pink heavens. Fortunately, they were far enough away to escape the chunks of falling masonry and the noxious gases and smoke from the explosion.

Jenna swallowed as grief tore at her throat once more.

It was all gone. Her brother. Mir-Brennan Tower. The Mir-Ferrins—and all those within the tower who'd served them.

Her stomach clenched then, as it occurred to her Tian and his father might not have even been inside the tower when it blew.

A moment later, she realized it was likely they were. Cathal's execution had been looming, after all. Neither of those bastards would have wanted to miss it.

Nausea rolled over Jenna, and she tore her gaze away from the smoke, focusing on the craggy landscape she was speeding over. She wanted to feel relief Tian and Mican Mir-Ferrin were both gone. But she just felt sick.

It wasn't supposed to go this way.

There had been a part of her that had feared they'd never rescue her family, a part of her that believed she'd be captured or killed during the attempt. However, this eventuality had never occurred to her.

Tears scalded her eyelids then, blurring her vision. Hurriedly she blinked them away.

As they sped through the outskirts of Melor, it became evident that news of the destruction of Mir-Brennan Tower had already reached the town. The tower was twenty klicks away, too far for the residents of Melor to see or hear anything.

Nonetheless, news traveled fast.

Cloaked figures gathered on the roads, and Malik caught the excited babble of various tongues. When they slowed to pass through a square, he spied a holo-image looming above one of the buildings, showing the billowing black cloud surrounding the ruin of Mir-Brennan Tower.

Malik ground his teeth.

He didn't need to see that right now, and neither did his companions.

Glancing left, Malik's gaze alighted upon Jenna. Crouched over the handlebars, her hood pulled forward, it was impossible to see Jenna's face. All the same, he noted the rigid set of her shoulders and the way she bowed her head forward.

She'd been furious earlier, yet sorrow had come for her.

Maybe once she weathered the storm, she wouldn't blame him—wouldn't hate him.

Right now though, she wouldn't even look his way.

As the streets narrowed and they neared the center, they slowed their hoppers.

There were Mir-Ferrin troops everywhere, although they didn't pay Malik or his companions any notice. Instead, the soldiers rushed around, shouting into their wrist-comms; they were frantic after receiving the news of the explosion.

Malik's mouth thinned.

He couldn't be sure Mican Mir-Ferrin and his son had actually been in Mir-Brennan Tower when it blew, but it was probable.

Their deaths were no great loss to the sector.

He'd wanted to kill Tian, for Jenna, but Cathal had saved him the trouble.

In truth, Malik was still reeling from what the clan-lord had done.

He hadn't wanted to sacrifice himself, and yet in a single stroke, he'd brought down his enemies. The Mir-Brennans had suffered recently, but they'd just hit the Mir-Ferrins where it hurt.

All the same, Malik would never forget the despair he'd seen in Cathal's eyes.

One rash decision had brought terrible consequences.

They crossed the sprawling town and headed for the spaceport—and the closer they got to their destination, the busier the streets became.

Tension thrummed through Malik, his gaze sweeping the crowds.

They needed to reach the sanctuary of *The Wayfarer*. Once they did, Jenna would be able to contact the Mir-

Brennan fleet and let them know they were ready for them to attack the blockade.

Reaching the spaceport, the party of six dismounted from their hoppers, pulled up their hoods, and joined the throng swirling in and out of the port.

Inside the cavernous departures terminal, chaos reigned.

Malik had already noted the crowds upon their arrival the day before. Many locals had been trying to get off the planet—largely Mir Brennans who feared persecution from their new overlords—but now swarms of agitated travelers jammed the massive space.

It was too early for the Mir-Ferrins to know who'd destroyed Mir-Brennan Tower. Instead of hunting for those responsible, they appeared to be focused on establishing order. The roar of panicked voices echoed high into the metal girders crisscrossing the ceiling. There was a brawl going on before one of the ticketing-droids, and Mir-Ferrin troops had just arrested three multi-limbed Lebbins who'd tried to jump the turnstiles.

Vic cut a path through the surging crowd, a cloaked Obsidian at his side.

The space was vast; it seemed to take forever to cross the floor. They'd almost reached the security gates when the cyborg cast a glance over his shoulder at his companions. Jenna, Isla, and Bea were right behind him, while Malik brought up the rear.

"Keep close to me," Vic instructed. "Pilots and passengers of private ships don't have to wait in the regular queues ... all the same, we'd better keep our heads down in here."

Vic headed toward the exit for non-commercial pilots and passengers, skirting a scuffle that had erupted between the Mir-Ferrin soldiers and a desperate family of humans. Angry shouts and sobbing cut through the din.

Malik deliberately kept his gaze fixed forward. Up ahead, Vic stopped in front of a security-droid and handed over the stack of fake IDs he'd procured before leaving Morith.

Halting, Malik resisted the urge to glance behind him. Being surrounded by Mir-Ferrin troops made the skin between his shoulder blades itch. It was taking a while to check their IDs. He hoped Vic had paid for decent ones.

Eventually, the security-droid waved them through the gate. Malik followed his companions out of the terminal, leaving the chaos behind.

However, the tangle of covered walkways beyond were busy too. Sweating travelers, hauling cases behind them, and shouting at hapless utility-droids, thronged the boardwalks leading out to the landing bays.

An announcement blared through the spaceport then, cutting through the roar of voices. "Attention please … all ships are currently grounded. Passengers are instructed to return to the departure terminal and wait until further notice."

Furious muttering echoed down the walkways. This was bad news for those desperate to leave this planet.

There would be no getting off Idral at present. The blockade wasn't letting anyone in or out.

Malik allowed himself a hard smile. *We'll see about that.*

31. A ROUGH RIDE

"YOUR FRIENDS MADE it." Vic swiveled around from where he'd been hunched over the console in the cockpit and removed his headset. He then met Jenna's eye. "I've just hacked a Mir-Ferrin channel … *The Star Tempest* and *The Star Monarch* came out of hyperspace fifteen minutes ago and have engaged the blockade."

Jenna let out the breath she'd been holding, hope breaking through the shroud that enveloped her.

As soon as she'd boarded *The Wayfarer*, she'd pulled out her tablet and opened a channel to *The Star Tempest*. To her relief, Commander Levi Mir-Brennan had been waiting for her.

"Good," she replied, her voice husky. "Now we just need to reach them."

"The Mir-Ferrins have grounded everyone," Vic reminded her. "They'll fire upon us if we try to take off."

"How sturdy are *The Wayfarer's* shields?" Malik asked.

Jenna tensed. Her bodyguard had risen from his seat, moving toward the cockpit. They hadn't spoken since leaving Mir-Brennan Tower, and she continued to ignore him now.

"Sturdy enough," Vic answered. "These freighters have the old-fashioned shields—durable Lazda steel. They'll take a bit of fire, but they won't handle a pyro-torpedo."

"Only the battle cruisers have those," Malik assured him. "How fast can you get us off this launch pad?"

Vic inclined his head. "Fast … although it won't be comfortable." He paused then, his hazel eye narrowing. "I'd rather not fly my ship into a fire storm."

"That can't be helped," Malik answered. "Let's go."

Irritation spiked through Jenna, and she cut Malik a sharp look. She was in charge here. It was up to her to give the orders.

However, glancing his way was a mistake. He was watching her, a stubborn glint in his eyes.

Her bodyguard was challenging her, daring her to lock horns with him.

Jenna swallowed down hot anger. She would—just not now.

"Strap yourself in then," Vic replied, swiveling back in his chair, and muttering an instruction to Obsidian. "This is going to get rocky."

Jenna fumbled with her harness. Isla and Bea were already buckled in. Her sister-in-law and niece looked as drained as Jenna felt; their faces were taut and pale, their eyes red-rimmed. Isla now had a stunned expression as shock settled over her. Reaching across, Jenna placed a hand over Isla's arm and squeezed gently.

Meanwhile, Malik took a seat at the end of the row.

A few seconds later, *The Wayfarer's* engines roared to life.

Shortly after, the comm on the cockpit console started bleeping.

"What's that?" Jenna called, alarm knotting under her ribs.

"Tower control," Vic shouted over the thunder of the engines. "We'll just ignore them." He shifted his attention to where Obsidian crouched upon the seat next to him. "Ready the shields," he ordered. "Raise them as soon as we're clear of the landing bay."

"Yes, Captain," the battle-droid replied.

The engines thrummed harder then, the noise increasing to a whine.

Jenna drew in a deep breath, her fingers wrapping around her armrests.

She hoped Vic wasn't overstating the durability of his ship's shields. She didn't want them to be blasted out of the sky before reaching *The Star Tempest.*

The freighter shot upward then, with such force that Jenna's belly dropped like a stone, and she was thrown back in her seat.

Bea shrieked, and Isla gripped hold of her hand, murmuring in an effort to soothe her terrified daughter.

The Wayfarer corkscrewed upward, in the fastest takeoff Jenna had ever experienced. The view beyond the cockpit window blurred, and the ship's fuselage creaked and shuddered as the shields raised.

Jenna whispered a prayer to the Gods under her breath then—all of them—wishing she'd been more devout over the years.

The freighter shuddered once more, violently, and Malik swore. "They're firing on us."

Jenna's grip on her armrests tightened. Those shields had to hold.

"Open a channel to *The Star Tempest*," she shouted above the whine of the engines. "Tell them to cover us once we leave Idral's atmosphere."

"One thing at a time, Lady Jenna," Vic answered as the ship rocked violently. "Let's get out of range of their guns first."

They rocketed upward so fast that a wave of dizziness swept over Jenna. Her ears started to ring.

She kept her gaze fixed forward, upon the captain and copilot of *The Wayfarer*. Both Vic and Obsidian looked as if they knew what they were doing. Cyborg and droid worked together, while Vic hauled back on the controls, guiding the ship through a barrage of fire.

A high-pitched wail cut through the roar of the engines then.

"Rear shields are failing," Vic muttered.

"We must almost be out of range?" Malik called out.

"Nearly."

Outside the cockpit windows, the view of the pink sky changed, turning pale blue and then dark purple.

And then Jenna spied the rust-colored curve of Idral beneath them, and the star-dusted black curtain of space behind.

The roar of the engines settled now that they'd broken free of the planet's gravitational pull.

It struck Jenna then that she didn't feel queasy, as she usually did during takeoff. Indeed, she'd been too scared, too preoccupied, to think about herself.

Vic bit out a curse, and an instant later, Jenna saw why.

Just ahead, a battle was in full flight. Four arrow-shaped Mir-Ferrin battle cruisers, including *Defiance*, one of the Mir-Ferrin flagships, had engaged *The Star Tempest* and *The Star Monarch*. Pyro-torpedoes detonated against the battleships' shields, the light from the explosions illuminating the emptiness of space.

"Vic … open that channel to *The Star Tempest*," she shouted. With all that fire, there was no way they'd get to the battle cruiser without being shot down. "Now!"

Vic complied, punching something out on the screen in front of him. Static then filled the cockpit. "*Star Tempest*, this is Vic Mir-Riorde, captain of *The Wayfarer*. Urgent request to board … I have Lady Jenna Mir-Brennan with us. Over."

A beat passed before a clipped voice responded. "Negative, Captain. You're flying a Mir-Ferrin freighter … unless you can provide proof that—"

Jenna swore under her breath. She'd forgotten to warn Commander Levi about that earlier. Unclipping her harness, she shoved her way past the others and launched herself at the console. She then grabbed hold of the back of Vic's seat and leaned forward.

"This is Lady Jenna Mir-Brennan," she snarled into the comm. "Open a landing bay ready for us and send out an escort immediately."

A shocked silence crackled back before the comms officer cleared his throat. "Copy, Lady Mir-Brennan." He paused then for a second before speaking once more, his voice all business now. "Make for Landing Bay C4 on the aft hull. An escort will be with you shortly … we will try to cover you until then. Over."

Jenna's breath gusted out of her.

"Strap yourself in, Jenna," Vic replied, his voice tight. "We're about to enter rough seas again."

She nodded, retreating to her seat—and had just clicked the harness back into place when *The Wayfarer* jolted, a graunching noise filling the cabin.

"That didn't sound good," Isla gasped, glancing around her, eyes wild.

"Two Arrows are on us," Vic reported. "We've just lost our rear shields."

Bea started to cry, her frightened sobs muffled as she clung to her mother.

Jenna swallowed hard. Arrows were Mir-Ferrin fighter planes. The arrowhead shape was a hallmark of the clan; they used it for all their craft, from utilitarian freighters like this one to their biggest battle cruisers. Arrows were fast, agile, and as deadly as Idralian sand-stingers.

Vic stopped speaking then, his entire focus on guiding his ship toward *The Star Tempest.* The crab-shaped vessel seemed too far away; it felt as if a huge gulf divided them. One filled with enemy ships.

The Star Tempest began firing on the Arrows then—white laser streaming from its guns. The fighters were nimble, and avoided it easily, although the diversion bought *The Wayfarer* time.

The freighter shuddered once more, and alarms went off, blaring through the ship, and drowning out Bea's sobs.

A moment later, smoke drifted into the cabin.

"The cargo hold is on fire," Vic announced. "I've sealed it off ... but the drive console in the passageway is in danger of melting. If that happens, we'll be dead in the water."

"I'll try and stop that from happening," Malik shouted over the wailing alarms. He unclipped his harness and pushed himself out of his seat. His gaze then cut to Jenna. "I'll need help."

Wordlessly, Jenna nodded. She rose to her feet, and as she wriggled past Isla, she glanced through the cockpit window and glimpsed fighter planes emerging from the belly of *The Star Tempest*. Star Kites—Mir-Brennan fighters—were coming to their aid.

They left the cabin, and Malik sealed the door behind them.

In the passageway beyond, he grabbed an extinguisher and a mask and thrust them at Jenna before grabbing some for himself. Donning their masks, they made their way down the passageway, past the exit hatch, and toward the cargo hold. The smoke grew thick here, making visibility difficult.

Something struck *The Wayfarer* then, and the freighter listed to one side.

Jenna flew sideways and would have collided with the wall if Malik hadn't caught her.

He hauled her against him, and then the freighter righted itself.

For an instant, their bodies were flush, and Jenna shoved herself away. Malik let her go, and they moved forward.

But when Jenna's gaze settled on the drive console—a large panel of counters, screens, levers, and buttons that controlled the ship's lightspeed and hyperdrives—she cursed. It was on fire.

They ignited their extinguishers, spraying a stream of blue foam over the fire. It took them both to put it out, and when they had, nothing but a tangled, melted mess remained of the console.

"Shit," Jenna muttered. "That doesn't look good."

"Come on." Malik's voice was muffled through the mask. "We'd better get back to the cabin."

They retraced their steps fast, their boots ringing on the metal floor, resealing the door behind them.

"The drive console is fried," Malik announced.

"Just is well *The Star Tempest* has locked us in a tractor beam then," Vic replied, glancing over his shoulder, his hazel eye glinting. "That's quite an escort they sent out. They want you safe … My Lady."

Jenna's gaze traveled past the cyborg to the view beyond the cockpit window. While she'd been helping

Malik put out the fire, the freighter had stopped shuddering. The attack had ceased. Instead, *The Star Tempest's* hull loomed before them, a hangar door yawning to receive them.

Jenna nodded. Hysteria twisted under her ribcage then. She'd reached her limit. Her skin prickled as the belly of *The Star Tempest* became the heavens.

Of course, they wanted to keep her safe.

She, Isla, and Bea were all that was left of the Mir-Brennan ruling family.

32. MY LADY

"FOR FUCK'S SAKE."

Halting in the doorway, Jenna glanced down the corridor to see Vic standing before the melted mess that had been the drive console, viewing the destruction.

"I'll see to it that your ship is fully repaired," she assured him. "And I'll give you double the price I promised back on Morith." She paused then, flashing him a brittle smile. "You've earned it."

Vic turned before favoring her with a respectful nod. "Thank you, My Lady."

My Lady.

For most of the rescue mission, he hadn't used an honorific with her. But now he did. It was a reminder of the responsibility that had been thrust upon her.

Jenna turned from the cyborg, her gaze flicking over her shoulder at where Malik, Isla, and Bea waited behind her.

Her bodyguard's expression was veiled, while her sister-in-law and niece clung together, faces drawn with grief.

Jenna shifted her attention outside the freighter then and down the ramp.

Rows of black and gold armored figures awaited her.

For a short while, she'd stepped out of her old life.

For a few days, she and Malik had been on the run, planning and executing a rescue together. The boundaries between them had blurred, yet the events back at Mir-Brennan Tower and the sight of Commander Levi Mir-Brennan, standing rigidly to attention at the head of the column, reminded her of who she was, of who Malik was.

And the things that divided them.

Glancing down at her soot and dust-covered tank top and cargo pants, Jenna's mouth thinned. It was as if she were looking down at herself from above, detached and a little scornful.

There had been moments over the past days when she'd almost believed she could be someone else—that she and Malik could reach across social class and be together against the odds.

But it had been a dream.

The man followed orders, and from now on, she would give them.

Squaring her shoulders, Jenna walked down the ramp into the landing bay. The hiss of extinguishers echoed through the hangar as droids hosed down the rear of the freighter, ensuring its smoldering hold didn't burst into flames again.

Levi Mir-Brennan watched her, his lean face tightening in surprise. Dressed in black with a golden cloak hanging from his shoulders, his dark skin gleaming in the austere overhead lights, Levi had been one of her brother's closest friends.

He glanced behind her then, his gaze taking in the clan-lord's wife and daughter, before his attention snapped back to Jenna.

"My Lady," he greeted her.

"Commander."

"The clan-lord ... is he—"

"He fell," she replied, confirming the concern in his eyes. "My brother set off a detonator inside Mir-Brennan Tower. He was responsible for its destruction." She halted then, swallowing as her throat tightened.

Levi's throat bobbed, his dark eyes guttering. "That is tragic news, My Lady." The commander's gaze cut behind Jenna once more, to the clan-lord's wife. "I'm truly sorry, Lady Isla."

The *Star Tempest* jolted then, a reminder that there was still a battle going on.

"We will grieve my brother soon, Commander," Jenna replied, forcing crispness into her voice. "But first, we have more pressing issues to focus on."

Commander Levi favored her with a brisk nod. "What are your orders, My Lady?"

"What's our status?"

"We're holding off the Mir-Ferrins for the moment … but we're significantly outnumbered." Levi paused then. "We came, as you ordered … yet this was always to be a diversion and a rescue … not a fair fight. Our shields are taking a battering."

Jenna's jaw tightened. She'd seen the size of the Mir-Ferrin blockade and the battle cruisers bearing down on them. "Very well … Commander, give the order to retreat. Our ships are to plot a course back to Staturine II. Make the jump into hyperspace as soon as you're ready."

The commander gave another nod. "Yes, My Lady." Levi swiveled on his heel then, his golden cloak billowing behind him. "I will see it done."

Jenna stood on the viewing platform, watching as *The Star Tempest* made the jump into hyperspace. The stars turned fluid, streaming over the clear bubble ceiling made of multiple layers of tempered glass overhead.

She tensed, yet dizziness didn't assail her. Nor did she start sweating or feel sick.

The irony of it wasn't lost on Jenna. Tragedy had cured her of a malaise that had always made space travel difficult for her.

Standing alone on the viewing platform, she waited for the sorrow she'd kept carefully banked ever since leaving Idral to hit her.

But the tears wouldn't come.

Her belly still felt twisted in knots, and the weight of losing Cathal crushed her chest, but her eyes were dry. Isla and Bea had retreated to their quarters, where they'd both been sedated after their ordeal.

But Jenna didn't have that luxury.

She was clan-lady now—ruler of her clan.

There would be no sedation, and tears would be shed in private only. Not here. Not now.

Not when she was waiting for someone.

A man she could no longer avoid.

The whisper of the doors behind her warned her of his arrival. However, she didn't turn, didn't look away from the stars streaming by. They'd safely distanced themselves from the Mir-Ferrin battle cruisers, even as the enemy continued to fire on them, and had made the jump into hyperspace.

Idral was behind them, but it wasn't lost.

Jenna's mouth thinned, and she made her brother a silent vow. *Cathal. I swear to you, I'll take back our home one day ... I shall see Mir-Brennan Tower rebuilt.*

Resolve surged through her. The intensity of it stiffened her spine and made her breathing quicken.

And she would.

"My Lady." Malik's voice, low yet firm, sounded close behind her.

Inhaling sharply, Jenna swiveled to face him.

He was standing nearer than she wanted, and she took a step back, stopping short when her spine hit the wall of tempered glass behind her. Curse it, she couldn't distance herself any farther from him.

Like her, Malik hadn't yet changed clothing since their arrival upon *The Star Tempest.* His cargo pants and close-fitting t-shirt were sweat-stained and covered in soot, grime, and red dust. His short black hair was disheveled as if he'd just raked his fingers through it.

Yet Malik's expression was composed, his gaze unwavering. "You called for me?"

Jenna cleared her throat. "I did, Captain."

Silence fell between them then, and Jenna drew in a few slow, deep breaths, to try and settle her suddenly racing pulse.

This conversation was necessary and couldn't be put off. But now that Malik was standing in front of her—her bodyguard, her lover—the resolve she'd felt when she'd sent a utility-droid off to fetch him faltered.

Damn him, the man sent her pulse wild, even now.

"Firstly, I wanted to thank you," she said, surprised at how cool, how controlled, her voice sounded. Good. At least, her years as the Mir-Brennan ambassador would serve her well now. "Your bravery ever since you saved my life on Aura Terminal will be recognized. You will be decorated for your service to my family."

Malik stared back at her, a muscle feathering in his jaw. He then inclined his head. "I thought you were angry with me?"

Jenna sucked in another deep breath, her belly twisting. "I was," she admitted, her voice betraying her. "But I realize now, you were only carrying out orders."

"I didn't want to leave him there," Malik replied quickly. "Any more than you did … but your brother was doomed."

"You swore an oath when you joined the Lord's Watch … I understand that."

His mouth tightened. "Do you? I'm not so sure."

Jenna folded her arms across her chest. It was a defensive posture, yet she had to create a physical barrier between them.

"I'll admit I felt betrayed," she said after a pause. That was the truth; as they'd made their escape from Melor, she'd promised herself she'd have her reckoning with this man. Yet now that the crimson cloak of rage had drawn back, she saw that the situation was more complex. "But I wasn't thinking at the time … I was too upset."

"As you had the right to be." He swallowed then. "I'm sorry, Jen … but don't think it was an easy choice."

"Don't call me that," she replied huskily.

His gaze snapped wide, his big body tensing. "Why not?"

Jenna stared back at him, nausea churning within her now. Finally, they'd gotten to it: the reason she'd called him up to the viewing deck. She'd felt brave earlier, still pumped with adrenalin after their escape from Melor. Now though, all she felt was dread and a twisting grief under her breastbone that wasn't just to do with her brother's loss.

She was about to lose someone else—someone she'd waited her life to find, someone that was never meant to be hers.

Malik Mir-Draven.

Dragging in another deep breath, she held his eye, even as sweat beaded upon her forehead. "The closeness we formed on the way back to Idral can't continue," she replied softly. "I'm discharging you from duty, Captain. From this moment forward, you no longer serve my family."

33. THE CHOICE IS YOURS

IT WAS AS if she'd just punched the air from his lungs.

Reeling, Malik searched Jenna's face, trying to see past that icy veneer she was wearing.

Ever since she'd set foot on *The Star Tempest*, it was as if they'd stepped back in time.

To how things had been before that fateful diplomatic mission.

He hated it: the cold formality, the distance.

It reminded him of all the years he'd observed Jenna from afar, wanting her but refusing to admit it to himself. Instead, he wanted to see her vulnerability, her passion. The woman behind that mask was warm and sensual, yet you'd never know it to look at her now.

Jenna held her chin high, and despite that she wore cargos and a filthy tank top, she still managed to look haughty, aristocratic.

She was reminding him of the chasm between them. She was of the ruling class, and he from the gutter.

And now she was firing him.

"Good," he growled after a few seconds.

A nerve flickered in Jenna's cheek. She hadn't expected that reaction. "You're happy about it?"

"Yes." He took a bold step forward, stopping when less than a foot separated them. "If I'm not captain of your guard, I'm a free man. Your equal."

She stared up at him, her deep-brown eyes widening. "You were always that," she whispered.

Malik fought a lip curl. "No, I wasn't … I was a servant, bound by an oath you've just released me from."

He stepped closer still and leaned in, placing a hand on the tempered glass next to Jenna's shoulder. It was ice-cold against his palm. The move was a dominant one, but he didn't care. He was sick of keeping his feelings leashed, of pretending nothing mattered—when the truth was, it did.

Jenna mattered more than anything, and he wasn't going to let her go without a fight.

"But now I'm just a man," he continued roughly. "One who will stand at your side, if you'll let me."

Jenna jolted as if he'd just struck her, her full lips parting. "What?" she whispered.

"I'll be your husband if you wish it … or your lover, if you don't," he ground out, his throat tightening as emotion threatened to choke him. "But be certain of one thing, Jen … I love you … and I'd lay down my life to prove it."

Their gazes fused and held, and for a few moments, the universe narrowed to just this one point.

Malik was keenly aware of the hard thud of his heart against his ribs as he awaited her answer.

"You love me?" she whispered eventually, her chest rising and falling sharply now.

Finally, the façade was crumbling.

Malik fought the urge to reach for her. "Yes," he answered softly. "Discharge me from duty Jen … I'll step down willingly … but don't send me from your side. You are the only thing in this universe that I want."

She swallowed. "But I'm the Mir-Brennan clan-lady now. Do you want everything that goes along with that?"

His mouth quirked. "I'd put up with it. You can do what society dictates … cast me aside and choose a high-born mate … but never forget that you make the rules now." He paused then, his gut tightening. "The choice is yours."

Jenna stared up at Malik, taking in every detail of his face: his straight nose, expressive dark eyebrows, penetrating violet eyes, strong jaw, and sensual mouth. It was a face she never wanted to look away from.

"You make it sound so easy," she whispered, her voice catching. "But if only it were."

"What are you afraid of?" he murmured back.

"I don't know."

His features tightened, his gaze darkening. "You don't want me, is that it?"

Her chest ached now, a steady throb in time with the beat of her heart.

Dropping her arms to her sides, she sucked in a shaky breath, just as a soft sob escaped her. "I want you with everything I am, Malik … I love you." Her voice choked off then.

Anxiety fluttered in her throat, and cold sweat beaded across her skin.

She'd hated being married to Tian, but at least her heart hadn't been at risk with him. She'd been able to protect herself from hurt, from loss.

Until now.

"I've lost everyone I ever cared about." She broke off then as her throat thickened and her eyes started to burn. "I don't want to lose you too."

His mouth curved before he raised a hand, his knuckles gently tracing the line of her jaw. "I'm not going anywhere, sweetheart."

And with that, he leaned in, his lips brushing across hers.

The kiss was slow and sensual, deepening gradually.

Jenna's pulse hammered in her ears, and her head swam. Reaching up, she grasped Malik's shoulders, anchoring herself against him. And when he stepped in, his long body pressing hers up against the glass, she let herself go.

Tears trickled down her face, a sob rising in her chest.

Malik lifted his mouth from hers, his lips skimming over her cheeks, kissing away her tears. "I'm scared too," he admitted huskily. "And I know what it's like to feel alone. But I'm not giving this up, giving *you* up. No matter what the future holds … we will face it together."

His words drew her in, wrapped her in warmth and safety.

Sinking against his chest, she let herself cry. Finally, she let go, let grief flow through her. Cathal was gone, and she had to allow herself to feel his loss—the memory of the last time she'd seen him.

The raw despair in his eyes.

"I'm sorry I lashed out at you over leaving Cathal," she hiccoughed, lifting her head. "It wasn't your fault."

Malik looked down at her, his smile tender. "I liked your brother … but he was always one to rush into situations without thinking. I wish he'd hesitated … that he'd told us what he was planning to do."

Jenna swallowed. "This was never meant to happen … he was supposed to rule our clan, not me."

"Jidea has decided otherwise," Malik replied, his expression growing serious. He paused then, his thumb sweeping away the last of her tears. "You were born to rule, Jen. Your brother knew he was leaving the future of the Mir-Brennan clan in safe hands."

Reaching up, Jenna's hand closed over his, holding it fast. "So be it," she replied huskily. "I'll rule, I'll take back what we've lost … but I want you with me, Malik."

A smile curved his lips once more, his eyes gleaming with emotion. "Always."

And with that, he kissed her again, and kept kissing her, until everything else disappeared.

EPILOGUE. YOUR CAUSE IS MY CAUSE

One month later …

JENNA SLUNG A cloak over her shoulders before venturing outdoors. Staturine II didn't have Idral's climate. Most days were cool and cloudy, with an icy wind gusting in from the north.

It was taking some getting used to. Her clan had originally hailed from this planet, yet she could see why her grandfather preferred Idral. Staturine II was rich in minerals, its mountainous surface pock-marked with mines, but it was cold and damp. She missed Idral's hot, dry air, laced with the tang of iron, and the sight of the sister moons every night.

Stepping out onto the balcony, a wall of noise met Jenna—cheering and applause from the vast crowd gathered on the wide square beneath her. The citizens of Briscay, Staturine II's capital city, had gathered here to witness Jenna Mir-Brennan take the clan seat. She now stood upon the public balcony of Castle Valnor. Before her, Briscay's skyline bristled with delicate dove-grey spires set against the backdrop of purple, snow-capped mountains.

Jenna had just come from the great hall, from a ceremony where she'd taken the clan ring.

Cathal's ring, a signet upon his right hand, had gone with him to his death, and so she'd had another made.

Jenna raised her right hand to greet her people. The gleaming gold signet, with her clan's emblem upon it, glinted in the pale sun.

The cheering grew louder, and the air trembled from the force of it.

Jenna couldn't help but smile at their greeting. It was a warmer one than she'd expected. She was the first clan-lady in six generations, yet her clan welcomed her.

Glancing right, at where Isla and Bea stood, Jenna caught her sister-in-law's eye.

Unlike Bea, who'd rallied in the way only children could after her father's death, Isla was thin and drawn these days, yet she managed a small smile. Dressed in flowing black, for she would be in mourning for a full year, Isla's skin was so pale it almost appeared translucent, and there were dark smudges under her eyes.

Jenna had been worried about her of late, yet Isla just needed time.

They all did. Cathal's death had sent shockwaves through the clan. There had been public scenes of grieving upon the streets of Briscay.

They needed a new leader—someone to give their people guidance and strength. Jenna had wanted to leave her swearing-in for at least three months, but a week earlier, Isla had come to her and suggested she move it forward.

"We can't wait," Isla had insisted, her blue eyes glinting. "Our enemy certainly isn't."

Like them, the Mir-Ferrins had lost their leader. The clan was rallying its strength, and Elijah, the eldest of Mican Mir-Ferrins's surviving sons, had recently been sworn in upon Platinum 5.

There were whispers of revenge, although those rumors just filled Jenna with resolve.

If there was vengeance to be had, she would be taking it.

Even before her swearing-in, she'd been to numerous meetings with the Mir-Brennan space fleet commanders. They were recruiting new soldiers, building new ships, and making new weapons.

The Mir-Brennan clan would rise from the ashes, even stronger than before; she'd see to it.

Gaze sweeping over the crowd of bobbing heads, Jenna spied a familiar face near the front: a well-built man with brown hair and a black metal plate over his right eye socket.

Stepping close to the balustrade, Jenna met Vic's eye and grinned.

An instant later, he raised a hand to acknowledge her, his mouth twitching.

Warmth suffused Jenna's chest. It was good to see the cyborg was still in residence here in Briscay, although she imagined he'd soon be moving on. Repairs on his freighter would almost be completed by now.

Vic was restless, a loner. She'd approached him a couple of weeks earlier, asking him to lead the Lady's Watch. However, he'd politely refused, and she hadn't been that surprised.

Vic had given his life to serving a clan-lord and had paid for it with his humanity. His transitioning had played a cruel trick upon Vic, for he was far too aware of what they'd taken from him.

All he had now was his free will, his ship, and a droid who'd follow him anywhere. Jenna understood his restlessness.

The crowd's cheering increased once more, waves of noise rolling over the wide square and reverberating off Castle Valnor's granite walls. Jenna glanced over her shoulder to see Malik emerge onto the balcony.

Like her, he wore a heavy black cloak about his shoulders, although, unlike Jenna, who wore a high-necked gown of shimmering gold, he was dressed in black and grey. They'd have to wait until the year of mourning for her brother passed before they could marry; as such, he didn't yet wear gold. Only members of the ruling family wore that color, but once they wed, Malik would.

As always, Jenna's breathing caught at the sight of him.

The past four weeks had been the most emotional, and the happiest, of her life. Her unhappy marriage was behind her. Tian was dead. And in his place was a man who loved her with an openness and courage that allowed her to face her fears and love him back with the same determination.

Reaching out with her left hand, she entwined her fingers through Malik's, drawing him to her side.

A slow smile stretched across his face. "They love you, My Lady."

"They love you, too, it seems," she teased back, squeezing his hand.

Indeed, the crowd was going wild at the sight of them standing upon the balcony together. News of Jenna's lover had rippled over Staturine II within days of her arrival at Castle Valnor.

She'd been worried about a backlash, that the Mir-Brennan governors, who held stewardship over the various planets and stations in this territory, and the members of the wealthy elite, would step forward and declare her relationship with Malik scandalous. But none had. Sure, there had been whispers, yet no one had been bold enough to criticize her publicly.

Eventually, the cheering died away, an expectant hush settling over the square. The biting wind buffeted the balcony; they were entering the northern continent's long winter. Many of the upturned faces were flushed with cold and excitement, and everyone was bundled up warmly.

"My people," Jenna called out, her voice carrying across the crowd. "Thank you for welcoming me as your clan-lady. I will do my best to serve you, as my brother did before me, with integrity and strength."

Cheering erupted once more, and Jenna waited until it settled down before she continued.

"We are weathering dark times. My brother is dead, Idral is currently under Mir-Ferrin rule, and our relations with that clan have gone back to the days of old. We are enemies once again."

Curses rang out, the mood of the crowd shifting in an instant. The Mir-Ferrins were hated here.

"We can't abandon the people of Idral ... both our colonists and those who welcomed the Mir-Brennans among them," Jenna continued, her voice cutting through the rumbling. "And we won't." She inhaled sharply then. "But we must look ahead. I'm currently seeking to rebuild trust with the Mir-Leliths." She didn't mention that their relationship with that clan had been poisoned by Mir-Ferrin lies. She didn't want a riot.

More cheering and applause erupted, and Jenna waited once again. She'd prepared this speech carefully. Her words walked a fine line between diplomacy and warmongering. Her people were understandably hungry for vengeance, as was she, but she didn't want to stir them up.

She wanted them to see beyond revenge; she wanted to work toward stability.

"We are currently rebuilding our space fleet ... so we can regain what has been lost." She paused a moment and then raised her right hand, palm outward, as she'd seen both her father and brother do countless times when addressing the masses. "The Mir-Brennans will rise again. Glory is the reward of valor!"

"Glory is the reward of valor!"

The chanting began then, and Jenna squeezed Malik's hand once more.

She wondered what he thought of all of this; he was a Mir-Draven, after all. However, when she glanced his way, Malik's gaze gleamed and his jaw tightened. Catching her eye, he squeezed her hand in return.

"Your cause is my cause, Jen," he said, as if reading her thoughts. "I, too, want to return to Idral one day." He paused then, smiling. "Good speech, by the way."

Her mouth curved. He knew that she'd been nervous about today, about how the masses would respond to her—to them.

But she needn't have worried.

The past weeks had shown her that many of the things she feared weren't worth her worry.

Loving Malik hadn't weakened her. Instead, she'd never felt stronger.

Her people weren't sitting in judgment of her. Instead, they looked to her for leadership.

Malik was right—she'd taken to this role naturally. Marrying Tian had eroded her self-confidence, had embittered her, yet he hadn't been her destiny—this was, and she'd embrace it.

Moving closer to Malik, she let him place his arm around her shoulders in a protective gesture that would be seen by all.

The chanting dissolved into cheering. Moments later, the clear call of trumpets rang out, and streamers erupted from cannons lining the square, spirals of color decorating the pale, wintry sky.

Laughter and gasps of awe joined the roar of the crowd.

Looking on, Jenna leaned in further to Malik. "This feels right," she murmured to him, her arm winding around his waist.

Malik's arm tightened around her shoulders, and she felt him plant a kiss upon the crown of her head. "That's because it is," he murmured.

The End

ABOUT THE AUTHOR

Samantha Charlton fell in love with Han Solo at an early age and began a life-long love of Sci-Fi adventure and Space Opera. This passion led her to write Space Opera—with emotional and steamy romance—of her own! Samantha is also the multi-award-winning author of Amazon best-selling Historical Romances, writing under a nom de plume.

Connect with Sam online:
www.samanthacharltonauthor.com
www.facebook.com/samanthacharltonauthor
Email: samanthajcharlton@gmail.com